A Turn-up for the Books

Rachael Gray

Print ISBN: 978-1-917449-41-0

For Steve, my rock

Chapter 1

Laurel

'I don't understand, does trouble find you, or do you find trouble?' he asked.

Dr Laurel Nightingale levelled a cool stare at the older man by her side, her friend and neighbour, Albert. 'You always know the right thing to say, don't you,' she huffed.

The third of their trio, Dorothy, gave a mirthless laugh.

The three of them peered into the room. It was a cosy, if old-fashioned bedroom with patterned wallpaper, a chest of drawers, an armchair, a rug, and a very dead body.

'I've called the police,' said Dorothy. She ran a hand through her short grey hair and shrank further into her chunky knitted cardigan. 'I knew it was a bad idea to rent Tulip Cottage to a media type, a journalist no less.'

They were standing in the hallway of Dorothy's holiday cottage, crowded around the doorway to the single bedroom. A body dressed only in a pair of blue and white striped boxer shorts lay face-down on the unmade bed. The rumpled sheets twisted underneath his bloodless limbs and his hands lay palms down by his head. That he was no longer living was obvious. The knife sticking out of his back being a dead giveaway.

'What do you have against journalists?' Despite the tremble in her voice, Laurel's tone was sharp. She didn't know Dorothy well but had witnessed the woman's judgemental and unpleasant character more than once. She took a deep breath. 'Sorry, this has been a shock for all of us. Who is he?'

The older woman's mouth turned down. 'That's really none of your business. You might have solved those murders last year, but you've no cause to be poking around in my affairs.'

'I'm only here because I was trying to help.' Laurel felt needled into defending herself. It wasn't her fault. She didn't seek drama; it was the very antithesis of what had driven her to move from Somerset to East Yorkshire in the first place.

Albert patted her on the arm. 'I thought you did a marvellous job last time and if you fancy trying your hand again, at least the cause of death is obvious in this case. No one can dismiss the knife in his back as an accident.'

'Don't encourage her, old man,' Dorothy said. 'We don't need some credulous fool running round thinking she's some modern-day Miss Marple.' She paused, head cocked at a sound of a vehicle outside. 'That'll be the police.'

Shooed back outside by Dorothy – Laurel glad to put some space between herself and the other woman – they watched a car crunch up the gravel driveway and come to a stop. After a breathless pause, the driver stepped out, the weak sun catching his silver hair as he straightened up. 'Laurel.' He smiled, his eyes crinkling at the corners. 'Why am I not surprised to find you here? We really must break this habit of meeting in such *grim* circumstances. Albert, Dorothy.' He nodded. 'Good to see you too.'

Laurel flushed. 'Ben, hi.' Uninvited, the memory of their last meeting claimed her attention. It wasn't a moment she wished to dwell on, when a killer had taken a pot shot at her outside her own front door. Sergeant Ben Templeton, being one of the first on the scene, had found her huddled in the hedge, snotty-nosed, red-eyed, and terrified.

'Anyway.' He cleared his throat and gestured to the cottage. 'What exactly is going on here? Dispatch said there's been a death?'

'A murder.' Colour bright in her cheeks, Laurel blurted the word, earning her a scowl from Dorothy.

He held up his hands. 'Whoa, let's not jump to any conclusions. Let's just take things a step at a time and see where we go from there, shall we?'

'Officer,' said Dorothy, 'this is my holiday cottage. I rent it out. The deceased is– *was* my current guest. His body is in the bedroom, and he most certainly was murdered. I'll show you.' To the others, she urged, 'You can go now.'

'Actually,' said Ben, 'I need all three of you to wait right here, please. Go nowhere, touch nothing and just... do nothing.' He gave them each a hard stare – though his lips quirked into the faintest smile when he got to Laurel – before disappearing through the front door.

They listened to his heavy footsteps as he made his way along the hallway. There was a pause and Laurel thought she heard a gasp before a burst of rapid, inaudible speech, a one-sided conversation reporting the crime. A swift tattoo of boots broadcast his return.

Dorothy folded her arms. 'I told you it was murder.' She looked smug. 'Do you think I don't understand what it means when a man has a dagger sticking out of his back?'

Ben ignored her as his radio squawked. He turned away to reply, making a request for a senior officer. Laurel felt relief to have someone competent, and official, in charge. Brow furrowed, he swivelled back, notebook in hand. 'While we wait, I need to get some details. Dorothy, Mrs Little, you're the owner of Tulip Cottage and the person who called this in?'

'*Ms* Little. When are you going to get him out of here so I can clean up?'

'I'm afraid, Ms Little, that we'll be here for some time and even once the deceased has been moved, we won't be able to release the cottage immediately. I'm sure that you understand there are procedures in this kind of situation. It is a crime scene.'

She sniffed.

'And I hope you don't mind me noticing, but for someone who has recently found a dead body, you don't appear unduly perturbed.'

'Officer,' she fixed him with a steely eye, 'before I retired, I was a nurse in the casualty department at Hull Royal Infirmary; I've seen more dead bodies than you've had hot dinners.'

'I see.' He jotted a note. Dorothy craned to look at the page and he adjusted his position to obscure her view. 'Now, I need to ask you how you came to find the deceased. Why were you in the cottage?'

'If you must know, I thought he'd gone to The Pleasant Pheasant for his breakfast as was his habit since he's been staying. So, I popped over to check that everything was okay and that he was looking after the place properly. I have every right to do so. I can't see the cottage from my house, meaning I have to come down here to check. When I came inside – I keep a spare key before you ask – I found his bedroom door locked.'

'How did you know he was in there?'

'Why else would the door be locked?'

'Perhaps he'd gone out and felt the need to lock the bedroom door behind him?'

She glowered at him. 'I'm no snoop, if that's what you're implying. Besides, I could see that the key was in the lock, on the inside.'

'You don't have a spare key to the bedroom?'

'No, there's only the one.'

'Then how did you know something was wrong? He might have been in the bath or the shower.'

'Young man, I am not daft! I was knocking and calling loud enough to wake the– for him to have heard me.'

Ben underlined something. 'Did you try looking through the window?'

'Of course, but the curtains and the window were tight shut.' Hands on hips, Dorothy watched him as he flipped back through the pages he'd just filled.

'Laurel, Albert, how did you come to be here? Albert, you first.'

Albert's attention was divided, his gaze fixed on something over Ben's left shoulder.

'Aroon! Damn bird, there you are!' he exclaimed as they all turned to see a cockerel disappearing round the corner of the cottage. 'That's why I'm here,' he called back as he hurried off in pursuit. 'I've been out looking for this little rapscallion.'

Unfazed, Ben looked to Laurel. 'Okay, Laurel, let's start with you.'

'It's not my fault. I was on my way back from the bakery when I ran in to Dorothy.' She felt a guilty twinge as she remembered how she'd been tempted to scurry off in a different direction when she'd first spotted Dorothy at the end of the driveway. 'She looked distraught, so I asked her what was wrong. She told me. Albert showed up. Here we are.' It was the short version but covered the basic run of events. It probably wasn't worth mentioning the bickering about whether they call the police first or try to get into the room.

'Yes, here we are,' echoed Ben. There was a pregnant pause. 'So, who can explain why the door to the bedroom is now wide open?'

Albert sauntered back, cockerel at his heels and cobwebs

sticking to his hair and clothes. 'Ah, that's my cue, I do believe. No doubt you're curious as to how we effected an entry?'

'If you would be so good as to enlighten me.'

'You'll want to remember this handy little trick.' He winked and nudged Ben in the ribs. 'Make sure you write it all down,' he added, prodding the notebook. 'The key was in the lock, you see, on the inside. I slipped a page from my newspaper under the door, then I poked a pencil in the lock to knock out the key, so it landed on the paper. I pulled the paper back from under the door bringing the key with it. Voila.'

'Lucky the door had a gap underneath,' Ben observed.

'Of course, dear chap. We might have had to resort to brute force otherwise.'

Ben finished writing and regarded Albert, Laurel, and Dorothy with a puzzled air. 'Let me get this straight: the door was locked with the key on the inside; there is only one key; and nothing and no one else was present in the room when you opened the door, except the dead body?'

'Precisely,' confirmed Albert.

Chapter 2

Laurel

'I need help to kill people again.'

Laurel blinked. 'Pardon?'

'Ah, you don't know who I am, do you?' His mouth was smiling, but his eyes were flat.

When she didn't respond immediately, he continued. 'I'm Hugh Quintrell, the author. Crime novels. I make my living killing people in ingenious ways. Or at least, I used to, but I've been suffering this wretched writer's block for months.' He slumped in his chair and rubbed his hands over his face.

Laurel sat facing him, her diary with his details lying discreetly in her lap. For fifty-three years old, he looked good, like someone who was a regular at the gym. Brown hair touched with grey at the temples and glasses that struck the perfect balance: intelligent and bookish, but stylish, too.

'Mr Quintrell, Hugh, if I may?'

He gave a curt nod.

'Naturally, I know who you are.' This wasn't strictly true. She'd thought his name sounded familiar but hadn't been able to place him. She was still distracted after the events of the morning. It would have been prudent to cancel her afternoon appointments, but she hadn't wanted to let down a new client, this client.

'However, I try not to pre-empt what a client might want me to know, and I would instead prefer to hear about you in your own words.' It was a weak cover, but she thought she might get away with it. 'And I'm curious, it matters to you that people know who you are?'

He was quick with his answer. 'When you've worked as hard as I have, then, of course it matters.' He pursed his lips for a moment. 'But I see your point about wanting to hear about me in my own words.'

'Why don't you start by telling me more about your writer's block?' she suggested, her voice low and soothing, relieved he was mollified.

He took a breath, sat back and straightened the crease in his trousers. 'Well, it began about three months ago, late November. I'd just had enormous success with *Death Dances with Destiny*.' He paused.

'Gosh, yes, tremendous.'

'But since then, nothing.'

'What do you mean?'

'The words have dried up. I'm Hemingway with his blank sheet of paper. I hoped that by coming here, to the middle of nowhere, where I could be alone with my thoughts and not hounded by the press and fans, here I thought I might be able to break through.'

It was interesting he compared himself to Hemingway. She made a note. 'I see. But that hasn't happened, the block is still there?'

'Of course. Why else would I be sitting here?' He gestured to the room. 'I would have booked in with my usual therapist, but he's unavailable and since you weren't fully booked...'

He is in distress, she reminded herself, but his insinuation stung. She fought the urge to defend her new practice, which, okay, wasn't that busy yet, but it would be. *Focus!* 'Has this happened to you before?'

She let the silence hang, giving Hugh time to decide what, if anything, he wanted to reveal. He'd stopped making eye contact.

'Once, but that's of no import, it's happening now, and that's what I need to focus on. There's no sense in digging around in the past.'

This felt a lot like avoidance. She knew to back off, though. This was only a first session. They'd get to the core issues in time. Therapy couldn't be rushed.

'Of course. So, if we focus on the here and now, you mentioned the success of your most recent book?'

He squirmed. 'Yes, well, the readers loved it, but my publishers aren't happy. Seem to think I'm *getting repetitive.* I believe that's what they said.' His face was red, his hands clenched.

'And how does that make you feel?'

'How do you think it bloody makes me feel?'

'I want to hear you put it in to words.'

He glared. 'Furious, incensed, outraged. For a start.'

'And?'

'Wounded.' He spat out the word, his face contorted as if in physical pain.

She waited a moment, letting the words hang in the air between them. When his face relaxed and his fists unclenched, she continued. 'And these emotions are impeding your writing?' This was where he needed to be for their work together, honest and vulnerable.

'They're wrong though, and I am not going to take it lying down. There's a journalist, a Simon Forster, very well regarded.

He's up here to interview me for a piece about my work, my craft.'

The mention of a journalist, a visitor to the village, gave rise to an image of a dead body clad only in blue and white striped underwear. Dorothy's media-type guest at Tulip Cottage. Oh dear. It couldn't be. Could it?

'You mentioned earlier that you'd come here to be away from all that?' It was a clumsy question, but Laurel needed a second to think. Even if her hunch about the identity of the body was right, she couldn't break the news to Hugh, could she?

He waved a dismissive hand. 'One can never truly disappear. Part of the job, I'm afraid.'

'Can we go back to those feelings you mentioned?'

Hugh sighed and steepled his fingers. 'Laurel, it is Laurel, isn't it? I see what you're getting at. In my ninth book, *The Therapy of Death*, my killer was a psychologist, so I understand a thing or two about psychotherapy. As such, I can tell you raking over the past is not what is required here. I would prefer if we were to focus on the here and now and tackle the issue of my writer's block. I'm sure you understand?'

Unconditional positive regard, she held the phrase in her mind. Being one of the core components of client-centred therapy, it was essential in her work. She looked around at her office. She'd taken weeks choosing the twin sage green armchairs, which were placed at just the right angle to encourage conversation. A low coffee table sat between with the obligatory box of tissues. The botanical prints for the walls, the use of natural wood, and the potted plants all selected to help smooth the edges of raw emotions. This was a space clear of clutter, apart from the hectic world outside, a safe place.

Apparently, though, it wasn't doing it for Hugh. His reluctance to be vulnerable with her might get in the way of forming a constructive, therapeutic relationship, no matter how emphatic and genuine she was with him.

She chose her words with care. 'Hugh, perhaps we're not a good fit and you might be better off waiting for an appointment with your usual therapist?'

'Oh, now don't be upset,' he said, offering her the box of tissues. 'Once we get to know each other, I think we'll do great work together.'

Chapter 3

Laurel

Maggie was waiting at their usual table in The Pleasant Pheasant. Her blonde hair, immaculate as always, was in an elegant French pleat and her cream and blue scarf complemented a dove-grey jumper. Laurel wove her way between the closely set tables and other patrons and slid gratefully into the waiting chair. Although Maggie was older by ten years, Laurel felt frumpy in comparison.

'I've gone ahead and ordered you a bacon and brie panini,' said Maggie with a grin. 'It's Wednesday, so I assumed you'd be having your regular?'

Laurel smiled back, then frowned. 'Am I that predictable?'

Jo, the owner of the café and wizard in the kitchen, was clearing the table next to them and piped up, 'Ah, Laurel, we all know your love for bacon and cheese.'

The Pleasant Pheasant, along with The Plump Tart, a sublime bakery run by sisters Hetty and Constance, and The Snooty Fox pub, meant that Elderwick locals were never far from a good meal or a piece of heavenly cake. Both of which Laurel and Maggie availed themselves of as often as their schedules – and waistlines – allowed. Laurel wasn't obsessive about her weight but had promised herself to look after all aspects of her wellbeing from now on, emotional and physical. It was what she'd told her patients to do for years whilst working in the NHS. But practising what she preached was a harder gig.

Maggie, Laurel noticed, had gained a little weight since ditching her bully of a husband, Nicholas, shortly before Halloween the previous year. It suited her, and she suspected it might have something to do with how often Maggie and Hetty were spending time together. She was happy for her friend, but piqued by just how much time Maggie was spending with the baker.

Knowing they'd have a wait for their food, Laurel was eager to update Maggie on the previous day's events, but Maggie beat her to it and leant forward to whisper, 'I heard you found a dead body yesterday!'

One of these days, Laurel vowed, she'd be first with the news. 'Albert?' she asked.

'Hetty, but she heard it from Constance, who heard it from Albert. They said it wasn't anyone local, thank goodness. Was it someone here on holiday?'

'Hmm. Yes, someone on holiday, I suppose. I'm not sure.' She had to be careful about what she said. 'All I know is what Dorothy told me, that he'd arrived four days earlier, booked for a month, and was from London.'

They paused in their conversation as Jo delivered their drinks. 'Two ticks and I'll be out with your food,' she said.

'Was it awful?' Maggie probed when she'd gone.

'It wasn't pleasant, but for a murder it was surprisingly... bloodless?'

'That sounded like a question,' observed Maggie, before picking up her mug of hot tea and taking a sip.

Laurel pictured the scene in her mind and shuddered. 'Well, he was stabbed. The knife was right there, sticking out of his back, but there wasn't a lot of blood. I didn't really clock it before, but you'd expect more blood. I guess.'

'Does this mean you're going to solve a murder again?' Maggie's eyes were wide.

'Oh no, I've already told Albert, I'm staying clear.'

'Very sensible.' Maggie sat back as Jo brought over their food. 'I know we dealt with those murders a few months back – and I still maintain we made an excellent team – but the idea of getting involved with such nastiness again... well, it doesn't bear thinking about. Besides,' her serious tone disappeared, and her eyes sparkled, 'I have something far more exciting, and glamorous, to talk about. You'll never guess who I saw in here yesterday?'

'Who?'

'Hugh Quintrell!'

Laurel made a non-committal noise. This could be awkward.

'You know,' persisted Maggie, '*Hugh Quintrell*, the author? He wrote *The Song of Death*, and *I Dance with Danger*. You must know him? I have all his books and he's here in Elderwick! I wonder what he's doing here, and how bizarre that the king of crime is here just as a murder is committed. I asked around and a little bird told me he's staying at that fancy place between here and Little Wick, so maybe *he* will solve the case.'

'I know of him.' She was deliberately vague so as to give nothing away. She hoped Maggie wouldn't pick up on her discomfort.

'Well, he was right here. I didn't speak to him or anything. I mean, you don't do you. And he's so handsome, very distinguished. He was sitting just over there.' She pointed to a table in the corner and the elderly couple enjoying their toasted teacakes gazed back in confusion.

Laurel gave them a wave. They returned wary smiles and went back to eating in studied silence.

'You've read his books, haven't you?'

'No, I haven't really come across his work.'

Maggie put a hand to her heart. 'How could you not? He's one of the biggest crime writers there is. Here.' She delved into her handbag and pulled out a book, which she placed on the table. 'You can borrow this. You must read it.'

The Murder of Innocents, Laurel read the title. 'It's a hefty book. Why on Earth are you carrying it around?'

Maggie blushed.

'Ha!' The truth was written all over her friend's face. 'You wouldn't be hoping for an autograph if you see him again, would you?' Laurel teased.

Maggie's colour deepened but she was saved from having to defend herself as the bell over the door was set jingling. She seized the advantage of the distraction. 'Oh look, it's Ben.' Swivelling all the way round to face the newcomer, she called his name and waved.

He turned at her voice and spotting her gave a hesitant wave back. Maggie beckoned him over. Behind him followed a tall, striking blonde whose hand he was holding.

'Hi, Maggie, nice to see you. Laurel, nice to see you again. That is, it's nice to see you today; yesterday wasn't... I mean. Never mind. Um, this is Elise.' He guided his companion forwards.

'Elise, hi.' Maggie beamed at her. 'You're not from around here, are you? Welcome to Elderwick.' She pointed to the two empty chairs at the table and encouraged them to sit.

Elise plonked herself down and grinned. 'Finally, I get introduced to some of Ben's neighbours. It's a pleasure to meet you.' She held out her hand.

As they shook, Elise spotted the novel sitting between them

and her lip curled. The expression lasted less than a second, but Laurel caught it and felt a beat of satisfaction; it was gratifying to know not everyone was enamoured with Hugh Quintrell's work.

'We can't stay long,' said Ben, still standing. 'We've just stopped in to collect a picnic that Jo's made up for us.'

'Oh, how romantic,' said Maggie.

Elise nodded. 'It really is.'

'It's a bit cold for a picnic, isn't it?' asked Laurel, peering at the smudge of grey outside the steamed-up café windows. A flash of reproval from Maggie made her cringe, she hadn't meant to rain on their parade. But really, it was February.

'It's more of a carpet picnic,' said Ben as a crimson flush crept up his cheeks.

'In front of a roaring fire and everything. He's planned it all, haven't you,' said Elise, smiling up at him.

'Ben, you romantic thing.' Maggie fluttered her eyelids. 'So, Elise, tell us about yourself. What do you do?'

Laurel remembered the first time she'd met Maggie for tea and cake and recalled Maggie's tendency to get stuck right in with personal questions. On her own arrival in the village, she'd quickly learned it was the modus operandi of all the locals. Luckily, Elise didn't seem to mind.

'I'm a chef. Only in a small restaurant in Beverley right now, but one day, I hope to open a place of my own.'

'How fantastic! Maybe you could open one here in the village. What kind of food do you like to cook? Do you live in Beverley?' Maggie peppered her with questions.

Elise's face lit up. 'No, I'm in Cherry Burton, and I cook all sorts of food, but Greek is my favourite, and...'

Ben, who had been looking at his watch, cut in to say, 'Elise, we should really get going.'

She smiled and stood to join him. 'Sorry, ladies, my

handsome prince calls. We must arrange a time to meet properly. I haven't been in the area long and really don't know many people down this way yet. It would be lovely to have a coffee together, if you would like to, of course?'

'That would be wonderful,' said Maggie, whipping out a pen and paper to jot down her number. Handing it to Elise, she explained, 'It's my home number. I don't have a mobile because the signal around here is non-existent. Call when you're free and we can arrange to meet back here for a good girly chat.'

Elise grinned. 'Let's do it soon.' Here, she scribbled her number twice on a napkin and ripped it in two, handing a piece to Maggie and the other to Laurel. 'Now you have mine too.'

She and Ben collected their picnic basket from Jo and slipped back out into the cold. Feeling the draft from the door, Laurel grabbed the scarf that was looped over the back of her chair and settled it snugly around her neck. She felt ridiculous sitting indoors wearing it, but the chill had penetrated her bones. She would have a long, luxurious bath when she got home. The best way to warm up in the bleak winter months.

Cosy Myrtle Cottage on Birch Lane was a world away from the utilitarian new build she'd lived in before moving to Elderwick in September of the previous year. Her first few months in the village had been terrifying and taxing, but it was home now, and she couldn't imagine ever wanting to leave. The dullest of winter days was no match for a fire blazing away in the wood burner, a mug of hot chocolate, and a good book.

'Is it just me, or did it seem like Ben was doing his best to keep his gorgeous new girlfriend away from us?' queried Maggie.

'Yeah, he was definitely in a rush to get her out of here.'

Maggie sipped her tea and placed the mug back on the table before saying, 'Elise seems delightful. Ben has done well for himself there.'

Laurel agreed, but it was the strangest thing, was that a twinge of envy she was feeling? What was that about? She was quite happy being single, *thank you very much.* Before she could interrogate her reaction further, a second blast of frigid air heralded Albert's arrival.

With wind-swept white hair and rosy cheeks, he peered through his misted glasses. Whipping out a large white hanky, he wiped them clear before setting them back on his nose and scanning the room. 'Ah, I thought I might find you ladies here,' he called as he located them. He bustled over and took the empty seat at their table. 'I have an update, but first, where's Jo? I am minded to spend some time here this morning indulging in both her sublime cooking and tackling this fiendish crossword.' He conjured a copy of *The Times* from a pocket, then shrugged off his coat to reveal an orange and brown argyle cardigan over a mustard shirt.

'Albert, my, you remind me of the seventies, and not in a good way,' said Jo, arriving to take his order.

He smiled, well-worn laughter lines creasing his face. 'Now, Jo, you know I love a spot of colour. Today's ensemble is new, fresh from the charity shop in Beverley. And in good durable fabrics.'

Having seen her away with an order for a full English breakfast with extra toast, extra beans, but no mushrooms, he leaned towards Laurel and Maggie, lowering his voice. 'Following the lamentable events yesterday, I was having a little tête-à-tête with an old friend of mine down at the police station. He tells me they have little to go on and many questions unanswered. Dorothy was asked to attend the station for some further questions pertaining to what the poor chap had been up to before he met his maker.'

'They haven't arrested her or anything though, have they?' Maggie's tone was somewhere between horrified and fascinated.

'Not at all. All routine. I do wonder if she had any knowledge that could aid them in their quest, but to that puzzle, I do not yet know the answer.'

Maggie looked from one to the other. 'Ben was just here, and he didn't mention anything. What questions were they asking?'

'I haven't a clue.' Albert shrugged, sitting back. 'And nor does my man on the inside. Incidentally, do you know that the phrase *don't have a clue* is thought to come from when *clue* had an entirely different meaning, and was in fact spelled c-l-e-w–'

'I have a question,' interrupted Laurel.

She saw Albert wink at Maggie. 'The Elderwick sleuth is back in action,' he teased. 'Ask away.'

She ran it through in her mind once more, checking her loose theory quickly before speaking. 'Albert, from what we saw from the doorway, how would you say the man died?'

'He was stabbed. It was hard to miss the knife in his back.'

'Exactly, the *knife* in his back. But Dorothy said *dagger*.'

'I don't understand the significance?' said Maggie.

'Most people would assume it was a knife – it certainly looked like a knife to me from where Albert, Dorothy, and I were standing. None of us had been into the room so Dorothy didn't get a closer look or anything, and Albert you talked about it as a *knife*. So, why did Dorothy say dagger?'

There was a long pause. Albert shifted in his chair and played with the menu on the table. 'Ahem, it's a curiosity indeed, and an interesting query, but I'm not sure it's...' he waved a hand in the air, searching, until settling on the word, '...significant.'

Laurel felt crestfallen. It had sounded good when it had popped into her head, but Albert was probably right. She wasn't even sure what the difference was between a knife and a dagger. 'I wonder if they'll want to speak to us again, too?' Her last visit to a police station had resulted in her being targeted by a killer, and she was in no rush to repeat the experience.

'Perhaps, but I don't believe there's anything we can tell them we didn't pass on yesterday.'

Laurel squirmed. 'Should we have mentioned that Dorothy insisted we open the door of the bedroom *before* calling the police? I assumed it was because she didn't want to call them out unnecessarily, but could there be more to it?'

'We could ask her some questions of our own when she's back,' suggested Maggie.

'Good luck with that,' snorted Albert. 'Dear Dorothy is not the sort to engage in twittle-twattle unless it involves people other than herself.'

Laurel nodded. 'She certainly won't tell me anything, but Maggie, she might...' she broke off. 'Oh, for goodness' sakes! Look at me, I'm doing it again. That's it, I'm stopping right now. You can do what you like, but I promise you, I am not getting involved. I'm leaving this murder to the professionals.'

Chapter 4

Laurel

The biting wind attacked Laurel and Maggie as they left the warm fug of the café. February had long been Laurel's least favourite month, the short, grey days and the lingering hours of darkness hung heavy after the colour of Christmas and the freshness of New Year. February was a chore to endure in the wait for spring.

'Have you heard,' said Maggie, 'Marcus and Petra have decided to sell Elderwick Hall? I can't say I blame them, especially now they're settled in the South of France.'

'No, I hadn't heard, but I thought they were moving to the United Arab Emirates?'

'Petra got Marcus to change his mind. She never did fancy the UAE.'

Laurel pictured the attractive couple who, until three months ago, had lived at the hall. 'I wonder if they'll have trouble finding a buyer given the history of the place?' She remembered the grisly stories she'd been told when she'd first moved to the village. Over the decades and through the generations of Hartfields – Marcus' ancestors – there had been enough murders and disappearances for the property to gain a morbid reputation. Marcus and his wife, Petra, had dismissed the old whispers warning of a curse until a few months ago when Marcus had been attacked in his own library and left for dead.

Laurel shivered at the memory. 'I wouldn't want to live there after what happened.'

'The reports don't appear to have put people off. They already have two buyers lined up. One is private – she didn't mention a name – and the other is a charity. They run centres in the countryside for inner-city and deprived children. I hope it goes to the charity, but it'll most assuredly come down to money.'

'Well, either of those options sounds better than the executive homes and hotel Marcus wanted to build. I liked the sound of...' she trailed off when she registered Maggie was no longer listening.

'Who's that?' Maggie nodded toward a lemon-yellow Fiat 500 parked across the village green. Standing by the vehicle, a figure swaddled in a bulky coat, hat, scarf and gloves was squinting towards The Pleasant Pheasant.

'No idea, but they're dressed for the Arctic. Oh, don't look now. I think they're coming over.'

'Hi,' called a voice, as the figure approached. 'Can you help me? I've got a bit turned around. Is this Elderwick?'

They could see now that it was a young woman beneath all the layers. 'Yes,' said Laurel. 'This is Elderwick.' She tried to make out the features of the speaker, but the winterwear and the flat light reflecting off the stranger's glasses kept her hidden.

'Oh, thank goodness. Honestly, I've been driving up and down the same lanes for what feels like hours trying to find this place, and the satnav in my stupid rental was no help.' She threw a withering look at the car. 'Are you local? I don't suppose you happen to know if there are many holiday cottages in the village? I think it's an Airbnb I'm looking for.'

Laurel hoped that the woman wasn't searching for the recently deceased journalist; she didn't want to have to break bad news.

'There are a few rental places. Do you have a house name or address?' asked Maggie.

'No, I, um... I'm looking for a person staying here somewhere. He told me he was coming here but not the exact address and I need to find him on quite an urgent matter.'

'Who is it you're looking for? It's not... oh dear, I'm so sorry if it is, but it's not a journalist, is it?'

Laurel braced herself, then breathed a quiet sigh of relief when she heard the answer.

'No, not a journalist, but erm, honestly, I'd better not say. He's here on the quiet.'

'Is this person famous, by any chance?' Maggie gave Laurel a not-so-subtle nudge. 'Because if so, we might know where you can find him.'

The pregnant pause was answer enough.

'Although if this person didn't give you their address, we really can't share that information.' The last thing Laurel needed was Hugh accusing her of a breach of confidence.

'Oh, I'm sure it'll do no harm to tell her.' Maggie turned to the woman. 'Maybe if you tell us who you are and why you need to find him?'

A flicker of indecision crossed the stranger's face as she looked around her again. 'Okay, I guess it can't do any harm, and it sounds like you know already that it's a gentleman called Hugh I'm looking for.'

'See!' Maggie said to Laurel. 'I was right, it's Hugh Quintrell, isn't it?'

'Yes. I'm Natalie Marwood, his literary agent at

Greenleaves Lit in London. I really need to see him. I know he came down here to hide out after his latest book reviews, but, what with the death and all, I want to make sure he's okay.'

'The death?' Laurel asked, keen to give nothing away just yet. Who knew if Natalie was really who she said she was?

'You know about that?' Maggie added, earning her a frustrated look from Laurel.

Natalie motioned them closer and bent her head to whisper. 'I only heard about it this morning, from a friend of mine who works for *The Guardian*. I don't think it's hit the news yet. It's so awful, isn't it. I was only talking to Simon last week! Do you know how he died?'

'No,' Laurel answered for both of them. 'We haven't heard much at all.'

Maggie asked, 'Hugh knows him? Knew him?'

'Yes, Simon's a very well-respected journalist. Was.' The agent sniffed. 'He was doing an important piece on Hugh's life and work. I guess Hugh invited him to come up here so they could keep working on it. I really need to find Hugh. He must be so upset. I know it must seem strange that he didn't tell me where he'd be staying, but that's how he is. He has such an amazing intellect that sometimes he needs to take himself off alone to concentrate on his art.'

It was quite a long trip to make from London to East Yorkshire without the certainty of a specific address as her destination. Laurel had a hunch it was personal and not professional concern that had brought Natalie to Elderwick.

'Oh my God, there he is!' Natalie exclaimed, waving as she looked over Laurel's shoulder towards the main road. 'Never mind, thank you,' she shouted back as she strode away across the winter-brittle grass. 'Hugh!' she called.

Laurel watched as Hugh, carrying a large box from The

Plump Tart, continued walking giving no indication he'd heard Natalie.

Determined to keep to her promise of staying out of the latest village intrigue – and not to muddy the waters with a client – Laurel was ready to get home and into the warmth with a good book, but Maggie was already drifting towards the couple.

'Natalie,' she heard Hugh say. His tone bordered on irritation rather than being an enthusiastic welcome, but Natalie didn't falter.

'Hugh, oh my goodness! I'm so glad I've found you. I've been driving around for ages looking for you. I just had to come and see if you were okay. Are you okay?' She hovered near him, arms held out as though offering a hug.

'Of course I'm okay,' he said, flapping his free hand at her. 'What are you doing here? I told you not to disturb me whilst I was away.'

With reluctance, Laurel trailed after Maggie and as they drew closer Hugh noticed he had an audience. 'Laurel, how wonderful to see you again.' He walked towards her and away from Natalie. 'And who is your radiant friend?'

From the corner of her eye, she could see Maggie's jaw drop. 'Hugh, this is Maggie. Maggie, Hugh.' It was always a delicate dance when she encountered a client outside of the therapy room, but since he'd taken the lead, she could hardly ignore him.

'Hugh, we need to talk about Simon,' Natalie interrupted, tugging on his coat sleeve.

'It's a delight to meet you.' He shifted the cake box to his left hand, dislodging Natalie's grip as he did, and held out his right to shake. His long fingers enclosed Maggie's.

Maggie beamed as Hugh held her hand and Laurel saw an opportunity to do her friend a favour. She lifted the weighty tome out of her bag. 'It's not mine,' she mumbled, handing it to Maggie.

Hugh beamed. 'My first book. Tell me, Maggie, are you new to my work?'

'Oh no, no, no, not at all. I've read them all. All of your books. They're amazing, you're amazing. I was lending this one to Laurel. She hasn't read any of them but I know she'll love them.'

Laurel winced. She couldn't remember if she'd claimed to have read Hugh's books. His face gave nothing away, but she was certain he'd noted the information.

'Pen.' Hugh snapped his fingers at Natalie, who produced one from the depths of her coat.

Turning his celebrity smile on full, he handed his cake box to Natalie, then took the book from Maggie and wrote a lengthy inscription. 'There we are, just for you, radiant Maggie.'

Maggie took back the book with reverence. Hugh left Natalie holding the box and slipped the pen into his pocket. 'Now, as much as I love meeting my fans, I had better see what my assistant here wants. It is most tiresome, but such is the life of an author.'

Laurel wondered how his *agent* felt about her demotion to assistant, but Natalie didn't comment.

'Hugh, I'm so sorry about Simon.'

'What about Simon? I'm on my way over to his place now. We were going to review the notes from our last interview.'

Natalie's free hand flew to her mouth and the cake box threatened to tumble. 'You don't know? Oh Hugh, he died. He's dead.' Her lip trembled.

Hugh gasped and stared at Natalie. 'No!'

'I'm so sorry.' She reached out and put her hand on his arm, where he let it rest for a moment before shaking her off.

Staggering to a nearby bench he slumped down and put his

head in his hands. His breath puffed out between his fingers into the frigid air. With glassy eyes, he looked up. 'How was he killed?'

From the corner of her eye, Laurel saw Maggie frown and open her mouth to speak. She nudged her and gave a tiny shake of her head.

Natalie answered, 'They don't know all the details yet, but what I heard is that they're treating it as suspicious. That's the only intel I have so far.'

'Who's your source?'

'Tim, at *The Guardian*.'

'He's a stand-up guy and usually on the money.' Hugh coughed and looked at the ground. 'I wonder if we can get them to publish what Simon had already written about me?'

Chapter 5

Maggie

Although desperate to talk to Laurel about the encounter between Hugh and his literary agent, Natalie – not to mention grill Laurel over how she knew Hugh – Maggie didn't get a chance before she had to rush off to the church to meet Dorothy Little and the vicar, Christopher Ibori.

Christopher was new to the parish and had generated a brief flurry of interest on his arrival two months previously. His predecessor having retired suddenly after a heart attack and moved away to live with a younger sister in Bournemouth.

Christopher was tall and angular, a quiet, serious man, in his early sixties. Single, so the grapevine said, with two adult children – both living in the southeast – and had found his calling early, straight from school, so he'd said. A significant cohort of the WI had declared him *dishy*.

'You're late.'

'Hi, Dorothy, I know, sorry.' Maggie puffed as she sat to catch her breath. Although now out of the wind, she found she was even colder in the church than she had been outside. She shivered and pulled her hat tightly over her ears.

Christopher appeared and strode down the aisle clapping

his hands. 'Ladies, lovely to see you both, and thank you again for volunteering. Shall we pop through to the vestry? I've got a heater on in there and it's far more convivial. I'll talk through what we need doing and then we can set to.'

'How are you?' Maggie whispered to Dorothy as they fell in behind him.

'Perfectly well, thank you.'

'Oh, I just wondered...'

'What did you just wonder, Maggie Wright?'

'You know, after what you found yesterday... and then being questioned by the police.'

'Maggie, unlike you, I'm not in the habit of gossiping, and exactly what are you implying by saying I was *questioned* by the police? I was helping them out of choice. So, I'll thank you for keeping your insinuations to yourself.'

A little stung, Maggie wasn't going to let it go that easily. 'I hardly think this is gossip; a man was killed! I'd say that it's something we should know about, for our own safety.'

Dorothy pursed her lips and gave Maggie a sour look.

'A man was killed?' Christopher stopped walking and turned to gape at them. 'What? Who was killed?'

With a huff, Dorothy explained how she found that her guest had *departed* in a rather unconventional and unscheduled manner.

'Oh Dorothy, are you all right? What a dreadful shock that must have been. Come, come, let's all sit and I'll put the kettle on.' He ushered them both into the warmth of the cramped vestry and filled a small kettle from the sink wedged into one corner.

In the face of the vicar's obvious concern, Dorothy defrosted slightly and admitted that it had been rather a shock. 'He'd only been there a few days, so I didn't know him well and certainly not personally. Even so, you don't expect your holiday cottage guests to be murdered in their own beds. I was in two minds whether to rent Tulip Cottage to him and it looks like I should have listened to my instincts.' She settled herself more comfortably in her chair and eyed the tin of biscuits at Christopher's elbow. 'Perhaps a little fortification would help if you're to insist on asking all these questions?'

Christopher took the hint and passed round the tin, which Maggie was pleased to find held an assortment of *good* biscuits: chocolate Hobnobs, Jammie Dodgers and even a couple of Bahlsen.

After snaffling two of the Bahlsen and a pink Party Ring, Dorothy continued. 'These city types they come up here and cause all kinds of problems. Doesn't matter if they're from London, Birmingham, or even Hull, they're all the same.'

'What sort of problems?' asked Maggie.

'Oh, you know.' Dorothy waved away the question. 'And journalists, well, you know what they're like. What do they call them, the liberal elite? Drinking and smoking, chasing their lurid stories and not worrying about the effect it has on decent folk. Why can't they write more about good Christian people who still know what proper values are? It's all sex and drugs these days. In fact, I bet there'll be a whole lot more trouble round here if that charity get the go ahead and buy Elderwick Hall. *Inner-city youths*, that's code for delinquents, you mark my words.'

'Now that's not fair,' Maggie protested. She wasn't surprised by Dorothy's outburst, but she was surprised that the woman knew about the potential buyers for Elderwick Hall. Gossip travelled at speed in Elderwick, but even by village standards, this was impressive.

'You said you didn't know the gentleman personally, Dorothy?' asked Christopher, raising an eyebrow.

'No, but he was renting my cottage.'

'Well, since none of us were well acquainted with him, I think we should refrain from speculation. Besides, the poor man is dead, so let's temper how we speak of him and think kindly towards a fellow human being who has been taken too soon from this world.' He closed his eyes for a moment and looked as though he were mouthing the words of a prayer.

'*You* seemed quite pally with him.'

Christopher's eyes snapped open. 'I don't know what you mean.'

'Did you know him, Christopher?' asked Maggie. 'Did he come to the Sunday service?'

'No, it was on Monday evening, wasn't it, vicar?'

Maggie detected an edge to Dorothy's words. For as long as she'd known the woman – a regular in the WI – Maggie had failed to warm to her. Dorothy could be friendly and was always one of the first to volunteer, but Maggie often had the feeling that everything Dorothy did was about gaining leverage. Not that she had any evidence, and maybe she should do what the lovely Christopher was suggesting and think more kindly of her fellow villager.

Christopher's left eyelid twitched. 'Monday? I don't recall.'

Dorothy was happy to refresh his memory. 'Yes, it was Monday, around 5pm. You and he were tucked away in here for almost an hour. Goodness knows what you were chit-chatting about. You might have been one of the last people to see him alive, vicar, since it was Monday night that he was killed. What did you talk about? You should tell the police.'

'Hmm, yes, perhaps. Now, we really should attend to the reason we're here today.'

But Dorothy hadn't finished. 'And vicar, I don't know how you can bear that author, either? The one that the journalist was writing about.'

This was too much for Maggie. 'What's wrong with Hugh Quintrell?'

'Have you read his books? And his personal life was no better! Divorced, seen out with women half his age, abandoned his only daughter, a fair-weather churchgoer, I'll be bound. He was here too, wasn't he, meeting with you last week?'

'Dorothy, enough,' the vicar snapped. 'I appreciate that you've had a terrible shock, but you can't go around casting aspersions and you certainly can't expect me to discuss the private conversations I have with anyone who comes to my church. Please end this speculation and these *fishing* expeditions.'

Maggie had never heard Christopher raise his voice, and from Dorothy's reaction, she hadn't either.

'Well...' was all Dorothy managed.

Christopher stood up and lifted a stack of leaflets from a shelf behind the door. He split the papers and handed half each to Dorothy and Maggie. 'Right, these need delivering to the houses on School Lane and West Street. If you have any left over, you can drop them back here when you get a chance. And yes, Dorothy, they're for the Dandelions charity for deprived youngsters. If you have a problem with that, you can leave the leaflets here and I won't trouble you any further. Thank you.'

They'd been dismissed.

Chapter 6

Laurel

'Hugh, it's nice to see you again.' Laurel held open the door to her office. 'Please take a seat.'

She'd been surprised when he'd called and requested they bring his second session forward. Usually, she would have said no to two meetings in one week, but the poor man had just found out a colleague of his was dead, murdered to be precise. Which was why it was unnerving her to see him looking positively jolly upon arrival.

'Laurel, how wonderful to see you again. Let's get down to business, shall we?' As he sat, he pulled out a Dictaphone and placed it on the table between them.

Laurel made a note on the pad on her lap: Hugh had taken the chair she had sat in last time. She didn't have a designated chair, and always allowed her clients to select whichever they preferred – they were equidistant from the door and identical in every way. With all her other clients, whichever chair they selected on their first visit was the one to which they invariably returned for all subsequent sessions. Not so with Hugh.

'You'd like to record our session today?'

'Not just this one, all of our sessions from now on. I'll need accurate records when I'm writing.'

'Writing?'

'My new book. I'm cured, doc.' He smiled wide, showing off his unnaturally white teeth. 'The writer's block is unblocked. I've already made preliminary notes and it's going to be my best yet.'

They were jumping straight in without the careful checking-in process she liked to employ before therapy proper began. But Laurel's curiosity was piqued, so she let it run.

'That's a quick turnaround, Hugh. We spoke on Tuesday and it's only Thursday now. Can I ask what's precipitated such a rapid resolution?'

'Why, murder, of course!'

Of course.

'May I?' He gestured to the Dictaphone.

'Can we have a quick chat about it first?'

Hugh pouted but drew back his hand. 'What's to discuss?'

'First, let me make sure I'm understanding you correctly. Your writer's block has gone because you've been inspired to write a book?'

'Yes. I've wanted to get into true crime for a long time, but I haven't found a sufficiently inspiring project... until now.'

'And the murder of Simon Forster is sufficiently interesting?'

'Inspiring. Absolutely.'

'That's Simon Forster, the journalist, who was writing about you?'

'It's rather meta, isn't it?' He chuckled, apparently impressed with his own wit.

Laurel put down her pen and regarded the man in front of her. She could appreciate that, as a writer, he was excited by new ideas, but he'd known Simon. Now, merely two days after

Simon was killed, Hugh was full of beans over the thought of writing about the man's death.

He pre-empted her. 'As an artist, I live to create. Even in death there is birth. Of course, I am shocked and saddened by my colleague's demise, but if I can build something beautiful and profound from that, it would be remiss of me to pass up the opportunity. And, just think, if I can solve his murder, the book sales will be through the roof!'

Laurel pursed her lips. She didn't know Hugh well enough yet as a client to be sure if she could push him on which was his true motivation, but she strongly suspected it was the latter: book sales. 'You understand the police are investigating and they're unlikely to allow you to be involved?'

'That, my dear little therapist, is where you're wrong. What police force wouldn't want a renowned author aiding them in their investigations?' He spread his arms and held out his hands as if inviting her to try and disagree. 'In fact, just this morning I had Natalie contact the senior officer in charge of the case and offer my expertise.'

'What will you do if he or she declines?'

'Declines? We've got a meeting arranged for tomorrow morning. From what I've heard, they're rather floundering. It's been two days since Simon's body was found and not much progress has been made. They're very grateful for my offer.' He flashed a triumphant smile then leaned in. 'I heard about your exploits last year, and I'm impressed. This is rather out of your league though, so I don't expect you to fathom how real investigations work.' Sitting back and crossing his legs, he continued. 'Through my many years of writing, I have consulted with and for several police forces and am known for my keen and insightful mind. It's only reasonable for your local police force to be delighted to have me on board.'

'Quite.' Though stung by another of Hugh's judgements,

Laurel's shoulders relaxed as she spied a way out of her uncomfortable therapy arrangement. 'Now Hugh, since your writer's block has resolved, I assume there is no further need for us to meet?'

'On the contrary, I hope to use these sessions to reflect on my progress with the case and to deliberate over strategy. That's why I need to record them, to document my process.'

'Ah, well, that's not a service I offer.' She tried not to look or sound relieved. 'I don't believe it would be appropriate for me to charge you for a therapeutic intervention when I am not providing therapy. So, perhaps there is someone else...'

'I'm also going to need support as I process Simon's death. We were working very closely together, he and I. It might seem to you I'm being unfeeling in planning to use this experience to write my next book. However, I can assure you, I am feeling his loss keenly. Hold on.' Without asking again, he depressed the switch on the Dictaphone. 'There now. So, it would be therapy because you see, I've known Simon Forster for years. We were at school together. Our therapy will be my exploration of my relationship with him and the bereavement I am suffering as a result of his death.'

'Oh, I didn't realise you knew him before this?'

'Indeed, I did. However, I trust the sacred tenet of therapist–client confidentiality will ensure this information doesn't leave this room until I am ready to reveal all in my book. It's going to be a killer hook: esteemed author solves diabolical murder of old school friend. Hugh Quintrell battles grief and, against all odds, brings a callous and calculating murderer to justice. I'm going to call it *Plotting a Murder*.'

Chapter 7

Laurel

'Cooee, Laurel, it's me.'

Laurel had left the front door ajar, knowing her friend was on her way round for their standing arrangement of Friday morning coffee and cake.

'I'm in the living room,' she shouted back. 'Come on through, I'm hanging my new curtains. You can tell me what you think.'

'Hi,' said a second voice.

Laurel wobbled atop her precarious perch as she tried to turn her head far enough to see the owner of the second voice.

'I hope you don't mind,' said Maggie, as she and her companion came into the room. 'I found Natalie in the lane looking lost, so I've invited her to join a meeting of our book club.'

'Of course not, the more the merrier.' Climbing down from the dining chair, she smiled at Natalie. 'This was originally meant to be a book group, but I don't think we ever got around to inviting anyone else, did we, Maggie? Or actually reading many books.'

Maggie shook her head. 'No, so it became more of a, umm...'

'Excuse to meet, gossip, and eat cake,' finished Laurel. 'As long as you like cake, you're very welcome.' She noticed Natalie's expression. 'Or, if you don't like cake, you're welcome too.' *Who doesn't like cake?*

'To be honest, I'm not eating sugar,' Natalie explained. 'I need to lose weight.' She pulled at the hem of her baggy jumper and made a face.

Laurel had to bite her tongue. Natalie was positively skinny and didn't look like she had an ounce to spare, but it wasn't for her to judge.

'Ooh, I love the curtains!' said Maggie, turning her attention to the windows. 'What a gorgeous colour.'

Laurel stood back and admired them again herself. She had been worried the rich, yellow-gold fabric would look out of place in her humble room, but it brought a cheery dash of sunshine against the soft cream walls. Being as thick as they were, they would also keep out some of the drafts that seemed to find countless ways in through the attractive but old French windows.

'Yes, I definitely approve.'

Maggie had a wonderful eye for colour and had been encouraging Laurel to add a splash of something to lift the room, so Laurel was pleased to get her feedback.

'Right, sit yourselves down and let me get you a drink.' Would it be rude, she wondered, to go ahead and eat the cake she'd bought, given Natalie was dieting? Her indecision melted the minute she was in the kitchen and within sight of the glorious chocolate sponge. She would have a search through her cupboards, though, to see what she could offer Natalie as an alternative.

Once they were all settled – and Natalie had accepted an apple – Maggie jumped straight into the two topics Laurel had hoped to avoid: Hugh and murder.

'Natalie, tell Laurel what you told me, about Hugh, about how he's going to investigate this murder and write about it.'

'Well, that's kind of it, what Maggie said. I spoke with Hugh, and he's decided that he's going to work with the police to solve Simon's... you know... and I suggested he write about it. It'll be his next book and I know it'll be a hit.'

Maggie picked up the thread. 'Natalie said Hugh has been suffering from writer's block, but this has been the inspiration he needed to overcome it. Isn't that amazing? Well, you know, it's very sad about Simon, of course, but something good will be coming out of it.'

Laurel had been worried Maggie would quiz her over how she already knew Hugh. Now she relaxed: either Maggie had forgotten, or she was being discreet. Either way meant she could avoid a tricky conversation.

Natalie was nodding. 'The press are here already, TV and newspapers. I've arranged three interviews for Hugh this afternoon alone.'

'The national press? I didn't realise they would come out here.' Laurel hadn't noticed any evidence of reporters when she'd nipped out to the bakery earlier.

'Yes, Simon Forster was a big name in journalism. I've managed to generate a fair bit of intrigue over what he and Hugh were doing, secreted away up here in the depths of rural Yorkshire.'

'It means Natalie has nowhere to stay now, though.' Maggie gave Natalie a sympathetic look. 'She'd only booked a couple of nights at the pub and the press people have snapped up all the rooms for the weekend. So, I've said that she must stay with me.'

'Maggie, you're too kind, but are you sure? I don't want to be an imposition?'

'You will be nothing of the sort, and if you need to meet with Hugh, he is welcome to come round, any time.'

Laurel turned away to hide her smile. Maggie had a generous nature and would help anyone in need, but it wouldn't hurt that this act of generosity tangentially involved Hugh Quintrell.

'Speaking of murders.' Natalie fixed Laurel with a wide-eyed stare. 'Maggie tells me you solved a couple yourself last year? Is it safe here? Do a lot of people get killed in Elderwick?'

'No, I don't think so. I mean, I've only lived here for about six months, but I don't think it's exactly Midsomer. It was an unfortunate– there was a– it was a one off– well, obviously not now but...' she trailed off. 'Anyway, I'm not sure we solved anything exactly. In fact, we got it all wrong.'

'Well, the way Maggie tells it, I think you're amazing and so brave. I hope you don't feel Hugh will be stepping on your toes this time?'

'Hardly. I shouldn't have got myself involved last time and I intend to stay well away from all of this.' Laurel meant what she said: she intended to mind her own business this time. Even if she had already made a note of at least three odd things about Simon's murder. Maybe she would pass the information on to Ben, just in case. 'I'm just a therapist who is building her private practice, and that's more than enough to keep me busy and out of trouble.'

Natalie's gaze sharpened. 'Wait, you're not Doctor Nightingale, are you?'

She feared what was coming but there was no way to deny her identity. 'Yes.'

'Ah, that's why Hugh knew you. You're his therapist. He told me he was seeing someone down here.' She sat back, a satisfied smile on her face.

Oh heck.

Maggie frowned. 'You didn't tell me that, Laurel. Wait, that means you must have already known he was here before I told you!' she scolded. 'I mean, I did wonder, but you might have told me.'

Laurel felt her friend's disappointment. 'I'm sorry, but you know I can't talk about someone who may or may not be a client.'

'I suppose.' Maggie looked glum.

Natalie piped up. 'It's okay, Hugh told me, so it's not a secret.'

'Let's change the subject, shall we?' No matter that Hugh himself had spilled the beans, she still couldn't, and wouldn't, say anything about a client to anyone else. 'Natalie, what's it like being a literary agent?'

Natalie wasn't deterred. 'Hugh tells me all about his therapy sessions. It's okay, honestly. He actually told me how *he's* helping *you*. That he's going to put you in his book. You'll be inundated with new clients once it's published! You must be thrilled?'

'So you *are* going to be involved in solving this case?'

'Maggie, no, that's not– I can't...'

'Sort of,' said Natalie. 'Hugh wants to use her as a kind of *blank canvas* on which he can try out his ideas. No offence,' she said to Laurel. 'It's just for the book. It's not what Hugh actually thinks.'

Laurel stood, needing to get out of the runaway conversation. 'I'll give him a blank canvas,' she muttered to herself back in the kitchen as she flipped the kettle on to boil again.

By the time she returned, Maggie was trying to persuade Natalie that Hugh should give a talk to the WI. Natalie didn't look thrilled with the idea but was saved from more of Maggie's barrage when her phone binged. With what Laurel was sure was relief on her face, she announced she was needed by Hugh and gave her apologies for having to leave.

As soon as the door closed behind her and she was out of earshot, Laurel let out an exasperated huff. 'The nerve of that man. Blank canvas!'

'Well, you would know more than me what he's like.' Maggie was peevish and avoided eye contact as she pushed the last bit of cake around on her plate.

'Maggie, come on, you know I couldn't tell you he was a client. It's against the most basic tenet of my professional ethical code.'

Maggie heaved a long sigh and said, 'No, I know. I'm sorry. It's just... never mind.'

'Just what? Come on, Maggie, you can tell me. I hate to think that something is bothering you and you can't talk to me about it.'

'Really, it's nothing. I'm a bit jealous, that's all. That you've been getting to spend such intimate time with someone I admire so much.' She put down her fork and brushed imaginary crumbs off her lap.

'I don't think he's as great as you think he is.'

'Well, we're going to have to agree to disagree on that.' Maggie was shaking her head. 'He is an artist, so I think you've got to allow him a bit of licence to be different. You should read his books first anyway, before making up your mind.'

It was a fair point. Laurel could admit – to herself – she was judging Hugh's books, and consequently Hugh, without having read his work. 'You're right, I will borrow the book. Thank you for the offer. Do you have it with you?' It was clear that she wasn't going to dissuade Maggie from her hero worship, but she could make this peace offering.

'As a matter of fact, I do. I was going to show it to Albert. Here.' Maggie lifted the chunky book from her bag and placed it onto the coffee table. She fidgeted with it, straightening it up to align with the coasters. 'So,' she asked, '*are* you going to help Hugh solve this murder?'

'You heard what Natalie said. Hugh doesn't want my help; he wants a *blank canvas*.' She couldn't help the disdain in her tone. Really, she was going to have to step back as his therapist. It had only been a couple of days and already she couldn't stand the man.

'I may admire Hugh, but I know you, Laurel, and I know you're not the sort to be a passive character in somebody else's story. I expect he simply doesn't realise yet what an asset you would be. You and Hugh together would be a formidable team.'

'If anyone's a team, it's you and me. We'd run rings around Mr Famous Author.' Seeing Maggie frown, she added, 'Sorry, sorry, I'll lay off the insults.'

'I know the deaths last year were awful, but it was a little bit exciting investigating them, trying to identify the killer. At least it was until we found out who was behind it all.'

Laurel thought long and hard before she spoke. There was no way she would involve herself in that kind of trouble again. Would she? 'I know it's a bad idea, but perhaps we could just ask around a bit? See what people know. There are some things that have been bothering me about Simon's death.'

Maggie laughed and stood up to walk to the window where she looked out at the winter garden. 'I knew you wouldn't be able to resist.'

Chapter 8

Laurel

'Albert! How are you?' Laurel was pleased to catch her neighbour as he passed her garden gate on his way home. She also spied Aroon, Albert's faithful cockerel, waiting a few yards further up the lane. She clucked her tongue at him, but the bird showed no sign of having heard. Knowing Aroon as she did, it was probably a deliberate snub; she'd chased him out of her garden a couple of days earlier when she'd caught him eyeing up her new brood of hens.

'Laurel, my dear, I am most cromulent, thank you, and you?'

'You know, keeping busy. Um, isn't cromulent just a word made up by *The Simpsons*?' She was familiar with Albert's love, and habit, of playing with language.

'That's where it originated, indeed, but it seems to be making the transition to an accepted term and I'm rather taken by it. Ergo, I'm doing my bit to help it along.' His eyes crinkled as he smiled. 'Now, I hear that one of the things keeping you busy is your investigation into this dreadful murder? You're setting out to compete with Mr Quintrell in a race to solve the dastardly crime?'

MI6 should send their agents to Elderwick for training, thought Laurel, not for the first time.

'Maggie and I were having a chat about it, that's all. We're certainly not competing with Hugh. Not that he is really investigating, is he? I mean, it's a murder, the *police* are investigating.'

'It gave me quite a shock, I can tell you, finding the poor man. Dorothy is made from stern stuff. She barely even blinked.'

'Speaking of Dorothy...' Laurel felt the heat creeping up her cheeks. She didn't want Albert to think she'd been lying in wait for him so she could interrogate him for more information. Even if that was precisely what she'd been doing.

He squinted at her. 'A more cynical man than I might wonder if this chance meeting isn't perhaps by chance?'

Damn it. 'Okay, you got me. Sorry. I wasn't going to get myself involved this time, but Hugh Quintrell is going round insulting me, calling me a "blank canvas" and spouting on about how the local police are "delighted",' she made air quotes with her fingers, 'to have him on board helping them out.' Her indignation simmered.

Albert leant against the rich red brick of her garden wall and scuffed his boot in the remains of autumn leaves. 'I'm not sure I followed all of that, but I can see you're working yourself into somewhat of a lather over this author chap. Naturally, this *is* best left to the authorities. However, if as a concerned neighbour, you wish to apply your brainpower to the mystery, who am I to impede? To wit, I may have had further conversations with my – nudge, nudge, wink, wink – associate in the local police force.' He tapped the end of his nose and cast a furtive look up and down the lane.

She beamed at him. 'In that case, can I offer you a cup of tea and a biscuit or two, over which you might update me?'

'What a marvellous idea.'

He chatted on as they made their way indoors. 'Do you know, I've been doing a bit of investigation into another matter, the sale of Elderwick Hall. Dandelions, the charity seems marvellous, but the other chap who's interested in snapping up the old place, Don Carter-Bell, my goodness, what an arleas man he is.'

'Arleas?'

Albert grinned. 'Old English, means dishonourable. He bought another estate a few years back, over in Lancashire, got a deluge of government grants for re-wilding areas previously used for intensive farming, and promptly blocked access to ancient rights of way, diverted the course of a river – can you believe it – and strung barbed wire across the waterway to prevent anyone traversing by boat! He shall not be welcome here. I have passed this on to Petra, who is of the same mind, but I'm not sure about Marcus.'

Laurel heard his words, and at any other time she would have been equally horrified, but her mind was fixed on the murder.

Albert chuckled. 'I can see, my dear, you have other things on your mind.'

Once the kettle was boiled and he was settled at the kitchen table with a mug of steaming tea and a Jammie Dodger, Albert picked up their original topic of conversation. 'My source tells me the detectives, having spoken to the deceased gentleman's employer, have discovered that he, Simon, was known for never being without his journal. Suspiciously, no such item was found at the crime scene or anywhere else they've searched. My understanding is they asked Dorothy in to see if she knew of its whereabouts or could shed light on anyone who had been in contact with Simon who might have taken it.'

'And did she tell them anything useful?'

'Evidently not.'

'Who is this source of yours? Are they involved in the investigation directly?'

'Now, you must know I can't reveal any names, but no, he's not involved directly. Nonetheless, I would bet a pretty penny there's nothing that goes on in that station he doesn't know about eventually.' Albert helped himself to another biscuit.

Laurel stood up and began wiping a dishcloth over the worktops as she processed the latest information. Despite all her protestations, she couldn't resist a good puzzle and this murder was a doozy: a locked room; a well-regarded journalist stabbed in the back; a famous author; and now a missing journal. There must be vital information in that book, maybe even a clue that pointed to his murderer. Why else would it have been taken? Simon had been in Elderwick working with Hugh. Did that suggest Hugh was involved somehow?

Another question occurred to her. 'Albert, Dorothy was awfully keen we get that door open before we called the police, don't you think?'

On his third or possibly fourth biscuit, Albert paused in his crunching. 'Mmph...' He stopped, swallowed and started again. 'Maybe. I'm not sure why you find that suspicious, though?'

'Nor am I really. She was just very insistent. Perhaps I should have a chat with her.'

'If you wish to try. Or, as previously discussed, you might want to enlist Maggie, as she may have more success. Not to cause offence, but you saw for yourself that Dorothy isn't your number one fan.'

Laurel pulled a face. 'Maggie is pretty busy these days. I don't know if she could fit me into her schedule.' She regretted her tone the moment the words were out of her mouth. She knew she was being childish.

Albert was watching her. He patted her hand.

'I know I'm being ridiculous, but you and Maggie are the

closest friends I've ever had. Before moving here, I spent so much of my life keeping people at a distance, I'm not sure I know how to find a healthy balance in friendships.' Heat burned in her cheeks. As a forty-one-year-old, it was embarrassing to admit she needed help making and keeping friends. She snagged the packet of biscuits and stuffed one into her mouth so she couldn't say anything else stupid.

'A friend is like a four-leaf clover, hard to find, and lucky to have. In no time you and Maggie will be getting on again like a house on fire, especially with this murder to solve. If anyone can solve this, my dear, I bet my boots it'll be you two.'

Alone again, once Albert had left to get on with planting his new stock of Brazen Hussys, Laurel collected the post that had just been delivered and went back into the kitchen. Tossing the envelopes onto the table she grabbed a glass and filled it from the tap then nudged out a chair to sit and sift through the mail. She put aside two bills and a leaflet about the Dandelions charity before coming to a nondescript white envelope. It was hand addressed and had a local postmark. Intrigued, she ran her finger under the flap and pulled out a single piece of paper.

You shouldn't be here and you need to leave because your getting everyone who knows you killed. Leave Elderwick

It wasn't assembled using words cut from a newspaper, but it may as well have been: it had the same poisonous feel. Naturally, there was no signature.

She re-read the menacing missive. Was it a threat, a

warning, or a command? She scrutinised the paper, the envelope and the handwriting, but there were no useful clues as to the identity of the sender other than a postmark from Beverley, the local market town.

Taking another sip of water, Laurel examined the words. True, there had been two murders the year before, but one had happened on her first day in the village. She'd never met the victim in life. The second was the murder of a local busybody with whom she'd had a couple of mild run-ins. She'd known him – very briefly – but so did the rest of the village. Simon was a complete stranger. The letter made no sense.

She was curious as to who had written it and why, but with a murderer on the loose, she had more pressing matters on her mind.

Chapter 9

Maggie

Maggie gave the eggs and mushrooms one last stir in the frying pan before spooning them onto the waiting plate. She reached the toaster just as the toast popped up, buttered and cut the slices, and placed them, just so, next to the eggs. 'Voila, a proper breakfast to get you started.'

Natalie, having only recently surfaced from bed, was still in her pyjamas. 'My goodness, this looks delicious, but I don't think I'll be able to manage it all.' She picked up her fork but made no move to eat, being more interested in whatever was on her mobile phone.

The wifi password had been the first thing Natalie had asked for when they were done moving her belongings over from The Snooty Fox. Nicholas, Maggie's soon-to-be ex-husband, was another one who'd always been glued to his phone. With a grim smile, she revelled in the knowledge that he'd be self-catering these days, and he was a useless cook.

'Don't worry, just have what you like and leave the rest. Though, at the risk of sounding like your mother, it is the most important meal of the day.' She knew it wasn't done to remark these days, but Natalie could do with a bit of meat on her bones.

Under the kitchen lights, the young woman looked unwell, with dark circles under her eyes and a cold sore coming in at the corner of her mouth.

'When you invited me to stay, I didn't expect you to cater for me, too. Honestly, a bit of cereal and a coffee will do me in a morning. Most days just coffee is fine.'

'The least I can do is to give you a good start, and it's my pleasure. I enjoy cooking. Today, all you need to do is relax, unwind, and let me take care of you after this nasty business with the murder.' It was a welcome change having company again too, Maggie thought. Not that she missed her bully of a husband, but another person in the house was a comfort.

'I hope you don't mind me asking,' she continued, 'but are you all right? Did you sleep well? I can get you a thicker or thinner duvet, or more pillows. Whatever you need.'

'I slept like a baby, and I'm fine. I think maybe the stress of Simon's death and how upset Hugh was, it all got to me a bit. But I'm good. I need to be as I won't be relaxing. I'm not one hundred per cent sure what Hugh has planned for today, but I'll bet it's going to be a busy one.'

'On a Saturday? That's a shame, but hopefully, you'll be able to finish early.'

Natalie gave a non-committal shrug. 'The media guys won't stick around, so I need to keep them in the loop, keep the story on their radar so we can build the hype for Hugh's new book.'

Maggie's heart leapt. 'His new book. Can you tell me more about it yet?'

Natalie frowned and sucked in her cheeks. 'I can't really say anything, but Hugh will be making an announcement in the press soon. Today, he'll want to discuss our strategy for launch, so I expect I'll be hearing from him soon.' She tapped a ragged nail on her mobile phone.

'I wouldn't rely on him getting hold of you that way; there's next to no signal in the village. But I suppose you can use WhatsUp instead?'

'App.'

'What?'

'It's App, WhatsApp.'

'Okay.'

Natalie tried some of the eggs and took a bite of toast. Chasing the mouthful with a slurp of her coffee, she sat back and asked, 'So, Maggie, have you always been a fan?'

Maggie settled herself into one of the other chairs at the table and reached for a banana. 'Of Hugh? Oh yes, I've been reading his books from the start. I like to try to solve the murders myself, but I never manage it. I imagine it's wonderful to work for him?' Thinking about it, she was a little surprised at how young Natalie was to have such a prestigious responsibility. Hugh must be one of the higher profile authors managed by the agency.

'It's a privilege, it really is. He's an amazing talent. I have other authors on my list, but none of them is a star like Hugh.'

'And he's here in our little village. I still can't believe it.' Maggie cleared her throat, wondering if she should ask again. 'You know I asked about Hugh possibly giving a talk at one of our WI meetings?'

'Oh yes, sorry, I nearly forgot. I didn't think he'd be available, and I'm not convinced he has the time, but I ran the idea past him and he's really keen. To be honest, I think he'd like to use the opportunity to ask around about Simon's murder. See if there's any information your ladies might have that would be useful to his consulting with the police. I mean, he'd like to give the talk too, it's not just so he can gather information.'

Maggie clapped her hands, her eyes shining. 'That's wonderful. Thank you, Natalie. I mentioned to one or two of the members that it might happen and they're all very excited. I shouldn't think they'll know anything about the murder, but Hugh's welcome to ask his questions. It'll be like we're all helping him help the police. How exciting.'

'Perfect. I'll finalise the details with you later. And now, I really should run. I doubt Hugh'll have got much food in, so I'll stop by the bakery and get him some pastries.' She stood up and glanced apologetically at her full plate.

Maggie waved her away with a smile. 'Go, it's fine.'

Natalie flashed a grin, pocketed her phone, and grabbed her coat. Maggie winced as she banged the front door closed behind her.

Waste not, want not, she thought, as she pulled the breakfast plate towards her. She was about to try the eggs when there was a knock at the back door. She wasn't expecting anyone. Maybe it was Hugh. The idea sent a shiver up her spine and made her hands shake. She checked her reflection in the side of the toaster.

'Dorothy, what a surprise,' she said, deflating. Standing in the open doorway, she felt the stiff breeze pulling at her hair and clothes and smelt the recent rain. With a fixed smile on her face, she asked, 'How are you? Would you like to come in?'

Hunched in a shapeless grey cagoule, Dorothy looked miserable. 'I won't, thank you. I've just come by to tell you I wholeheartedly disapprove of Mr Quintrell being invited to speak at the WI meeting next week.' She held up a hand as Maggie opened her mouth to speak. 'No, I'll say what I've come to say and then I'll leave it to your conscience.'

'Right...'

'The *Women's* Institute is about giving women a voice and being a force for good in the community.'

Maggie was familiar with the characterisation; Dorothy's words were straight from WI literature.

'Mr Quintrell is not a good man: he treated both his ex-wives abominably; he exploited his daughter; his books are full of awful characters; he glorifies death, torture, and drugs.' She sucked in a breath. 'Did you know he was involved in a very... unfortunate event when he was at school? I bet that's not included in his little *about the author* blurb in his books. In short, he is not the sort of person who should be given a platform by the WI.'

With each exhalation the cloud of vapour around her head billowed. Though she'd never say it aloud, Maggie thought it fitting for a dragon like Dorothy.

'That's all I'll say on the matter, I'm no gossip. If you go ahead with the invite, I and a significant number of the other women will boycott the meeting. You know, I thought you of all people would know better than to tolerate such a despicable man, Maggie.'

Maggie glared at her. 'Are you referring to Nicholas? You've no right.' Although she no longer jumped to an automatic defence of her crook of a husband, that didn't mean she was comfortable with other people making judgements and telling her how she should feel.

As for the attack on Hugh, she wouldn't stand for that. They say never meet your heroes, but Hugh had been so charming when she and Laurel had run in to him by the green. Plus, the poor man was only now coming to terms with the death of his journalist colleague. She didn't know why Dorothy was making up all this nonsense.

'You know nothing about Hugh Quintrell. Boycott all you like.' She stepped back into the house and closed the door in the other woman's face. It wasn't quite a slam, but not far off.

Heart racing, shocked by how bold she'd been, which wasn't like her at all, Maggie took a moment to be thankful Natalie had already left before Dorothy's arrival. She didn't want anything to jeopardise Hugh's WI appearance. No one was going to mess up this opportunity for her.

Chapter 10

Laurel

'Bloody Dorothy,' exclaimed Maggie the moment she walked in the door.

Laurel grinned. That was strong language coming from her friend. 'You'd better sit down. I'll make you a cup of hot chocolate and you can vent.'

It had pleased her immensely when Maggie had called to ask if she could come round. Just Maggie – no Natalie, no Hetty – just Maggie. Finally, the original crime-busting duo would have a chance to put together some initial thoughts about the murder. If she was going to beat Hugh, they needed to get ahead of the game.

Their foray into sleuthing might have to wait, though, if Maggie's opening salvo was anything to go by. From the kitchen, Laurel could hear pacing and muttering. It must be bad. She willed the kettle to get on and boil so she could go back in to hear all about it.

Once installed with her steaming cup of liquid chocolate, Maggie recounted Dorothy's visit with much vigour and invective. Ire eventually exhausted, she heaved a sigh and slumped back on the squashy sofa.

For once, Laurel measured her words before opening her mouth and decided to keep some of her thoughts to herself. She didn't agree with Dorothy's insistence that Hugh should not speak to the WI, but she concurred that Hugh was probably not the paragon of virtue and genius of Maggie's perception. That said, what was it about Hugh that had got so far up Dorothy's nose? It was curious. Perhaps he'd had a run-in with her when meeting with Simon at Dorothy's holiday cottage? It bore further investigation, but she wouldn't raise it while Maggie was already in a tizzy about the woman.

'You really don't like him, do you?' accused Maggie.

Her face hadn't got the message about being discreet if Maggie had read her that easily.

'I'm sure if you get to know him better, you'll see. His books are first class, and Natalie is devoted to him, so he can't be all that bad. Have you read the book I lent you yet?'

Stealing a guilty glance towards the corner of the room where, under a pile of scarves and gloves, the tome languished, Laurel remembered how she'd flung it down with little thought and left it where it lay. She should have taken more care with it. It was Maggie's precious signed copy. 'It's upstairs on my bedside table, ready for me to begin tonight,' she fibbed. She absolutely intended to read it but doubted it would change her mind about its author. The titles of his books alone left her nauseated.

The one saving grace was it was his debut novel, a work which had at least garnered decent reviews. Pigs would fly before she would subject herself to his ninth, *The Therapy of Death*. Particularly as Hugh had implied she could learn from it. *The nerve!*

'Let's talk about this murder, shall we?' She mentally crossed her fingers, hoping they could move the conversation onto safer ground.

'Good idea.' Maggie's eyes brightened and she sat forward on the sofa. 'I have so much to tell you. I think I already have a clue. I don't know what it means or if it's even significant, but I know you'll make sense of the information.'

It frustrated Laurel how often Maggie put herself down, even now that she was free of Nicholas's pernicious influence. 'You said it yourself we make a great team. We'll figure this out.' *And long before Hugh*, she thought, but didn't say.

'And I've got these.' With a flourish, Maggie pulled two brand-new notebooks from her handbag and held them aloft. 'What colour would you like? I rather like the yellow myself.'

'Then I'll go with green.' Laurel reached for the soft leather-bound book and flipped through the deliciously empty pages waiting to be filled with clues and theories. Last time there had been murders in the village, she and Maggie spent many a productive hour reviewing the evidence they'd gleaned, evidence which resulted in the unmasking of a disturbed killer. It had also led to a falling-out and an attempt on Laurel's life, but before that, it had been invigorating.

She ferreted out a pen from the junk drawer in the coffee table. 'Let's start with what we know, then go on to what you've discovered.' She printed carefully on the first page:

VICTIM - SIMON FORSTER

'So, Simon was staying in Tulip Cottage which is owned by Dorothy Little. He was found dead on Tuesday morning, also by Dorothy. Plus, Albert and me.'

Maggie copied the details into her own book. 'How long had he been staying there?'

Laurel turned to the next page. 'Wasn't it about four days? We can check.'

'Put down his occupation and the reason he was in Elderwick. Do you think it would be useful to look up some of the work he's done in the past? To get a sense of what he was like as a journalist?'

Laurel smiled. This was fun, challenging her brain with Maggie. *Talking* about a crime wasn't going to get them into any tricky situations. 'Good idea. Now, what clue have you winkled out without me?'

'I heard this from Dorothy, so we might need to question the truthfulness. Dorothy said she saw Simon meeting Christopher on Monday evening. They met for around an hour, apparently.' Maggie explained how she'd come by her information. 'In the vestry, on Wednesday, with the vicar. It sounds like a game of Cluedo!' She chuckled.

'That's pretty significant. Christopher could have been the last person to see Simon alive. But how did Dorothy know they met and for how long?'

'See, that's what I mean, I didn't even think about how Dorothy knew. I assumed she saw Simon heading into the church. But you're right, did she hang around waiting until he left? That would be strange. It's not like her house has a view of the church.'

Laurel was scribbling away. This was a solid start.

'Christopher was very reluctant to discuss it too. He looked positively distressed.'

'Well, Dorothy can have that effect on people, and I'm sure he doesn't want her running round the village spreading rumours. Especially if Simon was there for confession or whatever the Church of England calls that kind of thing. Let's make it an action to see if he'll talk to us about it.'

Maggie looked sceptical. 'We can ask, but I got the feeling he thought the meeting was a secret so I can't see him being keen to discuss it.' She tapped her pen against the page of her notebook. 'In case he won't divulge, do we have anything else to go on?'

'Albert had some useful information from his informant at the police station. Apparently, Simon was well known for having a journal in which he kept all his working before writing his articles. And guess what the police haven't been able to find? And guess who let herself into Tulip Cottage on Tuesday morning when she thought Simon was out? And if that was the first time she'd done it, I'll eat my hat.'

'My goodness. She wouldn't?'

Laurel got up. She was feeling a familiar fizz of energy. An excitement that they could do this, they could solve this murder. 'There's one more thing, we both noticed it. Remember when we first met Natalie and then Hugh showed up? Do you recall what he said when he found out about Simon's death?'

Maggie fidgeted but conceded, 'Yes, I suppose it struck me as odd.'

'Exactly. The first thing Hugh said when Natalie told him Simon was dead was, "How was he *killed?*"'

Chapter 11

Laurel

Notwithstanding the hard wooden seat and the chill seeping into her bones, Laurel felt herself nodding towards sleep. The gentle voice was a lullaby, soft tones sending her deeper, eyelids drifting, drifting closed.

A cough from nearby brought her head snapping back up. She stole a furtive look at her neighbours. No one seemed to have noticed. Better yet, the elderly gentleman beside her was emitting delicate snores of his own.

She'd sung along with the first hymn, the words coming back to her across the years from her primary school days, but the sermon was soporific. Despite the recent murder, the Reverend Christopher Ibori had pressed on with the topic of the upcoming season of Lent. Perhaps it was too short notice for him to have written a piece that spoke to the upsetting events.

'Now, if you'll permit me, I wish to say a few words about the sad passing of a man who most of you will not have known, but of whom you have no doubt heard, the late Mr Simon Forster.'

So, he was getting a mention.

Laurel sat up straight and edged forward in her seat,

listening to Christopher's words, searching for any sense he had known Simon personally. None was forthcoming. It was a generic address, noting Mr Forster's career, the work which had brought him to Elderwick, and the kindness he'd been shown by the local people. Christopher was eschewing any direct reference to murder.

'I urge you, each and every one, give thanks for those around you, those who love and care for you, and who you love and care for in return, whether they be family, friends, fellow Christians or not. I am available should you wish to speak in confidence about the events of this past week, or indeed any matters by which you are troubled. My door is always open.

'And speaking of open doors,' he continued, 'some of you may be aware of Dandelions. They're a charity for inner-city and disadvantaged children and they have made a bid to purchase Elderwick Hall.'

There were murmurs amongst the congregation.

'If successful, they have provisional permissions from the planning and local authorities. Their intention is to open a centre specifically for youngsters from cities and deprived areas in the north of England. A centre to which they can come to enjoy our beautiful countryside.

'They are an organisation close to my heart, having grown up on the Orchard Park Estate in Hull, and they've asked our local councillor and myself to be involved in liaising with you, the residents of Elderwick. Every house should by now have received a copy of their leaflet – thank you members of the WI for delivering them – giving details of their existing centres and their vision for Elderwick Hall. I encourage you to have a read and if you're interested in more information, go to their webpage or contact myself or Geoffrey at the council offices in Beverley.'

It sounded to Laurel as though Dandelions was lobbying for

support amongst the local populace. She made a mental note to drop Petra an email, offer her endorsement, and add her voice to those encouraging a sale to the charity over the private buyer.

The rest of the service passed quickly, and Laurel felt butterflies stirring in her stomach as the end approached. She wasn't religious but questioning a man of the cloth sat uneasily. She doubted he was a likely suspect for the murder, but, apart from the killer, Christopher could well be the person last to have seen Simon alive.

As the congregation were gathering coats and children, preparing to brave the cold Sunday outside the doors, Laurel looked around for Maggie and caught sight of her in the third pew from the front. She raised her hand but lowered it again when she spied Natalie and Hugh alongside her friend.

'Hey, it's Laurel, isn't it?'

A tall blonde came into view from her left, distracting her. It took Laurel a second to place her. 'Elise, hi.' Not someone she'd expected to see in the little church of St Stephen's. 'Is Ben not with you this morning?'

'Ben, no, he's a dyed in the wool atheist.'

'It's a bit of a schlep from Cherry Burton, isn't it, to come to Elderwick this early for a Sunday service?'

Elise squinted and cocked her head to one side. 'Not really, and besides, Ben lives two minutes up the road, so...' She flushed. 'I hope that doesn't offend you, what with us not being married?'

'Oh God no! I'm such an idiot, of course you stay at Ben's. I mean, not oh God ... sorry, I've probably offended you now?' Her cheeks burned.

'It'll take a lot more than that to offend me.' Elise smiled. 'I was worried there for a second.' She lowered her voice. 'I thought you might be one of those extreme Christians. You know, people must never live in sin and all that.'

'Hardly! I'm afraid I'm only Christian by upbringing rather than by practice ... or belief.' *Great, keep talking,* she thought, *see if you can insult her faith a bit more, why don't you.* 'What I mean is I'm here to um...' She couldn't think of a reasonable excuse. 'To meet with the vicar.' She left it there, trusting Elise would be too polite to pry.

'Ladies...'

Hugh appeared at her elbow, Maggie and Natalie hovering close behind. Maggie was beaming. This must be a dream come true for her. Natalie, though, appeared fraught. She had her phone in her hand, thumbs dancing over the tiny screen, a frown deepening on her forehead.

'What a delight to see you here,' said Hugh. He took Laurel's hands in his and held them. 'But Maggie tells me you're here for detection rather than the divine since Reverend Christopher Ibori may have been the last to see Simon alive. Interesting.' He squeezed and let go, reaching now for Elise.

Laurel cast a glare at Maggie who was studiously looking elsewhere. How would they get rid of him now so they could question Christopher in confidence?

As Hugh's hands brushed at Elise, the woman shrank back and shrugged him off, a grimace on her lips. 'I have to head out, I'm afraid,' she said already walking away. 'Laurel, ring me. We'll have that coffee.'

Hugh mimed confusion and a muscle in his cheek twitched. Presumably, he wasn't used to people who didn't fall over themselves to make his acquaintance. She'd have to quiz Elise about that if she could find an opportunity.

'Christopher's finished his goodbyes at the door. Shall we see if we can borrow a moment with him now?' suggested Maggie who hadn't been watching the exchange. 'Hugh thinks it would be enlightening to speak with him too. It makes sense that he joins us, don't you think?'

The deal was done. Laurel felt she couldn't refuse without being rude. It was infuriating. She'd bet he hadn't even known the vicar had met with Simon until Maggie had blabbed. Since moving to Elderwick, Maggie had become one of her dearest friends, but at times, she wanted to shake her.

'Since you're assisting me with my investigation, Laurel, you can take notes while I take the lead?' Hugh declared. 'And Natalie?' he cast around. 'Where's she got to? Oh, there you are.' He'd spotted her sitting in a pew. 'Come on, there's no time for sitting around. You take Maggie and work through that list I gave you. Dear Maggie, you don't mind accompanying Natalie, do you? I think she'll benefit from your input.' He didn't wait for an answer and shooed them towards the door.

Maggie blinked and looked from Laurel to Hugh. Laurel raised her eyebrows and shrugged. Maggie had invited Hugh into this; she'd made her bed.

As they left, Maggie and Natalie passed Christopher, who was making his way back down the aisle, head bowed. When he looked up, Laurel could see the strain in his face and tiredness about his eyes.

He reached them and held out his hands, thanking them for attending the service, and presumably waiting for them to take the hint and leave.

'We need to talk,' said Hugh.

Christopher's face fell. After a breathless pause he replied, 'You'd better come through.'

Chapter 12

Maggie

Feeling dazed at how quickly she'd lost control of the situation, Maggie trailed after Natalie. 'What is it exactly that Hugh wants us to do?' she asked.

'Hmm, I have a list, but to be honest, it doesn't really need the two of us. You've probably got your own things you want to be getting on with?'

Maggie pouted. 'I was planning to see Reverend Christopher with Laurel, so no. I'm at something of a loose end now. Besides, many hands make light work, and once we're finished, we could go to the tearoom for a spot of lunch?' Now she no longer had to produce a full Sunday roast for her husband, Maggie rather enjoyed indulging in one of Jo's vegetarian weekend specials. Her mouth watered at the thought of a leek and potato gratin or perhaps a lentil curry.

Natalie pulled out her phone and peered at the screen. 'Actually, I need to speak to the owner of The Pleasant Pheasant. That's the tearoom, isn't it? I suppose we could do that together, but I probably won't eat.'

Maggie agreed, hoping she might still persuade Natalie to stay for lunch afterwards. Not that she minded eating alone, and goodness knows, there was nearly always someone in the tearoom to chat with, but Natalie was interesting company. In a village the size of Elderwick, she'd heard the same few stories, the same gossip over and over. Natalie was young, and vibrant, probably had lots of salacious tales of life in the city to share.

'Is this the way?' Natalie was pointing to South Street to the right. 'I haven't got my bearings yet.'

'No, this way,' said Maggie, as she turned left onto North Street. Natalie had only been there a few days, but how she couldn't navigate between two of the most obvious landmarks – the church and the tearoom – was baffling. Though many visitors got confused by North Street changing into South Street halfway along. 'What do you need to ask Jo?'

'Apparently, Simon made a habit of having breakfast there, so Hugh wants to know if he mentioned anything to this Jo that could be useful in the investigation.'

Picturing the usual breakfast-time rush of locals and builders from the new housing estate on the edge of the village, Maggie doubted Jo would have had time to chat with Simon. She didn't want to dishearten Natalie, though, so she didn't mention it.

'What's Jo like? Fill me in before we get there.'

The image that came to mind when thinking of the cook and owner was of a whirling ball of energy bouncing from table to kitchen to table. 'She's the nicest person and the most efficient cook I know. She only has help a few days a week, and while she gets her baked goods from Hetty and Constance at the bakery, she makes everything else from scratch. She's a wizard with food.' Maggie's stomach rumbled just thinking about it. 'Can a woman be a wizard, do you think? Calling her a witch wouldn't sound right.'

Natalie was tapping away on her phone again. 'You'll need to introduce me,' she said as they walked across the green towards the brightly lit windows of The Pleasant Pheasant. 'What's with all the twee names around here, anyway? The Pleasant Pheasant, The Snooty Fox, and what's the bakery again? The Plump Tart?'

Maggie bristled. 'You're in the heart of East Yorkshire, it's...' She didn't get to finish her defence of her beloved village before Natalie bounded up the steps, hauled open the door of the tearoom, and swept inside.

It was early enough that only three of the seven tables were occupied but glorious aromas were coming from the kitchen. Maggie inhaled deeply: bacon, sausages, toast, and was that apple-cinnamon? She regretted having eaten breakfast already, especially when she stole a look at the chalkboard with the lunch menu, noting with delight that spanakopita was the special of the day.

'Where is she?' whispered Natalie.

Maggie indicated Natalie should sit at one of the empty tables whilst she went to see if Jo could spare a minute.

'It is a murder investigation. Remind her,' hissed Natalie.

Peeking round the door of the kitchen, Maggie caught Jo's attention and, in a low voice, explained the situation. 'If you're too busy, just say and I'll put her off. I don't think she appreciates how much you have to do.'

'It's fine. I can spare a couple of minutes. But first, taste this.' Jo proffered a sliver of spanakopita pie on a fork.

'Mmm.' Maggie closed her eyes and savoured the bite. 'I've died and gone to heaven. This is... wow!'

'I got the recipe from Elise, Ben's new girlfriend, the chef. Greek food is her speciality. We've been talking about doing a themed diner service once a week and she said she'd help out with a Greek night. Do you think people would come?'

'Without a doubt. You can put me down now, and Laurel, I bet she'd love it.'

'Excuse me.'

They spun round to see Natalie in the doorway, little frown lines around her eyes but not so much as pucker on her forehead. 'Sorry, I was hoping we could have a quick chat? About the murder. Honestly, it really is quite important.'

Natalie was smiling at Jo, but Maggie thought she heard frustration in her tone. It upset her. Jo was a busy woman, and Natalie shouldn't expect to waltz in and have everyone drop what they were doing. Then again, Natalie was only helping Hugh, and there was good reason. It was about a murder. Her annoyance quickly quashed, Maggie assured Jo they'd only take a few moments of her time.

Seated as far as possible from the other patrons, Natalie pulled out her phone, wiped the table with a napkin, and placed the handset between them. 'I'm going to record this so I can share it with Hugh later. I hope that's okay?' Without pausing for an answer, she launched into her questions. 'What can you tell me about Simon Forster?'

Maggie thought she caught a look of distaste flash across Jo's face.

'I don't think there's much I can tell you beyond he would come in for his breakfast, around 9am if I remember rightly. Every time he ordered a full English, extra toast, and he would read the papers as he ate. He was a crossword fan, so he'd have the actual paper, and he'd stay until he finished the cryptic one. Never took him long.'

'Did you notice–'

'Now hold on there, before you carry on down your list, I have a question of my own. Why are *you* here asking about him? Isn't this a job for the police?' Jo folded her arms and Maggie could feel her foot tapping against the table leg. She had Natalie in the full beam of her stare.

Jo could be a formidable woman and scary when so

inclined. Maggie remembered a recent afternoon when a new lad from the building site, had been getting loud, swearing and causing a nuisance. Jo asked him to calm down and when he upped the offence level of his language instead, she seized him by the earlobe and hauled him right on out the door. His more sensible colleagues – who had been enjoying their daily bacon butties and afternoon tea breaks at the café for weeks already – apologised and promised never to bring him back again.

'I'm here on behalf of Hugh Quintrell, and he is working alongside the police in their investigation. Isn't that right, Maggie?'

Feeling put on the spot, Maggie thought it was probably true, but she had no proof Hugh was officially working with the authorities. 'I think that's right,' she hedged.

'Fine. One more question, then I have to get on. Make it a good one.'

Natalie swiped away at her phone and made a couple of false starts before settling on her final query. 'Was he always here alone?'

Jo gave a tight smile. 'That is a good one.'

Natalie flushed and looked pleased.

'He was alone every day, bar one.'

No one spoke and seconds ticked by.

'Oh, now Jo, that's very funny, but you have to tell us who he was with.' Maggie was uncomfortable.

With a sigh and a frown, Jo relented. 'I expect you'll only hear from someone else if not me. If you must know, he was in here on Monday morning with Ben's girlfriend, Elise, but that's all I can tell you. Now, I've really got to get on.'

Chapter 13

Laurel

Christopher ushered Laurel and Hugh into the vestry and motioned for them to sit. The room was already stuffy and became positively cramped once the door was closed. Books covered most surfaces, and rugs of various sizes patterned the floor. A high, dusty window let in the weak February light.

'You don't mind if I change while we're talking, do you?' the vicar asked. 'Only, I can't stay long. I'm visiting parishioners this afternoon and before that, I've arranged to have lunch with Albert.' He removed the green stole from around his neck and placed it on a hanger in a narrow cupboard behind the door, taking his time to smooth it out, and keeping his face turned away from them.

'Thank you, Christopher, we appreciate your time, and we certainly wouldn't want to monopolise you or keep you from your flock.' Behind Christopher's back, Hugh mimed writing to Laurel. She knew what he meant, but she wasn't going to give him the satisfaction; she wasn't his secretary.

'You probably know we're here to ask about Simon.' Hugh let the question hang as Christopher lifted his surplice over his

71

head, messing up his hair. He remained resolutely facing the cupboard.

'And we believe you might have been the last person to see him alive.'

Christopher's shoulders slumped and his head dropped. He stood motionless for a moment before facing them. 'I suppose Dorothy told you?'

Whilst Laurel was positive it had been Maggie who let the cat out of the bag to Hugh, she didn't want to get her friend into any bother, so she made a non-committal noise and asked a question of her own. 'Can you tell us why Simon came to see you?' She could practically feel Hugh's glare, but she ignored him.

Christopher undid a couple of buttons on his cassock and subsided into the only remaining chair. 'Even if he came here – and I'm not saying that he did – surely, you know I wouldn't be able to talk to you about it?'

'We don't need to know specifics, but you need to give us the gist. You see that, don't you? It is a murder investigation.' Hugh held out his hands, palm up, appealing to the vicar. 'Have the police spoken to you already?'

'If the police need to speak to me, they know where to find me. I'm not comfortable with the two of you doing... whatever it is you believe you're doing.'

Laurel didn't know Christopher well. She'd seen him around the village, and they'd said hello once or twice. The longest conversation they'd had was when in line at the bakery sometime in January, where they'd discovered a mutual love of cinnamon buns. He seemed a likeable man, quite quiet. He wore black and his dog collar most of the time but hadn't tried to convert her over the cabinet of croissants, for which she was glad. The last thing she wanted to do was upset the man, he was new to the village like her. Plus, she didn't want to give Hugh further ammunition. Unfortunately, curiosity got the better of her.

'Do the police *know* you met with Simon?' She watched as he closed his eyes. It was all the answer she needed.

'You know, you're right, we should let the police handle this,' said Hugh, settling back further in his chair, eyes fixed on Christopher.

The vestry was warm, but Laurel felt the temperature drop.

When Christopher next spoke, his voice was flat but there was a vein pulsing at his temple. 'You are well within your rights to speak with the police and share your... gossip.'

She wanted to defuse the tension but couldn't find the words.

'That's a good point,' continued Hugh. 'We don't want to bother the authorities with *gossip*. If you were to give us more information, we would probably decide there's no need to take this further after all.'

She was watching Christopher's face closely. His eyes narrowed. She almost missed the bare hint of a twitch at the corner of his mouth.

'I am sure you, of all people, Mr Quintrell, would not wish me to breach the confidentiality constraints to which I am beholden?'

He's got something on Hugh, she realised. Hadn't Maggie mentioned Dorothy also seeing Hugh visiting Christopher?

Hugh's nostrils flared and his lips compressed into a hard line. 'Quite,' he snapped.

Round one to Christopher.

Chapter 14

Laurel

They left the church by the side door but had barely gone twenty yards when Christopher called to Laurel and beckoned her back, away from Hugh. Crunching along the gravel path, she shivered as she returned to hear what he wanted of her.

In a low voice, the vicar asked, 'Before you go, can I ask if you saw Dorothy in church today?'

Laurel thought back, picturing the people around her during the morning service. 'No.' There hadn't been that many in the congregation, if Dorothy had been there, it would have been hard to miss her. 'I don't think so.'

A frown appeared on Christopher's face.

'Is something wrong?'

'Dorothy never misses a Sunday, and this week she's on the rota to help with the tidying up. You know, collecting up the hymn books and so forth. Maybe she's unwell? I might pop round and check on her.'

Seizing the moment, Laurel offered. 'I'm heading in that direction now. Shall I call in and see if she's okay? I can pop round to Albert's afterwards and let you know.'

Christopher's smile lit up his face. 'That would be most helpful. If you're sure you don't mind?' He took her hand and held it between his own. 'Before you go, I hope you don't mind me saying,' he leaned in to whisper, 'I would think carefully about aligning yourself with Mr Quintrell.' He released his hold.

Taken off guard by Christopher's blunt advice, Laurel nodded and watched him disappear back inside. There was definitely something going on between Hugh and the vicar.

'What was all that about?' asked Hugh as she caught up to him. His eyes darted between her and the closed church door, the fingers of his right hand tapping against his leg.

'Oh, nothing.' Her mind was busy filtering the likely reasons for Christopher's words.

'What did he say to you just then? Was it about me?'

With wide eyes, she regarded him. 'No, what could he have possibly wanted to say to me about you?' It was unlikely she'd be able to draw him on whatever was making him so uneasy, but it was worth a shot.

'Nothing. Nothing at all. Look, I've got some things to catch up on. I have to go.'

'Okay, I'll see you around.'

'Yes. Yes, you will. We've got another appointment booked for tomorrow.' He'd rallied, he was back to confident Hugh. 'Don't go forgetting.'

As if she could.

She waited to see which way he was going. There was a weak sun struggling through the clouds. It offered precious little warmth, but it made the day that bit less depressing. The graveyard was pleasant enough, for what it was, the graves tidy and the foliage under control. Towards the back, she knew, away from the entrance, were the oldest headstones, many of them bearing the name Hartfield, the family who had owned, lived, and died at Elderwick Hall for decades.

Laurel shuddered, both the house and the Hartfields had a long and tragic history. She hoped Petra and Marcus could put it all behind them and find the new start they were hoping to have in the South of France.

Giving Hugh a head start, she meandered through the graves before lingering in the shelter of the lych-gate until Hugh was out of sight. Then she slipped away, heading in the opposite direction, up to School Lane, past the primary school, and onto West Street, towards Dorothy's house.

It was 11.45am. She pressed the button for the doorbell but couldn't hear anything inside, so she tried knocking instead. As she waited, the poison pen letter floated into her thoughts. This would be the ideal time to challenge Dorothy about it; it felt like the kind of thing the older woman might do. Since finding it on her doorstep the day before, no other suspects had come to mind.

Dorothy's car was on the driveway and all the curtains in the house were closed. In the trees crowding over the narrow entranceway, birds gathered, feathers fluffed against the bite of the February wind.

'Dorothy,' she shouted. Tendrils of anxiety crept up her spine adding an edge to her voice. She jumped as three pigeons startled into the air, their ungainly wings loud in the hushed air.

There was a letterbox in the door. She could look through it, check nothing was obviously out of place. She hesitated. *If I find another dead body, Ben will never let me hear the end of it.*

Taking a deep breath, she bent down and pushed open the flap. There was nothing to be seen beyond except an empty hallway. A relieved laugh burst from her mouth. Of course, it had been ridiculous to think Dorothy was dead.

While she was down there, she may as well give it one more go. Dorothy was getting on a bit and could have fallen or be injured somewhere inside. With the letterbox open, she might hear a faint call for help, if there was one to be heard.

'Doro–' The word died on her lips. Something was moving in there. She squinted. The light was dim, but there was movement near the floor in a doorway to the left. 'Hello? Are you okay?' There was an odd smell she now noticed. She didn't sniff too deeply.

A grey cat trotted into the hallway and fixed her with haughty green eyes. The tension in her body ebbed.

'Hello. What's your name?' she cooed. The cat moved closer. 'What's that you've got all over you?' Leaving a trail of dainty footprints, the cat came and sat in front of the door. Laurel's stomach sank. From close up, there was no mistaking the reddish-brown stains around its mouth, chin, and whiskers.

'Oh crap.'

Chapter 15

Maggie

Elise sat in the armchair by the window, the light from behind making her a silhouette. Ben hadn't been keen to let Maggie and Natalie into the house, but Elise had waved away his concern.

'What can I help you with?' She crossed her legs and folded her arms.

The small front room was cosy in a mismatched furniture way, and spotlessly clean. It was full, but not cluttered, with tidy towers of old DVDs by the large television, books on built-in shelves on either side of the fireplace, and a vase of daffodils on the coffee table. To Maggie's eye it was a masculine space, but then, Ben and Elise hadn't been together all that long. Observing Ben's protective stance by his girlfriend's side, she bet it wouldn't be long before the stylish young chef was adding softer touches to this home.

'Is this about the murder?' Ben asked before they could reply to Elise. 'You have zero authority to be going round asking people questions.' He stood rigid, glaring at them.

'Ben,' Natalie smiled at him, all teeth and dimples, 'sit down. Honestly, it's fine. The senior investigating officer has given Hugh permission to dig around and see what theories present themselves. We're his assistants, you could say, busy little bees collecting evidence for him.'

Ben glowered, unmoved. 'From what I understand, Natalie, you're Hugh's literary agent, not an investigator. And frankly, the way your boss has wheedled his way into this case is disgusting. The SIO had no choice. The higher ups have been well and truly seduced by the idea they're going to be in a book, that it'll make them famous or whatever.'

Elise put out a hand and rested it on his arm. 'It's okay.' Ben's face continued to say otherwise. To Natalie she said, 'What do you want to know?'

'Why did you meet with Simon Forster at The Pleasant Pheasant last Monday morning?'

Maggie caught the twitch in Ben's jaw. She didn't think he'd known about the meeting.

Elise didn't look surprised at the question. 'Everyone knows everything round here, don't they?' She gave Ben's arm a squeeze before placing both hands in her lap. Her knuckles were white, betraying her tension. 'I recognised him and wanted to ask if he would be prepared to do a piece on the restaurant. Any publicity would be great for us and he's such a well-respected journalist.'

'And what was his answer?' asked Natalie.

'He said no. Said he was busy with a big article and food wasn't his thing, even if he wasn't otherwise occupied.'

'And that's it?'

'That's it.'

'He didn't offer to put you in touch with any restaurant critic colleagues of his, even?' Natalie pushed.

Elise paused before answering. 'No. He said he doesn't... didn't really know any.'

'That's interesting. And you were okay with him not

helping you out? Only, we heard the two of you were very intense, maybe even arguing?'

Maggie shot Natalie a look. Jo hadn't said anything of the sort; she'd refused to be drawn on giving any details.

Whether Elise had caught the pointed glance or not, she didn't take the bait. 'It was a perfectly amicable conversation. We chatted a bit about Elderwick, Jo's amazing food, and that was it.'

'Did you arrange to meet or just bump into him?'

'I'd seen him there before, having breakfast, so I took a shot he'd be in on Monday.'

'How come your boyfriend didn't know what you were up to? He looked surprised just then, when I asked you about it.' There was a hint of smugness in Natalie's tone.

For the first time, Elise appeared flustered, but Ben came to her rescue. 'I don't know what you're insinuating. I knew Elise was hoping to catch Simon, and even if I hadn't, I don't insist on knowing where she is and what she's doing every minute of the day. She's a grown woman.' The muscles in his jaw clenched. 'I want you both to leave now, please.' It was an order, not a request, no matter how polite.

Maggie hoped Natalie wouldn't make a fuss. The agent was only a visitor in Elderwick, whereas these people were her friends and neighbours.

'We might have more questions for you later,' Natalie threw out as they got up to leave.

'Sorry,' mouthed Maggie to Elise as soon as Natalie's back was turned. Elise didn't respond.

Back on the pavement, the door having been closed firmly on them, Natalie gripped Maggie's elbow and steered her away down the lane. Once round the corner and far enough away there was no chance of them being overheard by Ben or Elise, she stopped, triumph in her eyes.

'She lied to us.'

'What? How do you know?'

'She said Simon told her he didn't know any restaurant critics.'

'And?'

'He's married to one!'

Maggie let the information sink in. 'He could have been lying to her.'

'His wife is *The Observer* food critic. Being a chef, Elise will know of her even if she doesn't know she's married to Simon. Chances are she'd have found out sooner or later. I don't believe he would have lied about it.'

'So, why did *she* lie?' Maggie knew she was missing whatever it was Natalie was driving at.

'I guarantee she was lying about their entire conversation. We need to find out why she lied and what they were actually discussing. Once we do that, we might have a suspect for Simon's murder.'

Chapter 16

Laurel

'Oh, thank goodness.' Laurel rushed over to Maggie and threw her arms around her friend.

'What's going on? What's the ambulance for?'

Laurel almost couldn't bring herself to say it. 'It's Dorothy. She's been attacked. She's in a really bad way.' Around them, a police officer and a paramedic were in a heated conversation, whilst another officer urged onlookers to move back, or preferably, 'move on.'

Maggie clasped a hand to her chest. 'No!'

Adrenaline and shock made the words rush out. 'If I hadn't found her when I did... I mean, she still might not make it. Oh Maggie, what's going on in this village?'

Laurel explained how she'd found Dorothy covered in blood with only the faintest signs of breathing. 'It was only luck I came round at all, and if I hadn't seen her cat through the letterbox...'

Maggie pulled her in for a hug again. Laurel gave in to the tears and wept on her shoulder.

'It's one thing, finding the body of a stranger,' she sobbed, 'but I know Dorothy. I can't believe it. Who would do this to her? It must be connected to Simon's death. I need to tell the policeman.' She wiped her eyes and fished for a tissue to blow her nose. The need to ensure the authorities knew as much as possible gripped her. Dorothy was a defenceless old woman. Mean and a dreadful gossip, yes, but she hadn't deserved what had been done to her.

Before she could go to them, a policeman detached from his colleagues and approached. 'It's Laurel, isn't it love? I'm sorry, but it's not looking good. They're taking her off to hospital now. They'll do the best they can.' Though bulky and intimidating in his uniform, his gruff voice was sympathetic. He paused, giving her a moment for the news to sink in. 'We're going to need to ask you some questions. It's routine, nothing to worry about. The quicker we get the details, the quicker we can determine what's happened here.'

'Can we do it somewhere else?' Laurel asked. There were too many looky-loos gathered at the end of Dorothy's drive, eager for any gossip.

'We can go down to the station if you like?'

Before leaving, she had a quick word with Maggie. 'Can you tell Albert and Christopher what's happened? Christopher's having lunch with Albert. He's probably still there. I'll call you, okay?'

'Of course. Do you want me to do anything else, call anyone? Should I tell Natalie and Hugh?'

'Where is Natalie?'

'We went to the tearoom and then to see Elise. Natalie wanted to update Hugh after that, but I'm not sure where they are.'

'No, don't tell them. Not right now. Look, I'd better go. See you soon.'

Laurel immediately recognised the two officers who bustled into the room to interview her. They'd questioned her over two deaths in the village a few months back and she didn't think she'd made a good impression. One of them started the tape recording, they gave their names and hers, and informed her she had the right to legal representation.

Laurel understood this was no casual chat. 'Have I been arrested?' Panic fluttered in her stomach.

'No, this is an informal interview and you're free to leave at any time. However, we have some questions about today, and with your permission, we would like to take fingerprints and a DNA sample. You were in the property, and we'll need them for comparison purposes.' It was Detective Sergeant Hill who'd spoken first. There were more frown lines on his face than when she'd seen him last. His colleague, Detective Inspector Coral, was observing her with a scowl.

'Why were you at Mrs Little's house today?' asked DS Hill.

'Ms,' she corrected him automatically. 'It's Ms Little. She's always very clear about that.' Laurel gave a half laugh, tears threatened.

'Why were you there?' He was polite, but insistent.

She told them about Christopher's concern and how, on arriving at Dorothy's house, she'd felt something was *off*. 'I was looking through the letterbox and I saw the cat. The smell, and the... I knew it was blood.'

'How did you know?' demanded DI Coral.

'I've worked in hospitals for years; I know what blood looks and smells like.' Laurel bristled at the woman's attitude. 'I was only trying to help.'

'That's the thing though, isn't it. You were only trying to help when you found the body last week, and here you are again with another person left for dead. Not to mention the murders last year. You must be some kind of bad luck charm.' She had files on the table in front of her. She opened the one on top and read out loud. 'Church Cottage, Elderwick. Deceased, Mrs Lily Armitage. Present, Dr Laurel Nightingale. Village hall, Elderwick. Deceased, Mr Derek Fisher. Present, Dr Laurel Nightingale. Tulip Cottage, Elderwick. Deceased, Mr Simon Forster. Present, Dr Laurel Nightingale.'

Whether it had been Dorothy who'd sent her that blasted letter or someone else, it now felt as though they had a point. The fluttering in her stomach became a band across her chest. Was she actually a threat to her friends and neighbours? Each breath was hard to draw, the bleach, urine, vomit miasma of the interview room stuck in her nostrils, leaving her nauseated.

'Laurel, is it okay if I call you Laurel?'

Hill was good cop then.

She nodded, not trusting herself with words.

'It must have been very upsetting for you on those other occasions? Now, we're not saying you were involved in harming anyone, but it does mean we need to hash out the details here because Ms Little is almost certainly the victim of a vicious attack, and we know you want to help us find the culprit. Right?'

She nodded.

'So, you saw the cat, identified blood on his paws and face. What did you do next?'

'I was worried the blood was from Dorothy because I know she lives alone. I'd already been shouting and knocking, so I tried the door, but it was locked. Then I went round to the back and the back door was open.'

'When you say open, do you mean standing open, or unlocked?'

She cast her mind back. It was hard to recall the details. 'It was unlocked. I tried the handle.'

DS Hill made a note. 'Did you see or hear anything

unusual, or see anyone else around when you went to the back of the property?'

'No, nothing.'

'Carry on.'

She pictured the scene in her mind and steeled herself to relay the facts. 'I called out again and the cat came running. I tried to stop him, but he got by me and disappeared into the garden. I thought I'd better go inside and check if Dorothy was okay. I went into the kitchen, and she was there on the floor, by the sink. And there was blood all round her head.' Her voice shook.

'Would you like a glass of water?'

'No, thank you. I'm fine. She was on the floor, and I've done my basic first aid training at work, so I did that. Checked for breathing, and she was, so I didn't do CPR or anything. I wanted to put her into the recovery position, but I was afraid I'd hurt her more. Then I called the ambulance.'

'On your mobile?'

'No, there was no signal. I had to use Dorothy's phone, her landline.'

'Did you go anywhere except the kitchen?'

'No. I stayed with her. I couldn't let her be on her own.' The tears fell then, and she swiped at them with the back of her hand. DS Hill pushed a box of tissues towards her.

'Thank you,' she mumbled. 'Is she okay, do you know?' She'd been afraid to ask but needed to know.

'I'm sorry, we don't have any news yet,' replied Hill.

'Is she safe? Someone attacked her. What if they try again?'

'The wards in the hospital all have locked doors these days. You have to buzz or have an ID card to gain entrance. She's safe and being well looked after.'

Laurel had lost count of the number of times she'd been buzzed onto a ward without being asked who she was or anyone checking her name badge. Once through the doors, everyone was always so busy she'd frequently been able to wander at will. She wasn't reassured about Dorothy's security at all.

When they'd finished grilling her over her whereabouts for the previous twenty-four hours, they told her they'd be in touch if they had further questions. They handed her over to another member of staff to oversee the collection of her fingerprints and a saliva sample.

'The cat, was it... do you think?'

The woman looked up from filling out various labels. 'Don't you fret, love. We see this from time to time. I expect the cat was nosing around his owner and got the blood on him. It won't have been more than that.'

'Thank you.'

Free to go, Laurel didn't want to spend a moment longer in the police station. She found a bench in the park across the road and called Albert. He said he'd be right over to fetch her. She only had on a jacket, no scarf or gloves, and it wasn't doing much to keep out the biting wind. Leaves danced around her feet as she shivered and pulled her hands up inside the sleeves.

Albert had barely stopped the car before she flung herself inside. He took one look at her and turned the heater on full. He offered to listen if she wanted to talk, but other than the basic details, she felt beyond words, and he let her be. As he dropped her off, he volunteered to keep her company, but she said she wanted a bit of time on her own. Promising to call him if she needed anything, and with assurances she'd update him soon, she spilled out of the car and rushed to unlock her door.

Safely inside, she waited a moment for the shakes to subside then opened her bag and took out Simon's journal. Thank goodness they hadn't searched her belongings.

Chapter 17

Laurel

'Hugh, hi. Sorry, didn't you get my message?'

'About rescheduling? Yes, I got it, but I needed to see you today.'

Laurel felt her cheeks flush. 'I'm not sure I'm up to this today. I only came in because you didn't reply to my message, and I didn't want you standing out in the cold waiting for me. I would appreciate it if we could meet tomorrow instead?' Phrasing it as a question was a mistake, she knew it as soon as she'd said it.

'Nonsense. Come on.' He didn't so much push her out of the way as nudge, but he wasn't going to take no for an answer.

I should stand up for myself and tell him to get lost, she thought. Instead, she followed him up the stairs and through the empty reception area into her consulting room. She'd only had two other people booked in and they'd both been happy to rebook. She wanted to meet Maggie so they could discuss the journal. She really didn't have time for Hugh.

He'd made himself comfortable on her desk chair. *The nerve!*

'Sit. We've got a lot to get through.'

She found herself sitting and cursed under her breath. He wasn't in charge here, so why was she letting him order her around?

'I'm sorry, but we can't meet today.' *Stop apologising.*

He ignored her. 'Tell me about how you found Dorothy and what the police wanted with you down at the station.' He put his phone on the desk and started recording. He hadn't even bothered to ask this time.

'Who told you?' For an outsider he'd been quick to tune into the village hotline.

'Your friend Maggie told Natalie yesterday, and she passed it on to me. I thought you might have had the decency to inform me yourself, if I'm being honest. You know I'm working with the police.'

Maggie, of course it was.

Laurel cast her eyes to the ceiling and zoned out for a moment, letting her anger crest and fall. She would remain in control. 'If you're working with the police, they can tell you.'

He paused the recording and sat back in the chair – her chair – hands steepled. 'Come now, I didn't mean to criticise. We're making progress here and your input is very important to me.'

'Making progress? Are you serious? Dorothy is injured, maybe dying, and it must have something to do with Simon's death. What if all this,' she waved her hand between the two of them, 'what if this contributed somehow?' The words of the anonymous letter pierced her with a shard of guilt. 'What if it's our fault? What if someone else gets hurt? And you don't want my input, you want me to be a *blank slate*, isn't that what you said? I wouldn't have even been round at Dorothy's yesterday if we hadn't been to see Christopher.' *Damn, now he'll want to know about that.*

'What did Christopher say to you as we were leaving?'

There was no point lying to him now. 'He said he hadn't seen Dorothy, and she should have been in church. I offered to go round and check on her.'

Hugh was toying with a pen from her desk tidy but as she bent to pull a tissue from her bag, she caught him leaning forwards to start recording again.

'That is interesting. The vicar is the reason you found her. What does that tell us?'

She wasn't sure if he was speaking to her or himself.

He continued, 'The facts as we know them so far are as follows: one, Dorothy saw Christopher meeting with Simon the night before Simon's death. Two, Christopher sent you to Dorothy's yesterday where you found her.'

Laurel wasn't convinced. If, as Hugh seemed to suspect, Christopher harmed Dorothy, why would the vicar have wanted Dorothy discovered? The longer between the attack and her discovery, the better, surely? She didn't bother saying any of this. She would discuss it with Maggie later. Or maybe not. Albert might be a safer bet. Why had Maggie blabbed to Natalie again?

Hugh continued, 'I believe we have a motive for our reverend. If he killed Simon, and Dorothy could connect the two, then it makes sense that he tried to kill her to keep her quiet.'

'How would it help to kill Dorothy? Maggie was there when Dorothy told Christopher she'd seen him and Simon, so Maggie knows too. Which probably means everyone else does by now, including Natalie, you, and me.'

'You and I.'

She huffed and refused to engage with his pedantry. It was okay when Albert did it; Albert wasn't a patronising know-it-all. Besides, she wasn't even sure the author was right.

'We can't say it's a motive without knowing the reason for

the meeting between Christopher and Simon. It could have been perfectly innocent.'

Hugh swivelled in the chair to look out of the window. It was a delightful view, and one reason Laurel had chosen this space for her office. She could look out over the village green with its neat beds of flowers across to The Pleasant Pheasant. Having no buildings immediately opposite meant the room was typically flooded with natural light despite being north facing. Dreary February days being an exception.

'You're right. I believe it would be useful to have another conversation with Christopher. See if he can't be pressed on the issue now that there's been this attack.'

'I'll come with you.' She wasn't sure it was worth pursuing. She couldn't see the Reverend Christopher Ibori offing a reporter, let alone a little old lady. Particularly a little old lady who was a member of his flock. She didn't mean to be flippant, but didn't churches need all the congregants they could get?

Hugh, facing her again, squirmed. 'There's no need for you to come. If it's man to man, I might get Christopher to open up.'

'Oh, that's right, you don't want me there in case Christopher lets slip what he has on you.' She hadn't planned on baiting him, but it was out there now. 'That's what Christopher was getting at, wasn't it, when you tried to press him to tell you about Simon?'

Hugh scowled, then fixed her with a withering stare. 'You don't miss much, do you? Fine, Christopher and I had a conversation last week, but it's not something I'm going to discuss with you.' He stood and stowed his phone away in his jacket pocket. 'That's enough for today. You're right, I should let you rest. We can pick up again at our next session.'

Chapter 18

Laurel

'Can I come in?' Laurel peered past Maggie, searching for any sign that Natalie was around. She hoped not.

'Of course. Get in out of the rain.' Maggie hugged her, before holding her at arm's length and studying her face. 'You poor thing. They kept you for ages yesterday. I'm glad you left a message telling me you were home. I was on the point of sending Albert down to the station with Aroon to terrorise the officers into letting you go.'

Ensconced at the kitchen table, Laurel gave Maggie a rundown of her time with the police.

'Poor Dorothy. Do you know what exactly happened to her? Is there any news?'

'She was hit over the head. I expect she lost consciousness straight away.' Hopefully, it was the truth. There was no way Laurel was going to tell Maggie that Dorothy must have been stranded on her kitchen floor throughout the night. 'There was a nasty wound, and it had bled a lot. No news though, I'm not family, so the hospital won't tell me anything.'

'Did you see what she was hit with? On second thoughts, I

don't need to know.' She flapped her hands as though trying to shoo away the unpleasantness.

Laurel answered her anyway. 'No, I didn't see a weapon.' She looked down at her hands, could almost see the blood that had taken so long to wash off. 'Actually, do you mind if we change the subject?'

'Let me get you a drink.'

'Alcohol?'

'I was thinking tea. I have a lovely camomile and lavender, very calming.' As she played host, Maggie filled her in on the conversations she and Natalie had had with Jo and Elise. 'I don't think we discovered much of any use, or not yet anyway. Natalie is convinced Elise was lying about the restaurant critic thing though.'

'It could be worth following up. Maybe without Natalie, and without Ben?'

'I suppose. We don't have much else to go on.'

'Funny you should say that.' Laurel placed the journal in front of Maggie. 'Don't judge me. I found this when I found Dorothy. I know I shouldn't have, but I took it.' Saying it out loud drove home what a terrible idea it had been. The moment she'd spotted it, she'd known what it was and its potential significance. She'd slipped it into her bag whilst waiting for the ambulance. Initially, her thought was to keep it safe, and she had intended to tell the police.

'Is that...?'

'Simon Forster's journal? Yes.'

'How did you find it?'

'I was sitting on the kitchen floor next to Dorothy,' she blinked to banish the image crowding her mind, 'and from down there I could see the baseboard was wonky under the cabinets. It was one of those things you do without thinking about it; I tried to straighten it but it fell down and behind it was the journal.'

'Why on Earth did Dorothy have it?'

'She must have taken it from Tulip Cottage, but I don't know if it was before or after Simon died. I assume she already had it when we found the body because as soon as we did, we called the police and then we didn't go back into the house. The police searched, and they looked specifically for this, but Albert's friend at the station said they never found it. Now we know why.'

'They probably think the killer took it.'

'Maybe.'

'You shouldn't have it. You could be in all kinds of trouble.' Maggie pushed the book away, back towards Laurel. 'What if it's the reason Dorothy was attacked? What if the killer suspected she had it and tried to kill her too?' Fear bled into her voice. 'You have to hand it in.'

'I know I do, but we've got it now. I think we should read it first.'

'Haven't you read it yet?'

'No. I wanted to wait until we could do it together. If you want to?'

Laurel could see a battle playing out on Maggie's face between curiosity and caution.

Rather than answer straight away, Maggie got up and occupied herself laying out jam and lemon curd tarts. She put one of each on plates with bright, Scandinavian patterns. They were new. *Nicholas would not have approved*, thought Laurel with delight.

'Here, brain food.'

'Goodness knows, I need it.'

'Goodness knows, you need it,' said Maggie, simultaneously.

Laurel grinned at her and was rewarded with a faint smile.

'Look, I will give it to the police. I'll say I forgot about it because of the shock, or something. I think I'm going to have to tread carefully though. I get the impression they believe I'm involved in Simon's murder.' She was downplaying it to Maggie, but the idea had kept her awake for much of the night.

'That's ridiculous!'

'Of course it is. And thank you for not doubting me.'

'Don't be silly. It's an insane notion that you'd be involved. We need to set them right on that. Hugh might help, he could tell them how unthinkable it is.'

'Maybe.' Laurel wondered if she should tackle Maggie over the information she'd shared with Natalie. 'Speaking of Hugh, he said you told Natalie about me finding Dorothy and the police and everything.' She tried to keep her tone neutral: she didn't want Maggie to feel criticised, but she wanted to know why she'd blabbed.

'I'm sorry. I know you asked me not to, but Natalie was home when I got back after you'd gone with the officers. She could tell I was upset, and it just came out. She said she had to tell Hugh, and like I say, he could help you.'

'You cannot tell them about the journal!' She was wishing she'd kept it to herself now.

Maggie came back over with the plates of pastries and put one in front of Laurel. 'Hugh could review it, perhaps. He is working with the authorities. He can tell us whether it contains anything pertinent.'

Laurel suppressed the urge to groan. Maggie had become so much more independent since Nicholas had been hauled off to jail, but here she was deferring to another man.

'Don't you dare.'

'What?'

'I know what you're thinking. Hugh is not Nicholas. This is different.'

'You're a witch!' Laurel burst into laughter.

'Well,' sniffed Maggie, 'you be careful then or I'll turn you into a toad.'

'You're right, I'm sorry,' said Laurel, serious again. 'I worry about you, that's all.'

'I'm never going back there, you know. I'm my own woman.'

'You are. So, what does this woman think? Shall we read the journal and solve these attacks?' She took a bite of the lemon curd and her mouth flooded with saliva at the delicious tartness.

'I don't think we should read it. It could be full of personal, private information. If you won't share it with Hugh, you should at least take it straight to the police.'

Laurel licked the crumbs from her fingers and looked around for a pair of rubber gloves 'I will, but it's here now, it won't hurt to take a quick look. Have you got some gloves, so I don't mess up any fingerprints?'

'More than you already have, you mean?'

'Quite.' The atmosphere in the room was rapidly cooling.

Maggie pursed her lips. 'If you want to read it, I can't stop you, but I shan't be looking at it myself.' She plucked a pair of Marigolds from the side of the sink and slapped them down in front of Laurel then turned to busy herself with wiping down the kitchen worktops.

Laurel rolled her eyes. She toyed with the idea of leaving, taking the journal back to read in peace at home, but her impatience got the better of her. Ignoring Maggie's increasingly vigorous cleaning and sighing, she paged through the book. It took her a while to reach the juicy stuff, but when she found it, there was no denying the implications.

'Simon wasn't going to write a favourable piece about Hugh at all.'

Maggie put her hands over her ears. 'I'm not hearing this.'

'Just listen, please. This is all about how Hugh exploited his daughter for his first book, his repeated affairs, a breakdown. Dorothy must have read it, that's what got her all worked up when she came to see you on Saturday, the day before she was attacked.'

Laurel could tell Maggie was listening despite her protestations. She turned another page. 'Oh blimey!' she gasped. 'That's not even the worst bit. Hugh might have been involved in a child's death!'

'What?' Maggie came over and reached for the book.

'There, it's what I assume is a copy of a police report. Hugh was questioned about the death of a fellow pupil when he was at school.'

In silence, they read and re-read the typed page taped into the journal.

'I'm so cross with you right now. You're behaving exactly like Dorothy. You're determined to dislike him.'

'That's not true,' snapped Laurel. 'But listen, he can't find out we know about this. Promise me you won't tell Hugh?'

'Tell Hugh what?' asked a voice behind them.

Chapter 19

Laurel

'Natalie! How are you?' Laurel cried with false brightness.

Maggie all but leapt up from the table. 'We didn't hear you come in.'

Laurel flipped the journal closed but knew Natalie had spotted it.

'What's that?'

'It's just an old notebook. Maggie and I use it to jot down our thoughts when we're trying to work things out.'

'Things like the murder?' Natalie suggested. 'Honestly, I thought we were working with Hugh on this?'

Maggie popped a jam tart onto a plate and offered it to Natalie. 'Oh, we are.'

'What can't you tell Hugh?'

Laurel knew guilt was written on her face but crossed her fingers and hoped Natalie wouldn't outright call her a liar. 'We've been trying out a range of theories about who could have killed Simon and assaulted Dorothy. We don't want to show Hugh what we've come up with in case it colours his investigation or sends him off down the wrong track.'

Natalie's narrowed eyes said she wasn't buying it, but she asked, 'What have you come up with?'

Out of Natalie's line of sight, Maggie was wringing her hands. Laurel knew she would have to field this question herself.

'There's Christopher. Hugh and I spoke to him, but he wouldn't tell us why he was meeting with Simon the evening before Simon was killed. Then there's um...'

Visibly gathering herself, Maggie added, 'There's Elise, who as we know, met Simon at breakfast in The Pleasant Pheasant last Monday morning. I was telling Laurel about how clever you were to realise she was lying about what she and Simon discussed.'

Laurel was ambivalent regarding Elise as a suspect. She'd warmed to the woman and couldn't picture her as a killer. Then again, why would she lie? Either way, she was going to keep her mouth shut in front of Natalie.

Natalie didn't look entirely convinced.

'Natalie, Hugh mentioned earlier that he also met with Christopher, before Simon's murder. If he has a rapport with the vicar, maybe he can get to the bottom of the clandestine meeting between Christopher and Simon. Remind me what was it Hugh spoke with the vicar about?'

There was every chance Natalie wouldn't know. She hadn't even been in Elderwick at the time, but Laurel had the feeling there wasn't much Hugh did that wasn't organised or overseen by his agent.

'I have no idea. You'll have to ask Hugh.' She smirked. 'And I don't think there's any need to share your theories with him. He's well ahead in his thinking.'

'I bet he's got it nearly all figured out.' Maggie beamed. 'Writing those murders in his books, he must be very skilled at working out motives and suspects and so on.'

'Anyway,' said Natalie, looking at her phone. 'Maggie, can we finalise how long you want Hugh to speak to the WI?'

Laurel seized the opportunity to escape. The minute Natalie turned to look at the agenda Maggie was showing her, Laurel slipped the journal off the table and into her bag. She was going to go home and read it from cover to cover. Then she would definitely let the police know about it.

There was one other thing she wanted to do: she was going to invite Elise for that coffee to see if she could get the chef to tell her what she and Simon had discussed. And she absolutely wasn't going to let Hugh know about her plan. With Maggie's recent track record of blabbing, she wasn't going to tell her either.

Chapter 20

Laurel

She double-checked the front and back doors were locked before settling on the sofa to delve back into the journal. She started again at the beginning which comprised multiple lists. Simon had made lists of Hugh's books; lists of people to interview; significant dates in Hugh's life.

Of those scheduled for interviews, she only recognised half a dozen names, among them Natalie, Reverend Christopher Ibori, a well-regarded literary critic, and three moderately successful authors. She grabbed her own notebook and was going to copy out the details long-hand but realised it would be better to photograph the pages instead.

Two names she did copy out were Holly Quintrell – Hugh's only daughter from his first marriage – and a Dr Peter Burton, identified in the list as a psychiatrist. She would look them up later.

As she read on, she felt tension building in her neck and shoulders. If what Simon wrote was accurate, Hugh had taken intimate details of his daughter's life and plundered them for the sake of his debut novel. Simon's preparatory work had led him to conclude all the details in Hugh's book were accurate and so little disguised that Holly, and anyone who knew her, could easily connect her with the character in the story. For a father to do such a thing must have been devastating to the then seventeen-year-old.

Unsurprisingly, going by Simon's notes, Hugh's daughter had changed her name and broken all contact with her father following the publication of *The Murder of Innocents*.

Laurel opened a browser on her phone and did a quick online search to find the publication date. Supposing it had taken around two years from being written to being published, and given the time elapsed since, Holly, she worked out, would now be thirty-two or thirty-three. Uncertain she'd be able to stomach it, she nevertheless thought it could be useful to actually read his book and see for herself how cruel he'd been to his only child.

Turning to the next page in the journal, she came to the police report regarding the death of a fellow pupil at Hugh's boarding school. According to the police, the boy had died in the grounds of the school. Hypothermia was given as the cause of death, but there was a question over why he was outside at night, in the dead of winter, wearing only his pyjamas. Reading between the lines, it seemed the teachers at the school believed Hugh and the boy were not on good terms – whatever that meant – and that must have been reason enough for the police to question him.

Hugh, who she worked out would have been fourteen, had claimed he didn't know anything about his classmate's death. He denied any animosity between the two of them and was adamant he'd been in his bed all night.

Simon's notes recorded the outcome of the investigation; the incident was ruled death by misadventure. There had to be more to the story, and the fact it involved both Hugh and Simon set all kinds of bells ringing. However, digging up details after all these years, and without the credentials of a journalist, or official of some kind, would be tricky. With more hope than optimism, she made a note to see what, if anything she could uncover.

Feeling dejected after reading about the death of a child, Laurel was ready to take a break. She was re-folding the police report to tuck it back into the book when she noticed writing in pencil on the reverse. She squinted, it was faint, scribbled in haste.

HUGH'S INVOLVEMENT NEVER MADE PUBLIC –
SURPRISING!? ASK DAUGHTER ABOUT THIS – WORK No.
01482 930055 (CAN'T FIND HOME OR MOBILE No.)

It would be unethical, Laurel felt, to contact her. The woman had gone to great lengths to escape her father and it wasn't Laurel's place to open old wounds, she'd leave that to the police. But she made a note of the number just in case.

Chapter 21

Laurel

In Beverley, Laurel lucked into a parking spot in a small car park round the back of the main shopping thoroughfare. Emerging into the cobbled marketplace, she saw the old corn exchange. Its modern iteration was as a charming independent cinema in which she and her mum had, many years back, indulged in a showing of *The Big Sleep*. They'd been heading up to Scarborough for a week at the seaside but had stopped en route for one night in the pretty little market town.

Laurel smiled at the memory. The feeling was novel. Until recently, the memory of her mum, and her painful death eighteen years ago from cancer, had brought only sadness and regret. Since *readjusting* her life and making such wonderful new friends in Elderwick, she'd been able to move forwards. She felt she was living a life again, not merely existing.

It didn't take her long to find the Minster Tearoom, being, as it was, within sight of the magnificent gothic masterpiece that was Beverley Minster. Through the window of the café, she could see Elise had already arrived and was sipping from a steaming mug.

'Thank you for meeting me,' Laurel said as she slipped out of her coat and took the seat opposite the chef.

'My pleasure. It's a shame Maggie couldn't join us.' Elise smiled.

Laurel didn't share her sentiment. 'Mm, I know she'd love to meet up with you another time, but she was busy today.' A white lie she'd pay for later if Elise should mention their meeting to Maggie.

The waitress came over and Laurel ordered a decaf coffee and a cheese scone. If they'd been in The Pleasant Pheasant, she would have ordered her usual bacon and brie sandwich, but she typically avoided bacon when eating elsewhere. She was very fussy about her bacon, it had to be streaky, not smoked, and grilled – her preference over fried – to crispy perfection. 'Would you like anything to eat?' she asked Elise.

'No thanks, I'll grab something before service this evening. Sorry, I can't stay long.'

'That's okay, I appreciate you finding the time. I know you must be ridiculously busy.'

'It's my pleasure. Did you say you're in town to do some shopping?'

'Window shopping mostly. There's a fab independent bookshop and I want to call in and see what author events they've got coming up. Then, if I happen to go past Dyer Lane, I might just have to call in at the chocolate shop.'

Elise grinned. 'Make sure you try their bittersweet chocolate truffles. Just thinking about them makes my mouth water.'

'Speaking of food, I'd love to come and eat at your restaurant one evening.'

'If you do, let me know ahead of time so we can give you the VIP treatment.'

Laurel didn't eat out often, so a professionally cooked meal *and* special treatment would be a rare treat. 'That would be amazing, thank you. Maybe I can persuade Maggie to come with me. She loves food and she would get a real kick out of eating food prepared by someone she knows who's a professional chef.' Perhaps once Hugh and Natalie returned to London and when life had returned to normal, she'd suggest it to Maggie.

Laurel's drink arrived along with a hot, buttery scone. She tore off a small corner and popped it into her mouth. *Perfect.*

Conscious of time and believing they'd had enough small talk to ease into the subject, she brought up Maggie and Natalie's visit. 'I blame Hugh for your grilling on Sunday. Maggie's not usually like that: she's lovely.' She watched a flurry of emotions sweep across Elise's face, anger, sadness, and was that distaste?

'I'm sure she is,' Elise replied, her voice tight. 'Actually, I do mean that.' Her face softened. 'She has a warm presence. I felt it that day we bumped into you in The Pleasant Pheasant. I didn't warm to Natalie, though.' She pulled a face and spun her almost empty cup around in its saucer.

Letting the silence stretch, Laurel broke off another piece of her scone and stole a glance around the chintzy tearoom. The patrons consisted mostly of a group of older ladies, drinking tea and chattering like a charm of goldfinches. Looking back at Elise, who hadn't spoken again, Laurel thought she detected dampness on the chef's cheek. 'Are you okay? I'm so sorry, I didn't mean to upset you.' She hauled her overstuffed handbag from the floor onto her knee and rummaged in it for a clean tissue. 'Here,' she said, offering the whole packet.

'No, it's not you, it's not anything you said. It's that bloody woman and that...' her nose wrinkled, '...that idiot she works for.'

'Natalie and Hugh?' Was Elise going to tell her why she disliked them so much?

'Yes. Especially him. Have you read any of his books?'

'Maggie lent me his first novel, but I haven't read it yet.'

'I wouldn't bother, it's crap.' Elise blew her nose and shoved the damp tissue into a pocket. 'Sorry, I'm being a bit over-emotional. It's been a bit of a week, bit of a month in fact. I don't know what Natalie was implying when she came round, but she's got me all stressed that I'm in some kind of trouble. Ben told me not to worry, but...'

Laurel gave her a warm smile. 'He seems like the perfect boyfriend. Organiser of carpet picnics, defender against Hugh's busybody agent, what more could a girl want?'

Elise's lip wobbled and Laurel worried she'd put her foot in it. Though what *it* was, she wasn't sure.

'Maggie probably told you, they asked about me meeting with Simon?'

Laurel nodded.

'Ben and I argued once they left. I'd lied to him about being at work that Monday morning you see, the Monday I met Simon in the tearoom. It was a stupid lie, goodness knows, nothing stays secret in that bloody village.' She gave a dry laugh.

'Does he have a problem with you speaking to other men?' Laurel's opinion of Ben teetered.

'No, not at all. It's nothing like that. It's because I lied to him. I think he had a bad experience with an ex.'

'Are things okay between the two of you?' She squashed the nasty little part of her that was hoping Elise would say no.

'I don't know. We've been having problems for a while. Our careers don't lend themselves to a relationship; we both work crazy hours and Ben's timetable is so unpredictable. I'm not sure it's a match made in heaven.'

'I'm sorry, I really am.' She was... and she wasn't. *God, I'm horrible.* 'Look, tell me to mind my own bee's wax, but can I ask what you and Simon talked about?' She didn't want Elise to equate her with Natalie, but perhaps she could make it sound as though she was doing Elise a favour. 'The thing is, Natalie doesn't believe you were telling the whole truth when you told her you talked about restaurant critics and I think you deserve a heads up. You see, Simon's wife is, was... whatever, a restaurant critic, a very famous one.'

Elise covered her face. 'And Natalie knows?'

'I'm afraid so. She told Maggie, who told me.'

Elise groaned. 'I panicked. I knew it was a stupid lie, but I hoped Natalie wouldn't know about Joyce Forster. Damn it. What should I do?'

'Natalie's not the police, so it's hardly against the law to lie to her. I wouldn't say anything.'

'I'm such an idiot. Yeah, why should I tell her anything? God, I need a break. My brain isn't working right these days. It wasn't even a big deal, what Simon and I were talking about. He'd seen me going to church a few times and he was interested in knowing a bit about the congregation here, the vicar, how I feel being a minority?'

'A minority?'

'He was joking, he meant under fifty years old and Christian. There's not many of us around these days.'

'Why lie about that?' Laurel wasn't sure she believed this version of events any more than the previous one.

'It was none of her business. I don't mean Maggie, she goes to church, but Natalie. I know her kind and I didn't want to put up with any condescending, superior crap if I told her what Simon was asking.' She rubbed her nose as she spoke.

From many years in therapeutic practice, Laurel knew that people who were lying were often compelled to touch their face, usually around their mouth. A subconscious *tell* that the words coming out of their mouth were false.

Elise picked up her cup and sipped. Another tell. 'I'm going to pop to the loo,' she said as she finished her drink.

Laurel used the time to replay the conversation. Elise had lied to Ben about going to meet with Simon, and she was lying again now. But why?

Chapter 22

Laurel

Bundled in her coat, scarf and gloves, Laurel rapped firmly, hoping her knock would be answered soon. It wasn't as cold as it had been the day before, but the flat leaden sky had chilled her spirit. 'Hey, Albert,' she said when he peered out at her. 'Are you free for a bit of a chat?'

'Laurel, my dear, for you I am always available.' He swung the door wide. 'In fact, was hoping we would have chance to catch up what with all that has transpired this last week. How are you feeling, after finding poor Dorothy?'

'I'm not sure, but I'm beginning to think I might be bad luck.' *And someone else in this village clearly believes so too.* 'It's so messed up I don't know whether to laugh or cry.'

'Well, don't stand out there in the cold. Come in and have a piece of cake. I've got the fire going in the front room so it's nice and cosy.'

Surprise cut through her turmoil. Until now, she'd never seen beyond the kitchen of Albert's house and had begun to think he had some dark secret he was trying to hide behind closed doors.

'Will Aroon or Lago be joining us?' She grinned at her

friend. The rabbit was fine, Aroon on the other hand... well, theirs was a strained relationship. When she'd first met her neighbour, Albert had warned her the cockerel had a habit of crowing every morning at 5am. He had not been joking. And that was the least of the bird's bad habits.

'When there's cake around? Not a chance. Aroon especially, he'd be off with it like a shot. No, they're both safely tucked away in their houses in the garden.'

Albert ushered her through to have a seat by the fire while he pottered off to the kitchen, giving her chance to have a good nosey. In her cottage, the sitting room was at the back; Albert's was the opposite. He had a bay window which bathed the room with light, even on a miserable day such as it was. The room wasn't large but big enough to contain two substantial bookcases partially filled with books. The remainder of space on the shelves was given over to... *objets d'art* was perhaps the best descriptor. Almost all the pieces were animals: a bronze hare; a group of three hens and a cockerel carved from a single piece of wood; a stuffed robin. She reached out a hand to touch the bird, unsure if it was real or not. It was real. Or the feathers were at least.

'Little Robin Red Breast,' said Albert, making her jump and snatch her hand away feeling guilty. 'I stuffed him myself.'

Laurel pulled a face.

'Delicate work. Tiny thing under all those feathers. He and I were friends nigh on four years before he passed. Found him stiff as a board couple of winters back. Death comes to us all in the end.' He handed her a huge piece of chocolate cake and sat down with a plate of his own. 'Now then, tell me, what's on your mind?'

Desperate to shove an immodest wodge of cake in her mouth, Laurel resisted for long enough to tell Albert about the journal and her conversation with Elise. She'd get to Dorothy later; first she needed to think through the implications of what she'd learned. Albert was sure to be helpful. She would have liked to discuss it with Maggie, but at that moment, telling Maggie was as good as telling Natalie, who would automatically tell Hugh.

'My goodness, what a tangled web.' Albert settled in his wingback chair and closed his eyes.

Laurel took the opportunity to try the cake. It was sinfully moist and chocolatey. There was another flavour in there too.

'Can you taste the beetroot?' asked Albert, without opening his eyes. 'It enhances the chocolate and keeps it from being too rich.'

'Mmmm...'

When he opened his eyes again, he was nodding to himself. 'Well, the journal has to go to the police. As for Elise, you have no proof of her lie so perhaps wait a little longer and see what else you may discover. Do you feel comfortable with such a course of action?'

'I guess. I'll probably get in trouble for withholding evidence, but I can't, in good conscience, keep the journal a secret. It raises so many questions though.'

'Do you want to enumerate them so we can see if there's any light we might discern? Two heads, and all that.'

'Okay. First off, how and when did Dorothy come by the journal? Why did she hide it? If she had it before Simon died, was the killer looking for it? Is that why Dorothy was attacked too? If so, how did the killer know Dorothy had it? If–'

'Woah, slow down. One at a time, and let's start at the beginning. You and I were both in Tulip Cottage with Dorothy shortly after she'd found Simon's body. His bedroom was locked until I opened it. Did you notice the journal whilst we were there?'

'No, but we only saw the hallway and the bedroom. Did you see it?' Laurel asked.

'No, no books of any kind if I remember correctly.'

'Dorothy had been in the cottage before we got there. I'm willing to bet she had a poke around before we arrived on the scene. She wasn't overly distraught about Simon being dead, so a few minutes looking through his belongings would not have been beyond her.'

'Why would she take the journal, assuming she came across it?' asked Albert.

'Why not? She didn't like Simon, and we all know she was the biggest gossip in the village. I think she must have taken it between finding Simon's body and us arriving. Any sooner and Simon would surely have missed it, and there was no opportunity once the police arrived.'

Albert bobbed his head.

'Having read the journal, I'd say it gives at least three people a motive for killing Simon. But if it was one of those three who killed him, and if Dorothy hadn't got her hands on it yet, they would have taken the journal at the time of the murder, wouldn't they?'

'Not if they didn't know what was in it, and not if they couldn't find it.'

'If they couldn't find it, how did Dorothy? And, it seems to be the obvious connection between Simon's death and Dorothy's attack. The killer didn't find it at Tulip Cottage. They assumed Dorothy, as the owner, must have taken it, so they tried to kill her too.'

'But Dorothy had hidden it, and they evidently didn't manage to locate it whilst in her house.'

Laurel put her head in her hands. 'My brain aches.' They sat, lost in their thoughts until an idea came together in Laurel's mind. 'Your *contact* at the police station said Simon *always* had his journal with him, right?'

'Right. Always, and that came from Simon's wife and was corroborated by colleagues.'

'Well, I know of two people who saw Simon last Monday. We can ask them if he had it with him at each of those meetings. If he didn't, it's possible Dorothy already had it by the time he was killed between Monday night and Tuesday morning. Ergo, it wasn't with him for his killer to find and take at the time of the murder.'

'Which two people saw him?'

'Elise and Reverend Ibori.'

'You'll have to be careful if you're going round asking questions. You know as well as I that nothing stays secret for long in Elderwick.'

The hairs on the back of her neck stood on end.

'If the killer is looking for the journal,' said Albert, 'you don't want them finding out you have it, or knowing you've read it. That could be very bad for your health.'

Chapter 23

Laurel

'You should have handed this in the instant you remembered you had it.'

Laurel was getting a dressing down from DI Coral, and she supposed she deserved it. She hoped to save her skin from any serious consequences though. 'I'm sorry, I genuinely am. It must have been the shock. I put it in my bag for safe-keeping and then it slipped my mind.'

'You found it on Sunday and today is Wednesday.' DI Coral paused, leaving a silence for Laurel to fill, but if there was anything psychologists are particularly skilled at, it is tolerating an uncomfortable silence. Laurel waited out the policewoman.

'Have you read it?' Coral broke first.

She tried not to let the victory show on her face. 'I skimmed it quickly, that's all.'

They were sitting in a room at the police station, not the interview room from her last visit, thankfully. She'd intended to hand the journal in at the front desk and beat a hasty retreat. However, fortune was not with her. She was turning to leave when she bumped into the detective inspector, literally. Coral recognised her, questioned her presence, and now here she was being interrogated once more.

'And?'

'And what?'

'When you *skimmed* it, what did you see?' The officer's voice dripped scepticism.

'Nothing really.' It was obvious to Laurel that the DI didn't like her. She didn't believe the police saw her as a serious suspect in the deaths, but for some reason, Coral had taken against her. 'You don't like me, do you?' She felt a direct approach might be the best way to provoke Coral into giving something away. Years of therapy with a number of reluctant patients made it easy for Laurel to cut to the heart of animosity or uncertainty.

Coral stared at her. In a tight voice she said, 'Since you arrived in the area last year, there have been three murders and a violent attack on a frail old lady. That's not a normal amount for such a small village.'

Laurel's heart was racing, and her palms felt sweaty. Nothing good could come from further conversation. She needed to get out. She stood. 'You know what, I'm leaving. I'm not going to sit here and listen to this.' Reaching the door, she hoped to goodness it would be unlocked.

Coral hadn't moved. 'I'll be watching you.'

Chapter 24

Laurel

She fell into step alongside the Reverend Christopher Ibori.

'Hello, Laurel. Are you taking advantage of this beautiful afternoon too? I should be writing my Sunday sermon, but who can stay indoors on a day like this?'

He was right, for the first time in weeks the sky was blue, the sun was shining, and the perpetual chill in the air was gone. 'I hope it lasts,' she said. 'You know, despite all the nastiness we've had around here, the sun puts me in such a good mood.'

'Yes, first Mr Forster and now poor Dorothy. Unfortunately, I received further bad news today. Nothing as serious, but nonetheless disappointing. Dandelions have heard about our troubles and are reconsidering their plans for Elderwick Hall.'

Laurel scowled. If they pulled out it would be a huge shame for the children who could have benefitted from the centre, and on a personal and selfish note, she dreaded what would happen to the estate if the other guy Albert had mentioned bought it. The public rights of way through the grounds were some of her favourite walks in the area.

'That's hardly fair. I can't believe the murderer is someone from Elderwick.' She watched his face to gauge his response.

'Indeed, and I am confident the police will resolve the matter with haste. Let us hope it is concluded in time.' His expression gave nothing away.

'Actually, I'm glad I've bumped into you. Can I ask you something? Don't worry,' she said, catching his frown. 'It's nothing confidential.'

They were on a gravel track heading up towards Elder Hill and Drumble's Hive, an off-grid woodland community that had existed in the area since the sixties. Christopher was tall and his long strides left Laurel slightly breathless as she hurried to keep up. It was invigorating to get out walking again and to feel the sun on her face. The winter had been too long, wet, and muddy. She hoped this change in the weather would last.

'I know you couldn't confirm to Hugh and me that Simon came to see you before he died, but,' she pressed on quickly, hoping to override any objections, 'Dorothy saw you and so I know you *did* see him. I just want to ask if Simon had his journal with him when you saw him on that Monday evening? It would have been a brown leather book about this big.' She held up her hands giving an approximation of the size. 'It's important.'

Christopher's pace slowed. There was a bench a few steps off the path, he made a beeline for it and sat with a groan. Laurel remained standing until he nodded at the space beside him.

'You truly believe it's important?'

'I do.'

He leaned his elbows on his knees and turned his face to the sun. 'I suppose it can do no harm to tell you that no, he didn't have his journal. In fact, he remarked on it. He said he hadn't been able to find it since getting back from breakfast at the tearoom. He was convinced he'd left it in his room when he'd gone out. He said he was never usually without it, but he'd been distracted and had left it behind – before you ask, he didn't say what was preoccupying him. Unfortunately, he was minded to accuse Dorothy of having taken it. I suppose she was the only person with access to Tulip Cottage but I can't imagine for the life of me why Ms Little would have been in the cottage let alone why she would wish to take the gentleman's journal. I'm sure he was mistaken. Does that answer your question?'

'It more than answers it, thank you.' The new information was slotting into place with what she already knew. A picture was beginning to take shape.

'Can you tell me why this is so important?'

She chose her words carefully, mindful of Albert's warning. 'I'd heard Simon always had a journal with him and as far as I know, the police didn't find it in the cottage after he was killed.' *Not entirely a lie.* 'I just wondered if you'd seen it.'

'This is part of Mr Quintrell's *investigation*, I presume?'

'Something like that. Can I ask another question?'

'I can't see as how I can stop you.' He sounded tired, but there was a lift to the edges of his lips.

Laurel liked the vicar. She couldn't say why exactly, but he seemed a fair man. Maybe it was because he'd got the best of Hugh the other day in the vestry. 'How come Dorothy saw you meeting with Simon and with Hugh? At first, I thought she must have been in the church when they arrived, but Maggie said you were surprised Dorothy had seen you. If she'd been there doing her volunteering, you would have known, wouldn't you?'

'She wasn't there on any official business, but in the past, I have… caught isn't the right word, too judgemental… I have *spotted* her in the church from time to time when she wasn't scheduled to be there and hadn't made her presence known. So, it's very possible she could have seen the various comings and goings. You understand I remain unable to confirm who may or may not have been to see me.'

'I understand. And that does explain how Dorothy saw, I guess. I wonder what she was doing? Was she spying deliberately?'

'Personally, I suspect she's lonely.'

A heaviness settled around Laurel's heart. She knew what it was like to be lonely. She should have made more of an effort with Dorothy.

'Now it's my turn, I have a question for you. You said the police didn't find the journal. Has someone else found it?'

He's sharp. His deep brown eyes were locked on hers. *Can I lie to a vicar? Could he be a suspect?* She chose to trust him, a little. 'I found the journal, by accident. I wasn't looking for it. The police have it now.'

Christopher cleared his throat, and blinked rapidly.

He is afraid, she realised. This wasn't only about the confidentiality between vicar and a member of his flock, this was personal.

'I have to go now.' The words burst from his mouth. 'I'm... I apologise for rushing off.'

There was no way she could follow and keep pace, so she watched him disappear up the lane and round a bend, shoulders hunched, head down. What was he afraid she had seen in the journal?

The moment she saw the envelope waiting for her when she arrived home, she knew what it was.

This time, she left it on the mat until she'd put on her rubber gloves. If this became more serious, and she wanted to report it to the police, there might be a chance of fingerprints, if not on the envelope, then perhaps on the paper inside.

Touching as little of the paper as she could, she eased it out onto the coffee table.

Dorothy is in hospital because of you! LEAVE ELDERWICK NOW

The postmark was Beverley again, and it had been posted on Tuesday, two days ago. Two days after she'd found Dorothy. Dorothy wasn't the letter writer.

Chapter 25

Laurel

Hugh lowered himself into his chair looking like the cat who'd got the cream.

Laurel was in no mood to care what he was so smug about, but there was something she needed to say, 'Hugh, I think we need to end these... I'm not even sure I can call them *sessions*. I can't, in all good conscience, continue to take your money; you're not a patient, and this isn't therapy.' It wasn't helping that the more time she spent with him, or even talking to other people about him, the less she liked him. She'd lost her ability to be non-judgemental.

'Don't worry about it. I told you before, it's not therapy we're meeting for. I'm writing like the Dickens now. My writer's block is completely cured. I've already got 30,000 words down on the page. I start with the discovery of his body and I'm coming on to back story now.'

'Does that mean I'm going to be in your book?' She wasn't sure how she felt about that.

'No, you're fine. I know the details from the police, and no, you're not in the book. No offence.'

'But I was there. I was one of the people who found Simon.' Why was she arguing? She didn't want to be in his book.

'I'm writing it from my perspective, so it was easier to say I was the one who found him. You understand, of course. But don't worry, I still need you to help me hone my ideas as I'm conducting this investigation. You're an intelligent woman and I'm sure we can work well together. We've had a rocky start, not quite found our groove, but we will.'

It was the comment about her intelligence that gave him away. She understood him now. His motivation for keeping her around was so he could pick her brains and appropriate her story. Fine, she would play along for a while, but the information flow needed to be a two-way street.

'You are looking rather pleased with yourself today,' she commented. 'Have you made a break-through?'

His smile stretched wider. 'I suppose it won't hurt to tell you. The police have located Simon's journal and have invited me to read it tomorrow morning. As a writer, they want my insights into Simon's notes. They haven't said as much, but I think they believe the motive for his murder will be found in those pages.'

This was interesting. The officers involved in the investigation – the real investigation, not Hugh's version – would have read the journal themselves by now and would have seen what Simon had written. Were they setting Hugh up? Waiting to gauge his reaction, to see if he knew Simon had been writing such a scathing profile? If Hugh had prior knowledge, it made a good motive for murder. Judging by Hugh's present mood though, it would be easy to assume he had no idea what Simon's journal had in store for him. That, or he was an accomplished actor.

Laurel walked round to sit at her desk, putting her a head

above Hugh. 'Did the police tell you where they found the journal?' *Keep it light, nice and casual.*

'Very good question. Yes, it was at Dorothy's house which rather suggests...'

It took her a moment to realise he was waiting for her to complete his sentence the way a teacher would encourage their class. 'That Dorothy took it?' *Let's see how he handled her being deliberately obtuse.*

'Obviously.' He rolled his eyes. 'But more to the point, it suggests Simon's death and the attempt on Dorothy's life are connected, that the same person must be responsible for both. There must be something in the journal the killer doesn't want us to see.'

'Won't it just be full of notes about you? Was Simon killed because of you?'

'Don't be ridiculous. He'll have been working on other stories too. Certainly mine was the most prestigious, but I believe he was also working on a companion piece about the publishing industry which could throw up some suspects, I can tell you.'

That caught her attention. 'I wasn't aware the publishing industry was a hive of murderers and criminals?'

'You'd be surprised. They're all out to make a killing.' Hugh laughed at his own joke. 'Natalie's boss, Charlotte, is a piece of work for starters. No, what I'm saying is there will be all sorts in his notes and the SIO – that's the senior investigating officer – is aware it will take someone like me, who understands Simon's world, to decipher any relevant entries.'

She didn't recall seeing anything in the journal about publishing or publishers. It was interesting, though. From what little she understood, it was becoming an increasingly cut-throat industry. Maybe Simon had stumbled onto something someone felt was worth killing him over.

'The article about you... Did he approach you with the idea?' She wanted to poke Hugh a bit more.

'In fact, yes, he did. It must have been nearly six months ago now.' Hugh crossed his legs and steepled his fingers.

Here we go again, lecturing professor mode activated.

'He gave me a call and said he'd like to do a piece to celebrate my thirtieth book. He wanted to get into the mind of "the author who thinks like a serial killer" – his words.'

'That doesn't sound like a compliment?'

'If you understood my writing, you'd understand.'

'And what, he followed you up here to Elderwick? That's above and beyond, isn't it?'

'This story, *my story*, was very important to him.'

She wondered how he'd feel about Simon digging up the old police report on the death of a fellow pupil at his boarding school.

'So, you'll let me know if you find anything useful in the journal?'

'I'm not sure I'll be permitted. It's need-to-know, you understand.'

'How can we work together if I don't know what you know?'

Hugh waved away her question. 'Natalie tells me you and Maggie were working on some theories of your own the other day. Care to share?'

She'd prepared for this question and knew it would come up sooner or later. Hugh wouldn't want to miss out on any ideas that he could steal for himself. 'We haven't come up with much, I'm afraid. We were speculating again over what it could have been that Simon discussed with Christopher. Did you manage to speak with the reverend again, you know, *man to man*?' She couldn't help the sarcasm in her tone.

His eyes narrowed. 'Not as yet. I did have Natalie do a bit of digging, however, and she turned up some interesting information.'

He was going to make her ask for it. 'What is it? Or is it *need-to-know?*'

He tutted. 'You know what they say about sarcasm.'

Ugh.

He paused, no doubt savouring knowing something she didn't. 'It appears our Reverend Christopher Ibori had some trouble in a previous parish and was moved on. I suspect Simon uncovered this secret and challenged Christopher over it, perhaps getting himself killed in the process. Sadly, we haven't yet been able to uncover the nature of the trouble.'

'That's twice you've suggested Christopher might be behind Simon's death. What do you have against him?' What Hugh was telling her fit with Christopher's behaviour when she'd seen him the day before. He was afraid. But she *still* couldn't see him as a murderer. Was she being blinkered? Should she add him to her list of suspects?

With feigned wide-eyed innocence he said, 'I don't have anything against him. I'm simply following the evidence. To that end, I've tasked Natalie with making a few calls to see if we can uncover the dirty little secret of Elderwick's vicar.'

Chapter 26

Maggie

The village hall was packed. Maggie was pleased to see so many faces. Her plan was to ensure Hugh received a rapturous reception. She had two chairs set out on the stage, one for Hugh and one for herself. She'd be introducing him and fielding the questions. She'd even placed a small table beside his seat with a bottle of water, just like she'd seen done for author Q&A sessions at the Hay Festival.

It pained her to have the thought, but she was relieved Dorothy wouldn't be there. The poor woman hadn't deserved what had happened to her, but goodness, she had been a pill. Every time she attended a WI meeting – and she only did when it suited her – she would find something to quarrel about with the other members. Last month it had been an issue with their planned outing to see *Chicago* at Hull New Theatre. Dorothy had argued it was indecent and not the kind of entertainment the WI should be consuming. *Filth* was one of the tamer words she'd used.

Maggie had been dreading what Dorthy would spring on them when Hugh came to speak to the group. Dorothy always claimed she was simply speaking up for others, but in Maggie's experience, Dorothy only ever spoke for Dorothy.

'Are we all ready?' asked Natalie, striding up the aisle pulling a plastic trolley. 'Have you got a table ready for these?' She indicated the contents of the trolley, copies of Hugh's latest book.

'Maybe at the back where there's–'

'Give me a hand and we'll move that table down here,' ordered Natalie, mounting the stage and dismantling all Maggie's hard work. 'This little one will do, I suppose.' Once she'd finished re-arranging the furniture she looked around and asked, 'Where are you sitting? I'll need you to hold on to the cash box and be ready to take the money.'

Maggie wasn't sure which issue to address first, but if she wasn't assertive soon, she'd be manoeuvred out of her special night. 'That's my chair, next to Hugh's. You'll need to be the one in charge of the money and the books. You can sit on the end of the row, here.' *Well done, Maggie!* Nicholas was gone; she wasn't going to start letting someone else push her around, house guest or not.

Natalie looked like she was about to object but shrugged instead. 'Whatever.'

'I didn't realise you'd expect to be selling books tonight?' *Issue number two.*

'We... that is, Hugh thought it would be a good opportunity for your ladies to buy copies and have them signed.'

That actually was a good idea. 'Okay, but after the talk, not before. I don't want there being pandemonium and people not going back to their seats so we don't start on time.'

'Sure. Honestly, Maggie, be calm, Hugh's done this loads of times. He'll talk for a bit about his work, his life, his newest book. Then he'll take questions. Plus, don't forget, he wants to appeal for any information your members might have about the murders. Then the book signing. Simple.'

'He won't dwell too long on the murder and attack, will he? Dorothy is one of us, and after what's happened to her, it could be quite upsetting.'

'He'll be very tactful, I promise.'

There was no time for further reassurances; the front doors squealed open, hinges protesting the damp evening air. The Elderwick WI had arrived.

Hugh's talk was a resounding success. The audience had hung on his every word and the author had clearly been in his element.

'Now I have a favour to ask of you,' he said, leaning forwards in faux intimacy. 'You all know there have been two violent incidents here in the last fortnight. A murder and a bludgeoning. I understand that Mrs Dorothy Little is a member of this very WI. My dear ladies, you have my sympathies.'

A couple of people in the crowd sniffed and one or two wiped away a tear.

To call it a bludgeoning was a little unnecessary, thought Maggie. It rather brought to mind blood and... she shuddered and tuned back in to what he was saying. She kept her fingers crossed he'd avoid any further brutal language. She opted not to correct him for calling Dorothy Mrs. Dorothy could do that herself if he ever did it within her earshot.

'What I wish to ask is this: did any of you see or hear anything, or anyone, suspicious or out of place on the evening of Monday 18th February? This is when we understand Mr Simon Forster was murdered. Or on Saturday 23rd through to Sunday 24th when Dorothy was attacked?'

Whispered conversations broke out around the hall.

Sick with the thought of discussing the violence further, Maggie stood and raised her voice. 'If you did, please see Natalie before you leave, and she will take your details.'

'Actually,' said Hugh, 'I have time now.' His eyes roamed the audience. 'Any information you have could help to catch this crazed killer preying on you, the unsuspecting residents of this delightful village.'

He was trying to stoke fear. Maggie felt a flash of annoyance. 'I think we should say, there's no evidence anyone else is in danger.'

'Dear lady, do we know that?' Hugh challenged. 'I for one will not be walking these streets alone at night.'

Gasps and shuffling spread through the hall.

'I have some information,' called a voice.

Maggie searched for the speaker in the crowd. 'If you could see Natalie—'

'You know what,' interrupted Hugh, 'people are afraid, and rightly so. Let's hear what you've got to say.'

A woman stood up. Maggie recognised her as one of the less frequent attendees of the weekly meetings.

'From what I've heard, the journalist who was killed, he was here to muck-rake. I'm not saying he deserved to be killed, heavens no, but it was nasty of him to be up here bothering you, Mr Quintrell.'

'That's not really information, Agnes,' said Maggie.

'It's what I heard,' she shot back, sitting down.

A hand went up over to the left of the stage.

'Yes, Vera.' Maggie was glad to move on.

'I'm pretty sure I saw someone hanging around Tulip Cottage on the Monday evening before the murder. I can't remember what time it was, but it was getting dark, and the streetlights were on. I would have said it was a he, but then again, they looked like they were wearing a long dress. I could have been mistaken. They were all in black, they were, so it was hard to tell.'

'Could you see what this person was doing?' asked Natalie.

'Nothing much, just standing there; then they walked off. I rather think they saw me.'

'Which way did they go?'

'They went off down West Street, that's all I can remember. I wasn't paying much notice. I had to get home and get the tea on.'

'Thank you so much, this is all exceedingly helpful,' said Hugh. 'Anyone else?'

'Um, I have something.' A hand was waving at the back.

'Yes, at the back.' Hugh called on them before Maggie had chance.

'Thanks. Full disclosure, we're not members of the WI, but we wanted to hear Hugh tonight.'

Maggie recognised the voice now, it was Constance, one of her favourite people in the village. In large part owing to her skills with pastry at The Plump Tart.

'Hetty and I, we thought we saw someone going up North Street towards the green at fivish on the morning of Tuesday the 19th. We're always in the bakery early and we're used to seeing a couple of early risers, but this wasn't anyone we knew.'

'Whoever it was, they could have been coming from Tulip Cottage,' added a second voice.

'Hetty?' queried Maggie.

'Yes, hi.' Another hand waved.

Natalie was scribbling in a notebook as Hugh asked, 'Could you make out any distinguishing features?'

'No, it was dark and there aren't many streetlights along that section. The best we can tell you is they were probably average height, dressed in black or dark clothes, and fairly slim.'

'Man, or a woman?'

'No idea.'

'Did you get all that, Natalie?'

She nodded.

'Anyone else have any other information?'

'Wait, I just thought of something else.' It was Constance again. 'I don't know if it's relevant, but whoever it was, they paused when they got to the pond. I don't know why, and it was only for a second. I'm sure I heard a splash, but it could just have been that they'd disturbed the ducks.'

'Maybe they threw the murder weapon into the water?' suggested a well turned-out lady in the front row, clutching the string of pearls at her throat.

'No, the murder weapon was a knife, and it was still in the body when he was found,' said Hugh, as casually as if he were discussing the price of fish.

From all corners came expressions of horror.

Undeterred, he continued. 'No, I imagine he, or she – I'm not sexist, ladies–' he winked '–paused to get their bearings or check they weren't being observed. They would have been covered in blood from the stabbing. Their hands probably, certainly their clothing. They would have wanted to avoid interactions with any early risers.'

Maggie felt a pressing need to move them on before someone got the vapours. Quite a few of her members were elderly and frail. In a no-nonsense tone she spoke above the hubbub. 'We do need to end there. Please see Natalie if you have anything else to report.' Standing, her arms held out toward him she continued, 'Hugh, thank you for a wonderful talk this evening, we appreciate you giving your precious time. I'm sure we'll all be racing home to read, or in most cases, re-read, your fabulous books.' She began the applause and thankfully, the audience followed her lead. Hugh raised his hand in thanks.

As the clapping faded away, she added, 'One final thing, Hugh will be signing copies of his latest novel, *Death Dances with Destiny*, if you would like to purchase one before you leave.' The stampede to the table started before the final syllable left her lips.

Chapter 27

Laurel

Laurel waited until a crowd of five or six women were squeezing through the door and slipped out behind them, head down, and escaped into the night.

She wasn't a member of the WI, but that wasn't why she'd hidden away behind an old screen at the back of the hall. She wanted to be there to hear and observe the meeting without Hugh knowing she was present. She didn't want to stroke his ego – he was getting more than enough of that – but she did want to hear what, if any, information was garnered when the subject of the murder came up.

The first bit of actual information, about the figure near Tulip Cottage on the Monday evening, was vexing. The woman had said she thought it was a man, but also that they seemed to be wearing a dress. Christopher in his cassock had come immediately to mind, and she was sure the same thought would have occurred to Hugh. More grist to his mill.

What Constance and Hetty had reported was even more interesting. At five in the morning, there wouldn't have been many people out and about, so it was probable the figure they observed was Simon's murderer. Was there a reason this person had paused by the pond? And the splash? Were they disposing of incriminating evidence in the murky waters?

It was too dark to go looking straight away, but perhaps tomorrow she might happen by the pond with some frozen peas for the ducks, and she might happen to have a big stick with her to poke around in the reeds and the mud. It couldn't hurt, and it didn't sound as though Hugh was going to follow up on the tip. She wondered if he would even inform the police.

It had got her thinking again about the manner of Simon's death. Either the police hadn't shared all the crime scene details with Hugh, or he'd been exaggerating for effect, because there had been exceptionally little blood on the body. True, there was some around the knife – or dagger, as Dorothy had suggested – but not as much as you would expect. She'd seen death from a similar wound, close up. There'd been a great deal of blood. She swallowed hard. It wasn't a pleasant memory. Was Simon already dead when the knife was plunged into his back? Why would someone do that? If it wasn't the stab wound which had killed him, what had? Could the answer be in the pond?

She had no idea whether a post-mortem had been carried out yet. Albert's contact might know, but she wasn't sure he'd be able to share that kind of information. As a last resort, she'd have to ask Hugh. A post-mortem would confirm cause of death.

Musing on the grisly possibilities, she let herself into her cosy cottage and locked the door. Turning the key, she was reminded of the locked room in which Simon was found. It was a significant element of the mystery and one she was determined to unravel. Maybe the police had already figured it out, but there would be a certain satisfaction in knowing she'd solved the conundrum for herself.

She had the inkling of a theory, but there were two things she needed to check before she could pronounce it plausible. In the kitchen, she poured herself a glass of Chardonnay – a large glass – and went through to the living room where she nestled into the sofa and opened her laptop. YouTube was her first stop, where she found exactly what she was looking for. So far, so good. Second, she crossed her fingers and searched for *Tulip Holiday Cottage Elderwick East Yorkshire*. Bingo.

She'd hoped for photos of the interior of the cottage, so was elated to find a video walkthrough. It showed everything she needed. But to be one hundred per cent certain, she would run a real-life test. All she needed was a hammer and a screwdriver, and luckily, she had both of those around somewhere.

Chapter 28

Laurel

'Fancy coming with me to feed the ducks, Albert?'

He gave her a quizzical look. 'Not your usual Friday morning activity.'

'No, but it's not every day you find out there might be a murder weapon in the village pond.'

His eyebrows shot up. 'No, indeed, that is not an everyday occurrence. What murder weapon is that exactly, and why is it in the pond?' He was on the doorstep in his slippers, Aroon fussing at his feet.

'Hetty and Constance said they saw a suspicious character loitering by the pond the night Simon was murdered. It got me thinking about how he died, and I think we're missing something, and that something might be in the pond.'

'I'm not sure I follow your reasoning, but I don't doubt it's sound. You'd best be taking gloves with you though, if you're going fishing in that muck. It needs a proper clean out. Perchance in summer the council will get round to it.'

Laurel held up a pair of yellow Marigolds.

'And where's your usual partner in crime-busting?'

Laurel scuffed the toe of her boot against the stone step by Albert's door. She felt transported back in time to her eleven-year-old self, calling for a friend and being told they were already out with someone else. 'She's busy with Hetty this morning. I think Hetty invited her to go on a supplier visit or something.' It was ridiculous to be envious. She and Maggie had developed a close friendship only a few weeks after Laurel's arrival in Elderwick and nothing had changed. So, Maggie was seeing a bit more of Hetty, and now spending time with Natalie too. Of course, Maggie had other friends. If anything, Laurel needed to do the same for herself, meet new people, get out of her comfort zone. Until then, she could at least count on Albert.

'I see. That's a shame. Unfortunately, I'm unable to accompany you either. I have a prior engagement this morning. The vicar is coming to tea. Isn't that terribly English?' He chuckled.

Her smile slipped, but she tried to mask her disappointment. 'That's okay. I'll let you know what I find – if there is anything to find.' She turned to go.

'Laurel.' Albert held his hand out to her. She felt the calluses on his palm and his strong fingers gripping her own as she took it. 'You must come for tea, the meal not the drink. Tomorrow evening, seven o'clock. We'll have a proper catch up.'

'I guess.' She sounded like an ungrateful brat. 'Sorry. Thank you, Albert, that would be lovely.'

He squeezed once more, then let go.

Walking away, Laurel could still feel the warmth of Albert's hand. She was lucky to know such wonderful people. She should be grateful and not behave like a sulky teen. Her cheeks flared with heat; Albert deserved better. She'd make it up to him. She'd pick up a special dessert from the bakery and she would make a point of telling her host how much she valued his friendship.

Resolved to do better, she turned her thoughts to the pond. Passing her garden, she reached over the wall to grab the broom handle she'd fashioned as a poking stick. Suitably prepared, her wellies made ppfftt sounds as she continued up the lane. They were a bit tighter around her calves than she'd like. *No more cake for you.*

Laurel had banked on 10.45am on a Friday morning being a safe time to go treasure hunting: the children at the primary school would be back in class after their break; the early commute would be long over; and the tearoom should have emptied of the breakfast crowd and not yet be filled with the lunch rush. What she'd failed to account for was the 11am seniors' tai chi class in the village hall. There was already a crowd of bobbing, blue-rinsed heads outside the hall. She had an audience.

She came to a halt by the unfenced bank of the pond. It was bigger than she'd thought, having never really paid it much attention, and she didn't know where to begin her search. She could run up to the bakery and ask Constance where the mysterious figure had paused when passing, but in the dark, it had probably been hard to pinpoint. Besides, if something had been thrown in, it could have ended up anywhere.

May as well get prodding around in the reeds. No sense coming all this way and not giving it a go.

Using the broom handle for support, she shuffled down the shallow bank, slippery with mud.

'You won't catch many fish in there,' called a voice from over the road, followed by laughter.

She raised her hand without looking round and grinned. Goodness knows what they thought she was up to.

When she felt safely balanced, she lifted the stick and gave a couple of trial swipes through the greenery. A disturbed duck set off a cacophonous quacking, fleeing into the centre of the pool and upsetting his fellow fowl.

'Not many fish in there.' It was a male voice this time.

'Someone already used that one,' she called back.

There was a long pause, and she thought the owner of the voice must have moved on.

'What do you call a fish with no eyes?'

'I don't know. What do you call a fish with no eyes?'

'Fsh.'

It was a terrible joke but she laughed and turned to look for the voice on the bank. As she did, her left foot slipped further into the water, she dropped the stick, and landed with a teeth-jarring thud in the slimy, noxious ooze.

'Damn it. I'm sorry, that was my fault. Are you okay?'

Her pride damaged as much as her tailbone Laurel saw who it was behind her. 'Ben.'

He planted his feet firmly and reached out towards her. 'Grab on, I'll pull you out.' Out of uniform, he cut an attractive figure in jeans and a navy North Face jacket.

Why was it she always met Ben at the most unflattering moments? If there wasn't a dead body, then she seemed to be covered in mud and tangled in greenery of some description.

'Here.' He helped her over to the bench where she lowered herself cautiously. 'Dare I ask? What are you doing?'

She explained what she was looking for, and why, and though he nodded, she could see the scepticism in the line of his lips. The tai chi ladies had disappeared into the hall and they were alone, other than the ducks and a lone goose. The cold muck was chilling her, she stood and stamped her feet to get the blood flowing.

'It's a long shot, but what if it was the murderer and they threw a weapon into the pond? You saw the body. Do you think he was stabbed to death? Because I don't.' She hadn't ever looked at Ben long enough before to properly appreciate his eyes, hazel with flecks of gold. She looked at him now, searching for a sign he shared her theory.

He took his time in replying. 'This goes no further?'

'Absolutely.'

He scrubbed his hands over his face. 'The stab wound didn't kill him.'

It would have been unseemly to celebrate, but she allowed herself a glow of satisfaction at being right.

'Before you ask, I can't tell you the cause of death. Sorry. But we are looking for... other evidence. I'll need to let the SIO know what you've told me. Why didn't Constance or Hetty report what they saw?'

She was about to answer when a shout distracted them. A group of three teenagers were slouching their way towards them. Laurel frowned, she would never admit it, but she'd been enjoying Ben's undivided attention.

'It's PC Benny-Boy,' called the tallest. Clad entirely in black, he led his gang to the bench where he performed an elaborate greeting ritual with Ben, or possibly it was a handshake.

'Laurel, these fine, young citizens are Ivor, Seb, and Penelope... sorry, Pen.' He corrected himself quickly when the third member of the collection shot him a hurt look. 'They must have an inset day at school because no way would they be skiving in front of an officer of the law.'

'Skiving?' mocked Seb. 'The 1990s called, they want their lame words back.' The three fell about laughing as Ben shared a smile with Laurel.

'You know you're covered in mud, right?' asked Pen. 'It stinks.'

Laurel bit back a smart-alec retort. They were just kids being kids. She'd been insufferable at their age too. 'I am aware, thank you.'

'Are you Ben's girlfriend?'

The tilt of the chin, the challenge in her tone. Laurel hid her amusement. Pen had a crush on Ben. 'No, Ben was just helping me out after I slipped.'

'What were you doing in the pond?'

She looked to Ben, not sure if she should say anything.

He helped her out. 'Laurel thought someone threw something in there the other day. She was trying to get it back.'

'What is it?'

'I don't know,' she admitted.

'If it's shiny, the duck'll have it.'

'Pardon?' Laurel was flummoxed.

'Watch.' Seb took a pack of gum out of his packet and removed the silver paper from one stick. He folded it carefully, keeping from scrunching it too small, then threw it towards the middle of the pond. It was too light to go far, but it landed and floated on the scummy surface.

'Hey,' cried Ben. 'You can't litter.'

'Look,' said Laurel, pointing in disbelief.

One of the ducks was haring towards the paper. She grabbed it in her bill and swam off to a patch of the bank on the far side.

'Stupid duck thinks she's a bloody magpie,' said Seb.

'You've seen her do that before?'

He blushed. It wasn't cool for teenagers to watch the ducks.

'You should look over there.' He pointed to where the duck was re-emerging from the reeds and back out into the water.

A bus pulled up across the road and, as one, the kids grabbed their bags. 'Gotta run, can't be skiving off all day.' Ivor gave them a smirk and they ran for the bus.

'Thanks,' yelled Laurel over the cough of the diesel engine.

'Shall we go and look?' she asked Ben.

As they poked around in the glutinous mud, Laurel's mind turned to the letters she'd been receiving. She wasn't worried by them as such because she couldn't believe anyone intended to harm her. However, since the attack on Dorothy, she was upset at the accuracy of the sentiment expressed by the notes. She *was* a danger to people who knew her. Even the police who'd questioned her when she'd found Dorothy had pointed out how many people with whom she was acquainted had died or been hurt.

'Can I ask you about something, Ben? But off the record?'

'Okay.' He lifted his head from inspecting the sludge to look at her. 'What's on your mind?'

She planted her stick in the muck and removed her filthy gloves, dirty from examining various items of detritus.

'I've had a couple of letters sent to me anonymously. They're not threatening, but they tell me I should leave Elderwick. I'm not scared, but should I report them, do you think? Officially, I mean.'

Ben straightened up and gave her his full attention. 'How many letters?'

'Only two.'

'Do you still have them?'

She nodded.

'If you like, I can come round, take a look, and file a report for you down at the station.' A lock of hair fell over his eyes, and he swiped at it, leaving a smudge of dirt behind. 'If there's no threat in what's written, I'm not sure we can do much about it. But it would be good to have a record, just in case. After what happened to you last year, we shouldn't take any chances.'

Her eyes widened. She'd expected him to dismiss the letters as a prank, but he was taking them seriously.

'I'm sure they're nothing. It'll be kids messing with your head.' He hurried to reassure her. 'But if you're ever scared, you can call me, day or night.' He fished out his wallet and produced a card on which was printed his name and number.

Laurel accepted it and stowed it away safely in the inside pocket of her coat. 'Thank you, yes. Don't worry if you're busy, but if you could come round sometime, that would be nice.'

Feeling her cheeks colour, she unstuck her stick and swiped at the reeds, feigning complete focus on the search for a clue. Within a couple of sweeps, she spotted a heap of shiny objects collected by the scavenging mallard. 'Ah, look, I've found her stash.' She poked, separating out the different items. Most of them were silver pieces of paper, like the one thrown by Seb, but then her stick hit something solid.

'That must be it.' She pointed to a metal canister. 'The rest is just litter.'

Ben squatted to take a closer look. 'There are lots of reasons that might have found its way into the pond, you know.'

'Well, I know young people erm... use it, and I hear it's easy to get hold of, but you're going to collect it and check it out, aren't you?'

He pulled a plastic bag from his jacket and, using the bag so as not to touch it with his fingers, he plucked the canister from the duck's treasure trove. 'It's not something we've had much of a problem with in Elderwick. The kids–' he nodded in the direction the bus had taken, '–they keep me up to date.'

'That's remarkably responsible of them.' She couldn't imagine any of her group of friends from school would have been so keen to be police informants.

He laughed. 'It's part of our agreement, I defend them when the older residents of the village get themselves het up over a party, loud music, or the youngsters congregating at the bus stop. In return, they help me stay abreast of the latest trends in recreational narcotics. Community policing at its best.'

'Fair enough.'

His face turned serious. 'For now, best not mention what we've found to anyone. Is that okay?'

'They'll never *drake* me talk,' she quipped.

Chapter 29

Laurel

'What can I get you? A nice bacon and brie sandwich perhaps, for fortification?'

'You know me too well.' Laurel smiled at Jo.

'You on your own today?'

'I am.'

'It looks like you've got yourself some work?'

'Just some notes and a bit of reading I need to do.'

'I'm going to bring you a chocolate chip cookie straight from the oven too. You look like you could do with a bit of cheering up.'

Jo was right, she'd been home to change after her fall in the mud, but her bottom was bruised, and she was feeling sorry for herself. She missed Maggie. It wasn't the same sitting in The Pleasant Pheasant on her own thinking about one person who'd been killed and another hit so hard they might die. Alone, there was no gratification of clues uncovered and solved, theories deliberated over with her friend, feeling like she was helping, even in a small way. Instead, just sadness at the brutality and loss.

As Jo disappeared back into the kitchen, Laurel opened her

green notebook and looked at the lines already written. The entries were sparse. She and Maggie hadn't had many opportunities to discuss the cases so far, but she couldn't sit around waiting. Going on what she'd gleaned from Ben, she concluded the police weren't making great strides in identifying the attacker – or attackers – of Simon and Dorothy. Hugh was convinced Simon's journal would light the way, but having read it herself, Laurel was still at a loss as to who the culprit might be. Unless it was Hugh. It was possible it was Hugh.

Nearly two weeks had passed since she, Albert, and Dorothy had found Simon's body, and it was almost a week since she'd found Dorothy. How could they know so little after all that time?

Jo brought over her sandwich and a drink. 'There you go, love. Enjoy.'

Between bites of oozing, salty, crispy deliciousness, Laurel worked through her thoughts and jotted down the key points for each victim. Next, she made a list of questions yet to be asked. Principal amongst them was what Simon had spoken to the vicar about, and what was in Simon's journal that could have led to the attempt on Dorothy's life? The journal had to be the reason she'd been attacked.

After her adventure in the pond, and based on what she and Ben had found, she had an idea about the true cause of Simon's death and her internet research the night before meant she had a working theory as to how he'd been found in a locked room. But these insights only raised further questions: why go to the trouble of killing Simon, making it look like he'd been killed in an entirely different manner, and then set up a locked room mystery? It was bizarre.

With such scant information, she could identify few suspects. Hugh was the most obvious. He knew Simon, had known him at school in fact. He had visited Simon at Tulip

Cottage. If he'd known what Simon was planning to write, that was motive. And, on the village green, the day after Simon's death, Natalie had arrived to tell him about it, and he'd asked how Simon had been *killed*. Had he assumed Simon had been killed or did he already know?

Christopher could be a suspect, but only in as much as he'd met with Simon and refused to say why.

Then there was Elise. When asked about her meeting with Simon, she'd lied to Maggie and Natalie. Then she'd lied again when Laurel had asked her the same question.

Of those three suspects, any one of them could have been Dorothy's assailant. There'd been no sign of forced entry at Dorothy's house. Dorothy would have opened the door to Christopher without thinking twice. He was the vicar, and she knew him well. She probably wouldn't have been anxious about seeing Elise on her doorstep, but what about Hugh? From what Maggie had said, Dorothy disliked him intensely. If Hugh had knocked at her door, might she have opened it to give him a piece of her mind?

'Got room for that cookie?'

Laurel yelped. 'Sorry, Jo, you surprised me.' She closed her notebook. 'And, yes, there's always room for a cookie. Or two,' she added, seeing the plate. 'Thank you.'

'Are you Miss Marple-ing again?' Jo asked. 'We were all so impressed when you solved those murders last year.'

'More luck than judgement.'

'Nonsense. Maggie told me how you worked it all out. Then for that brute to drug you, heavens above! What a to-do. I would bet a week's worth of cookies you'll be solving this case too, and long before the police or that author fellow.'

She couldn't help her lips lifting. Great food *and* compliments.

'When you solve this one, I hope we can get Dandelions to

reconsider. I heard from Petra the other day, the charity have withdrawn their offer for the hall and that nasty Mr Carter-Bell is pestering Marcus at all hours to sell to him instead.' She pulled a face. 'Do you have a suspect yet?'

'Not yet, but maybe you can help me with the case.'

Jo beamed. 'Fire away.'

'The day before Simon was found dead he was here with Elise, Ben's girlfriend. Did you happen to hear what they were talking about?'

Jo pulled out a chair and sat. 'That's what that Natalie was asking about. She was here with Maggie the other day. I would have told Maggie, and I don't mind telling you, but not that young madam.' She beckoned Laurel towards her and said in a low voice, 'I didn't catch much of the conversation, too busy, but I did hear Elise ask, no, beg is a better word – beg Simon not to involve her.'

'In what?'

'I don't know.'

'Did she seem angry, upset? Was he?'

'She was, and afraid, I think. He wasn't fussed at all.'

Laurel scribbled a note. 'Anything else you can remember?'

'There was one other thing. He said nothing and no one would stop him from writing the story.' She shrugged. 'I guess he was wrong.'

Chapter 30

Laurel

Hugh was sitting on a bench by the war memorial, phone in one hand, newspaper in the other. He was squinting in the low sun in the washed-out sky.

'Hugh, I'm glad I've bumped into you.'

He grunted. His eyes were red rimmed, Laurel noticed, and his skin had an unhealthy pallor. He barely glanced at her.

'Can I sit?' She knew he wanted to say no, but she wasn't prepared to miss this opportunity. She sat.

'It's not a good time.' He was sharp.

Laurel recalled their last conversation. By now he would have read Simon's journal. She experienced a momentary flare of sympathy but squashed it. If he was the murderer, he might be using his influence to interfere in the police investigation in all kinds of devious ways. 'I have a couple of questions, then I'll leave you be.'

'I can't tell you what's in the journal. I explained that to you already.' His nostrils flared and he continued to avoid eye contact.

'No, it's not about the journal. Hugh, do you remember the Wednesday when Natalie arrived? I was with Maggie right about here, on the green. Natalie was here to break the news to you about Simon's death, and you asked her a question.'

'So?'

'So, you asked her how he'd been *killed*. Why?'

Now he looked at her properly. 'You don't miss much do you.'

Well, duh. He wasn't the first to underestimate her and he wouldn't be the last. Being a diminutive five-foot-four brunette with glasses and an unimaginative wardrobe, she was used to people assuming she was some meek little nobody.

She waited him out.

'Fine,' he sighed. 'I can explain. I heard on Tuesday that he'd been found dead, murdered. I was coming out of the... what's it called?' He looked round and read the sign above the tearoom door. 'The Pleasant Pheasant. It was late afternoon, and I overheard that Dorothy woman telling someone about it as they walked in.'

Frowning, she asked, 'Why would you lie about that? Why pretend you didn't know?'

'I felt bad for Natalie. She'd driven all the way down here to tell me, to break the news gently.' He stared across the road towards the pond and shoved his hands into the pockets of his thick – expensive – winter coat.

Laurel recalled the way he'd treated Natalie, then and since. His account didn't ring true. Hugh wasn't the type to be mindful of the feelings of others, especially not someone he considered a member of staff.

Why is everyone lying about everything? She shook her head. 'I'm not sure I believe you.'

'That's how I found out. What more do you want me to say?' His jaw clenched, pulling the skin around his mouth taut. 'Bloody woman,' he muttered.

Laurel didn't know if he meant her or Natalie. 'Shall I tell you what I think? I think you wanted an audience. I get it, it's okay. You're a big-shot author; he was the journalist writing about your wonderful life and career.' She caught him wincing. 'You felt it was only right and proper the news was broken to you in an appropriately *respectful* manner. Overhearing it doesn't fit with the image. And you wanted to have your reaction witnessed so we could all see how upset you were. How shocked.' She was being very blunt and confrontational but wanted to see how he'd react. Would he admit to the truth now? She was 99.9 per cent sure she'd read him correctly.

'Get lost, will you.'

'I've got one more question.'

'Of course you do.'

'Now you've read his journal, was Simon going to write the article you thought he was going to write?'

Hugh Quintrell turned his head sharply and glared at Laurel. Then, without another word, he stood and stalked off.

I love the internet, she thought twenty minutes later as she tapped away on her laptop. It was so easy to find out all kinds of information. With the photos she'd taken of Simon's notes in his journal, she'd found some old newspaper reports of the boy who'd died at Hugh's school; Xavier Houghton was his name. She presumed it was due to his age that Hugh wasn't named in any of the newspaper reports on the death. In fact, there were only four mentions of the incident at all.

The thought had crossed her mind that Simon might have been related to Xavier, and that he had wanted to expose or take revenge on Hugh through the profile he was writing. There was no evidence of a familial link, though.

She could understand Hugh wouldn't want it dragged up,

but would it be motive enough for murder? Scandal surrounding public figures wasn't what it used to be.

The world on social media would share some new hashtags, then shrug and move on. A piece on Hugh speculating over his connection to the boy's death might be personally uncomfortable for him, but the news cycle churned past stories within days, if not hours. And there was the old adage about all publicity being good publicity.

Next, she looked up his childhood school and trawled through reams of photos and records, searching for any mention of him, Simon, or the boy who had died. On the school's own website, there was a section detailing famous alumni; both Hugh and Simon were included with brief profiles. It told her nothing she didn't already know.

Simon's back catalogue of work was well documented and easy to follow via LinkedIn, Facebook, the website of the magazine he'd been working for most recently, and in the lists of awards he'd won for his writing. His focus had changed over the years from interviews with the stars of British film and television, to increasingly in-depth and intimate portraits of the darlings of the UK literary world. Authors, editors, agents, publishers, all were included, or should that be targeted? The majority came out well, but on occasion, Simon had crafted razor-sharp exposés intended to draw blood.

Laurel liked the Reverend Christopher Ibori and didn't want to discover anything to change her opinion of the man. Hence, it was with a twinge of unease that she searched for his name. It was only too easy to imagine the sort of behaviour which would get a vicar moved on from one parish to another. She fought to keep her anger in check as she considered the number of times she'd read about an adult in a position of responsibility who had abused the vulnerable in the worst possible way. Perpetrators who, unbelievably, weren't then subject to justice, but instead were quietly shunted off to visit their abuse on other unsuspecting victims. Nothing to see here.

As far as she could ascertain, Christopher was not one of those predators. He *had* moved from his previous parish, and she couldn't find out why, but she had found a photo on the diocesan website of his leaving party in which he was flanked by his local bishop and the Archbishop of Canterbury. An unlikely photo-op had Christopher been leaving in disgrace.

The very last thing she did before shutting down her laptop was to search for silver metal canisters. The results were illuminating. True, many people found nitrous oxide fairly easy to come by – and to use to get high – but there was also a professional group who routinely used the gas and would have ready access. By her count, at least four people in Elderwick were members of that profession.

Chapter 31

Laurel

Laurel had avoided it for as long as she could, but the time had come: she needed to read Hugh Quintrell's book.

The author was the obvious suspect in Simon's murder – and therefore, Dorothy's attack – and reading his early work might give her a deeper insight into the man's personality. According to Simon's journal, in his first book, Hugh had liberally appropriated the experiences of his daughter and his then wife for the sake of his 'craft'.

After she'd stoked the fire in the woodburner she pulled a blanket over her legs and got comfortable on the sofa. Resting the book on her knee she studied the cover. It showed a young woman silhouetted by a streetlight on a dark and empty road. She noted the dedication – To the great authors of the world who inspired me to become the writer I am today – and began to read.

THE MURDER OF INNOCENTS

Chapter One

I'm the person they call in for the worst cases. I'm the person you don't want to see at a crime scene.

'What've we got?' The hangover burns in my stomach and fogs my concentration, but the coffee is helping. I need to focus. I was on leave. I was promised there'd be no calls, but they need me for this one and I need to be on point. I recap what I was told on the phone, a young girl, raped, left for dead. No one's saying it, but I know in my gut it's the same guy.

'DCI Steerforth, good to have you on board. What we've got is a seventeen-year-old female, IC1. Name and address from driving licence. Polly Irving. She lives two streets away. Same type of location, same injuries visible on the arms and torso. But there's one big difference to the other cases.'

I haven't got time for games. 'What?'

'This one's still alive.'

Laurel tasted bile. Was the victim the character based on his daughter? The ages matched, and Polly was not a million miles from Holly. He hadn't even tried to disguise her identity.

This is the break we've been praying for, and dreading, another victim of The Trash Collector. Even thinking that name makes me sick. It's the name he chose for himself and some bastard in the media ran with it. Now it's all over the papers, the internet, the TV. He debases his victims, treats them like trash, considers them to be human garbage. What's with the word 'trash' anyway? There's been debate over whether he's a Yank, from the US, but I don't believe it. He's home grown. He's a brother, son, father, neighbour of someone in this city, and his luck is about to run out.

She skipped through the following chapters, skimming a line here and there. Her appetite for reading the novel had well and truly departed.

Then, a passage on page 187 caught her eye.

I know, without a doubt, I would kill to protect my own daughter. It would be as instinctive as breathing. If ever she was in harm's way, I would do whatever was needed. And if I needed to kill someone, I'd be able to do it and get away with it. No one knows crime scenes like I do. I wouldn't make mistakes.

Quite aside from what this told her about Hugh, she was surprised at Maggie being such a fan. In the half-hearted book group they'd formed only a few months back, the flavour of books was very much cosy murder-mystery: Agatha Christie to Agatha Raisin. The fact they hadn't managed to read or discuss many books before becoming embroiled in two real-life murders was beside the point. What did Maggie see in this gratuitous police procedural?

Perhaps, she reflected, she was being unfairly judgemental. Knowing Hugh had exploited his daughter's horrific experience so blatantly was colouring her view. She had no reason to suspect Maggie knew this side of the story, and if you didn't know, the book was just like many thousands of others.

Was any of this useful information, though? That was the pertinent question. Earlier, she'd reasoned that any negative effect on Hugh's career as a result of Simon's article was likely to be short-lived. But what if Simon had finally woken Hugh to the reality of what he'd done to his daughter? Was that not sufficient motive for murder? In Hugh's own words, albeit spoken by his character, DCI Steerforth, it was.

She recalled seeing the name of a psychiatrist in Simon's journal and paged through her notebook until she found it. Hugh had mentioned having a therapist when they'd met for his first assessment sessions. She could call this Dr Burton and ask about Hugh. Chances were the doctor wouldn't tell her anything, but it was worth a shot.

She cleared her throat as she waited for the phone to be answered. Friday afternoons weren't the best time to catch people in the office, but it wasn't yet five o'clock.

'Hi, my name's Dr Laurel Nightingale,' she said when the phone was answered. 'I'm calling about Hugh Quintrell. Is it possible to speak with Dr Burton, please?' She crossed her fingers and to her surprise, she was put through.

Dr Burton, when he came on the phone, didn't waste any time getting to the point. His words were delivered in a rapid staccato. 'I have nothing to say about Hugh Quintrell. Please stop calling my office.'

'Wait, please. I haven't called you before. It's important, a man has been killed and you might be able to help.'

She heard a long sigh down the phone and could almost see the doctor debate whether to hang up on her. Curiosity must have won out. 'Did you say you were a doctor? Are you with the police?'

'No, I'm a clinical psychologist. I'm calling... that is... have you heard of Simon Forster?' She should have planned what to say before making the call.

'He's the journalist who's been calling here, harassing my staff. I told him we have nothing to discuss. You said someone's been killed. Was it him?' Burton's anger had subsided, but he sounded wary.

'Yes, I'm afraid so. He was murdered a couple of weeks ago in Elderwick, a village in East Yorkshire.'

She thought she'd detected an intake of breath when she gave the name of the village.

'Well, I'm sorry to hear that, but I don't know what you want from me.'

In that moment she decided to bend her ethics a little.

Sweat broke out under her arms. *This is not who I am!* 'Hugh Quintrell is a patient of mine and I'm concerned about him. Are you able to tell me if he is, or was a patient of yours?'

There was a long pause. 'Who did you say you were again?'

She was tempted to hang up the phone before he accused her of lying. Then she remembered she hadn't blocked her number when she'd called, and she'd given her name. 'Doctor Laurel Nightingale,' she said in a voice that shook.

'Hold on a moment, please.'

She could hear typing.

'What's you registration number with HCPC?'

She recited it, thankful she knew it off by heart. More typing.

'I see from your webpage you're in private practice? There's a phone number here. I'm going to call you back on that number. Are you in your office now?'

'No, but I can be in ten minutes.'

'I'll call you in ten minutes.' He hung up.

She was out of breath as she raced up the stairs of her office building and jammed her key in the lock. She could hear the phone ringing already. *I have to get in shape!*

'Hello, Doctor Burton?'

'I nearly gave up on you.'

'Sorry,' she panted. 'Thank you so much for calling me back.'

'That's okay. I probably wouldn't have done, but I've heard of you. You were in *The Psychologist* a few months back, weren't you? You solved those murders last year and nearly died yourself?'

She cringed. She regretted doing that interview.

'Hugh Quintrell is your patient, then. Lucky you.' The way he said it told her he thought she was anything but lucky. 'Hugh isn't and never has been a patient of mine.'

'Simon Forster wasn't calling you about him?'

'No.'

'Oh. I see.' She thought she knew now who Simon had been calling about.

'Yes.'

'And you didn't tell him anything, Simon, that is?'

'Absolutely not. Do you think this has some bearing on the murder?'

'I'm not sure, but if it does, Hugh's daughter might be involved.'

'She's not a suspect, is she?'

'Oh no, not that I know of. My understanding is she's had nothing to do with her dad for years, and I can see why. No, Hugh and Simon were both in Elderwick for work and I see no reason for Holly Quintrell to even know they were here. My theory is that Simon was killed to prevent him from publishing an article that could be damaging to Hugh, and probably distressing, if not traumatic, for Holly.'

'And you're wondering if Hugh might have been the one to silence Simon?'

'It has crossed my mind.'

'I'm sorry I can't help.'

'It's okay, and I think you have actually. If you're still seeing your patient, I hope she's okay. It can't be easy–'

'No. I have to go now. Take care, Dr Nightingale.'

'You too, and thank you again.'

She hung up and stared into the middle distance as she replayed Doctor Burton's words, and unravelled what he hadn't said. Holly was his patient then, not Hugh. Or she had been. Simon had done his homework.

Chapter 32

Maggie

Maggie had enjoyed her morning out with Hetty. The woman was a lot of fun, and just what she needed after the turmoil of recent months. It had taken her many years and her new friendship with Laurel to finally admit to herself that her husband was a controlling bully. Ex-husband now. Leaving him had been easy, figuring out who she was without him, however, had not been so straightforward.

Revelling in her good mood, she pulled onto the driveway in her baby blue Mini. Two months after taking delivery of her first car in fifteen years, she still enjoyed the thrill of going where she wanted, whenever she wanted.

She lifted shopping bags out of the boot, all the ingredients for a delicious supper for her and Natalie. Juggling the groceries, she slotted her key into the lock and with her foot nudged open the door.

'Let me help you with that,' said Natalie, appearing in the hallway. 'You've got enough here to feed an army,' she commented, as she carried over-filled bags through to the kitchen. 'Are you expecting company?' She began removing packages and placing them on the countertops.

'No, just you and me, but I wanted to make something special.'

'What's the occasion?' Natalie was eyeing a bottle of wine.

Maggie worked methodically, putting the shopping away in her neat cupboards, fridge and freezer. She paused with a bar of chocolate in her hand, biting her lip as she battled the temptation to tuck in. Restraint won out and she stored it safely out of sight, ready for making chocolate sauce later.

'No occasion, I think it's nice to treat yourself to a fancy dinner every once in a while for no reason, don't you agree?'

'I suppose, but Maggie, you know I'm not a big eater. I honestly don't think I'll be able to do your cooking justice.'

Maggie put her hand to her mouth. 'I'm so sorry, you must think I'm awful. I'm not trying to feed you anything you don't want. I should have thought... I should have checked with you.' She hoped she hadn't offended the young woman. Food was how she showed love and care for those around her. It was her way of giving to others. She shouldn't have been so wrapped up in herself that she forgot Natalie was trying to lose weight and wasn't a big eater.

'I can do you a simple supper if you'd prefer? In fact, let's do that. The other stuff will save for another day.'

'I've got a better idea. How about I give Hugh a call and see if he's free for dinner? Between the three of us, we should be able to put away a fair amount.' She waved her phone at Maggie.

With butterflies in her stomach, at first, all she could do was squeak out a 'Yes'. She took a deep breath. 'Do you think he'd come?' It was one thing having Hugh speak at the WI meeting, but to have him in her house, eating food she'd cooked, at her table. 'I can set the table in the dining room. It's a touch formal, but we can't eat in the kitchen, and I'll get the best china for us to use, and the crystal glasses. They'll look lovely. What else?'

'Maggie, calm down.' Natalie giggled. 'Hugh won't want you going to any trouble. Your delicious food will be all he cares about. Let me message him. I keep forgetting I can't call from here on my mobile. Shall we say 7.30pm?'

'That was incredible, my dear Maggie,' said Hugh as he placed his spoon on his plate, having eaten the last profiterole. 'I am stuffed.' He patted his trim stomach.

Maggie allowed herself a beam of pride. He'd already polished off a large slice of quiche lorraine to start then two helpings of her tarragon chicken with green beans. 'It was a privilege to cook for you.' She offered round the last of the wine and sighed with pleasure.

'Now, I hear you and Laurel have been theorising as to the identity of Simon's killer. Care to share what you've deduced?' He leaned his elbows on the table and gazed at her.

She blushed and stammered, 'We've talked things over, but we're strictly amateurs. I'm more interested to hear what *you've* discovered.' With a pang of regret, she realised how little time she and Laurel had found to speculate over the murder and the attack on Dorothy. She resolved to call her in the morning, and they could arrange to meet for a proper case discussion. In the meantime, hearing where Hugh was up to would be useful.

The author glanced at Natalie. 'We have some avenues we're exploring. I'm afraid I am limited as to what I can tell you. The police have put their confidence in my discretion. I'm sure you understand?' He tapped the side of his nose and winked at her. 'The information from your WI ladies was most useful, though, and has been passed on to the senior investigating officer. Unfortunately, there are no CCTV cameras in this village, so beyond interviewing each of the witnesses, there's little for them to go on.'

Maggie made a mental note to ask Hetty and Constance if the police had spoken to them about the figure they saw by the pond. Hetty hadn't mentioned anything. She did hope the investigating team were taking the reports seriously.

'Can I confide in you, Maggie?' Hugh took her hand and held it lightly.

Hugh Quintrell was holding her hand! She couldn't speak.

He smiled at her. 'Natalie... that is, Natalie and I are concerned about Laurel.'

Maggie tuned back in fast, all hand holding forgotten. 'What's the matter? Is she okay?'

'Natalie tells me Laurel continues to be terribly upset over finding Simon and then coming across Dorothy. She... we fear she is becoming too involved for her own good in seeking the guilty party.' He turned to Natalie who bobbed her head like one of those nodding dogs.

Maggie digested his words. They didn't ring true. 'She's very good at this kind of thing, you know.' She thought back to the disagreement they'd had at their last meeting, when Laurel had insisted on snooping in Simon's journal. Had she missed signs Laurel was struggling?

'I'm sure she is, but this is serious business, best left to the professionals. I'd hate for her to find herself in bother or to mislead the police in any way.'

Maggie opened her mouth to protest. Laurel would never do such a thing. Then again, last year she and Laurel had accused the wrong man of two murders. She closed her mouth.

Hugh pushed on. 'Only the other day she intimated she thought *I* may have something to do with all the nastiness. Of course, I don't hold it against her; she is out of her depth and distressed. Natalie has offered to have a discreet chat with her but what... I wonder... it might sound better if it's coming from you. You're obviously close and if she understands you're concerned for her, she's more likely to take notice. My relationship with her is a little complicated since I was seeing her in a professional capacity. Do you understand?' He released her hand and sat back in his chair.

From the corner of her eye, Maggie could see Natalie watching her closely. She took a sip of her wine that she struggled to swallow.

'We only have her best interests at heart. Do say you'll help us.'

'I suppose Laurel has seemed out of sorts lately.' Stealing Simon's journal from Dorothy's kitchen was out of character. Maggie picked at the corner of her nail and shut her eyes to think for a second. Opening them, she said, 'If you believe it's for the best...'

Hugh smiled. 'I knew we could count on you.'

Chapter 33

Laurel

It was early for someone to be calling, but the knocking was insistent.

'Hello?' It was Natalie on the doorstep. At least she thought it was Natalie; it was hard to tell under the bulky coat, scarf and hat. 'Do you want to come in?' she asked, more to keep the heat in than from wanting to spend time with Hugh's agent.

'Sure. It's freezing out here.' The woman shuffled in and closed the door behind her. In the living room, Laurel took the armchair and Natalie perched herself on the edge of the sofa, holding her hands out towards the wood burner. 'I'm so glad I caught you. I need to talk to you about Maggie. There's something I think you should know.'

Laurel's heart thumped. They might not have seen much of each other lately, but Maggie was her best friend. 'What's happened?'

'Can I speak to you in confidence?'

'Of course.'

'Maybe I shouldn't say anything.' Natalie pouted, shrugging her shoulders. She shuffled back on the sofa and unzipped her coat.

Laurel was tempted to shake her. *Get to the point!* 'It's obviously bothering you and if I can help…'

Natalie's pout intensified, but she relented. 'Maggie told Hugh she's worried about you.'

'About me?' Laurel was mystified.

'She told him you seem to have become fixated on him and you're starting to suggest he might be responsible for Simon's death. She thinks you're overwhelmed after finding Simon's body and then discovering Dorothy after the attack.' She tilted her head to one side and gave her a frowny face.

Laurel heard the blood rushing in her ears.

'I can see you're upset now,' said Natalie. 'That's why I'm here and not Maggie. She was afraid you'd be upset with her for mentioning her concerns. Also, I hope you don't take offence, but Laurel, speaking as Hugh's agent I need to reassure you, Hugh isn't responsible for Simon's death or the attack on Dorothy. Honestly, it was most likely a stranger or someone Simon upset with one of his articles in the past.

'Maggie is worried about you. She doesn't want to see you get into trouble over this and Hugh is too polite to tell you himself, so I'm here to give you a gentle caution.'

'Hold on.' Laurel's heart was racing, and sweat was forming along her hairline. She focused on the smell of the fragrant smoke from the fire, reminiscent of her childhood. She heard the wind rustling the dead leaves outside, and she watched a blackbird through the window skipping across the lawn. Only then was she able to unclench her hands.

'What are you doing?' Natalie's voice broke her concentration.

'I'm grounding myself. I'm feeling very strong emotions and I need a moment to get perspective on what you've said.'

'Okay.'

Thoughts were buzzing in her head. How could Maggie

have said those things to Natalie and Hugh? This was worse than her blabbing about the case. This was personal in the worst possible way.

Whether it was self-preservation or the look on Laurel's face that prompted Natalie to leave so soon after delivering her message, Laurel was relieved to see her go.

***

'Hetty and Constance have invited me to join their new business venture. The Plump Tart is going to offer baking lessons one afternoon a week and they want me on board. Isn't that fantastic?' Maggie was barely through Laurel's door, chattering away bright as a robin on a winter's morning.

'That's great.' Laurel tried to sound enthusiastic; cooking and baking were Maggie's joys in life. 'Are you going to do it?'

Maggie's grin told her the answer. 'Abso-blummin-lutely. I can't wait to get started. Hetty told me all about their plans yesterday when we were out visiting her suppliers. They're going to keep the classes small, but they expect to be fully booked right away. People will pay for the class and the ingredients then get to take home a delicious cake or pastry at the end. Hetty and Constance are so busy in the bakery they won't have time to lead the tutorials themselves, which is why they asked me. They're going to train me up and everything. I'll be learning all their secrets. Prepare to eat more cake than ever before!'

'Do they use nitrous oxide in their work?' Laurel heard the bluntness of her question, but she was in no mood to pussy-foot around. She hadn't intended to say anything about the gas, knowing it would undoubtedly filter back to Hugh, but it was germane, and he'd hear it from the police soon enough anyway.

Besides, she wouldn't mention the canister or where it had been found.

'Nitrous oxide?'

'I think it's also called noz. You find it in those things for making whipped cream and foams... I think. I'm not sure.'

'I don't know. I can ask. Why?'

'Just a theory I'm exploring.' She wasn't going to explain further.

In the living room, Laurel took her usual place in the armchair while Maggie walked to the French windows and looked out into the barren garden. Laurel fidgeted, searching for the right words to bring up Natalie's visit.

Maggie turned and sank onto the sofa, her smile dimming as she looked at Laurel. 'Sorry, I'm getting all caught up in my good news. Are you okay after Dorothy and everything?'

So, Natalie was right, Maggie was concerned. But it didn't excuse her betrayal. Laurel picked up a pen, needing something to occupy her hands. 'I'm doing all right, but it's upsetting not knowing how Dorothy is getting on. I tried calling the hospital again, they still won't tell me anything. But I'm fine.' She stressed the last word.

'Christopher's been in to visit her, I'm sure he can be persuaded to share enough to put your mind at rest.'

'That's not a bad idea.' It would be a good excuse to speak to him again, too. The way she was feeling, she might warn him about Hugh's suspicions. If Hugh was going to have her warned off, then it was only fair.

She was conscious she was holding back. All the people she'd spoken to over the last few days, all the lies. She desperately wanted to chew it over with Maggie. 'Speaking of Dorothy, have you heard anything from Natalie or Hugh about the investigation?' She was aiming for nonchalant but held her breath as she waited to see how Maggie would reply.

Maggie looked everywhere but at Laurel. 'Could I have some water?'

In the kitchen Laurel filled two glasses with cold water from a jug in the fridge and took them back to the living room, placing them on coasters on the coffee table. Maggie reached for hers and took a long swallow.

'Hugh's not saying much, even though he roped us in with questioning people earlier. I think he still has Natalie chasing around. How about you? I bet you've not been sitting idle?' Maggie was smiling a rictus grin.

Laurel picked up her own glass of water and ran her finger round the rim, avoiding her friend's stare. Taking a sip, she played for time as she ran through her options. 'I'm not sure how to ask you this,' she said, eventually, 'but Natalie came to see me earlier.' She paused, trying to gauge whether Maggie knew about Natalie's visit. 'She told me about your conversation with Hugh, how you told him you're worried about me and that I'm fixated on him being the murderer.'

Maggie's mouth dropped open. 'Natalie told you that?'

Laurel nodded.

There was a long silence.

Maggie sat up straight on the sofa, her cheeks flaming. 'What else did she say?'

Laurel related the conversation as well as she could remember it. She'd been distracted by anger for most of it.

'*Do* you suspect him?'

'He was on my list of possibles, and this stunt has promoted him right to the top.'

Maggie didn't respond at first. When she did, it was with sorrow in her tone. 'Natalie was right then. You are blinkered over this. I know you don't like him, but I can't believe you suspect Hugh. He's a famous author, he's...' She threw her hands in the air. 'Oh, I don't know why I'm bothering. Maybe we can catch up another time, when you're being less prickly.'

Laurel groped for a pithy response, but Maggie was out of the door before she'd settled on one.

'I guess I'm on my own again then,' she announced to the empty room.

Chapter 34

Laurel

Whatever Albert was cooking, it smelled amazing, and her stomach rumbled loudly.

'Voila,' said Albert, placing their plates on the table. 'Creamy vegetable pie with a little garlic mashed potato on the side. Bon appetite.'

Laurel's knife splintered the puff pastry as she cut into her pie. Individual pies versus one large pie were always best; it meant more pastry, and that was never a bad thing. Broccoli, carrots, peas, and leeks spilled out in a rich, silky sauce. She gathered up a forkful, blew across it gently to cool, and lifted it to her lips.

'Oh my God,' she said, when she'd swallowed. 'This is divine. I have to hand it to you, Albert. Does this village have a secret cordon bleu school that everyone attends but no one has told me about? Someone around here must be a bad cook. It defies the law of averages.'

Albert's face creased into a map of wrinkles as he chuckled. 'I'm delighted you're enjoying it.' He tucked into his own food and for a while the only noise was the scrape of cutlery against ceramic and the notes of a soft piano concerto from the CD player.

Between courses – she couldn't tear herself from the food to speak whilst eating – Laurel brought Albert up to date with the progress of her unofficial investigation and mentioned Natalie's visit, and warning.

'Have I understood correctly: Natalie cautioned you against suspecting Hugh?' Albert clarified.

'Yes.'

'Well, Natalie isn't here, so how about you lay out your evidence against him and we'll see what we've got?' As he spoke, he proffered a selection of after-dinner mint chocolates. When she'd chosen, he selected one for himself, lifted it from the paper envelope, and popped it into his mouth.

Her mouth also full of chocolate, Laurel had to wait before she could speak. 'I'm not sure there is any *evidence* exactly, but we have two motives for him to have killed Simon. First, Simon was going to write an unflattering profile which could have caused Hugh embarrassment and might have affected his career. Second, Simon knew things about Hugh that I don't think Hugh would want raked up or to become public knowledge. Namely, how he exploited his daughter for his first book, and the fact that he was questioned over the death of a boy he was at school with.'

She went on, 'Then there are the things that make him seem guilty. He and Simon went to the same school, but I don't think he's told the police. He knew Simon had been murdered before Natalie told him, but pretended he didn't. The vicar, Christopher, knows something about him that Hugh wants to keep under wraps. And finally, Hugh knew where Simon was staying and that he had a journal.'

'Do you have any other suspects?'

'I'd say Christopher is a possibility.' Laurel explained what she knew about the vicar, and what Hugh had disclosed. 'Perhaps Simon had something on him? At the WI meeting on Thursday, a woman called Vera – I don't know her – said she saw a figure near Tulip Cottage on the night of the murder. She was reasonably sure it was a man, but also said the figure looked to be wearing a long dress. A cassock looks like a long dress, especially in the dark.'

'Christopher is a good man. I don't believe he is in any way involved.' Albert's tone was firm. 'And Vera is as blind as a bat. She very nearly trampled my poor rabbit, Lago, when I was out walking him the other day.'

Laurel was surprised. 'Why not Christopher?'

'I've come to know him quite well since he moved here and there is no one less likely, in my opinion, to have committed murder or harm to Simon, or Dorothy.'

It wasn't an answer backed by evidence, but Laurel reasoned Albert was a good judge of character... usually.

'Lastly, there's Elise, Ben's girlfriend. I don't think she's much of a suspect because I can't think of anything that links her to Simon, other than she met with him in the tearoom the day before he died, but she does keep lying about their conversation.'

'I'm afraid to say, it doesn't sound like you have any definitive evidence against anyone. Only a list of people who had some contact or relationship with Simon.' Albert reached for a second mint and ate it whole. 'Where do you go from here?'

Maybe she couldn't convince him of her suspects, but she could demonstrate the party piece she had planned for the evening. 'Let's forget about the who and think about the how for a moment, can we? Aside from identifying the killer, the most perplexing aspect of this murder is the locked room element. I have an idea how it was done, but do you want to hazard a guess?' She appraised Albert; he'd shown himself to be adept at solving similar puzzles in the past.

'This one has me flummoxed, I'm afraid,' he admitted.

Pleased, Laurel said, 'Then watch this and see what you think. It's a bit complicated, but I'm almost certain our killer could have used this method. Don't panic at what I'm about to do. I'll put everything back how it was, I promise.'

'Have at it. I am fascinated. How can I assist?'

'Let's go into the front room.' She continued to outline her scenario as they decamped into the cosy room warmed by a smouldering fire. 'You be Simon. I'll be our bad guy. Right, we're both in the room, you're dead, the door is open and unlocked.'

'And you have to get out and lock it behind you, with the key in the lock on the *inside*.' Albert ticked off the points on his fingers.

'Yes.' She hesitated. 'Actually, can you come with me into the hall?' Her jacket was hanging on a coat hook in the entrance. She fished in the pockets and produced a screwdriver and a small hammer. 'I had a look at your doors when I got here earlier and they're the same as mine, and more importantly, the same as the bedroom door in Tulip Cottage. Now, this is the tricky bit.'

She had Albert steady the door before using the screwdriver to force up the pin in the middle hinge on the door. The hammer helped her tap it up further before she jammed the screwdriver into the underside of the hinge and pushed the pin all the way out. She did the same with the pins in the bottom and top hinges.

'Now we can lift the door off entirely.' With some difficulty, because the hall was narrow, she and Albert lifted the door clear.

'Step one done. Next, we engage the lock.' She turned the

key, leaving it in the lock on what was the inside of the door. 'And we go again, but in reverse.'

It took a lot of manoeuvring and grunts of dismay from Albert as the large chunk of wood threatened to take bites out of his wallpaper, but they were able to angle the door so the deadbolt slotted back into the bore hole, as it would when the door was locked. At the same time, they had to line up the parts of the three hinges. Once done, Laurel popped the pins back in and the door was rehung.

She wiped her sweaty palms on her jeans. 'There you go: door locked, key inside, killer outside.'

Ending up on the wrong side of the locked door was an issue Laurel had overlooked, and it took Albert a couple of minutes to perform his trick with a pencil and a piece of paper so they could unlock the door and get back into the front room. Back inside, the fire was dying down. Albert nursed a glass of whiskey and Laurel pretended her elderflower cordial was a sophisticated cocktail. Between them, they'd agreed Laurel's trick with the door was possible, though it wasn't a very elegant – or physically easy – solution to the locked room mystery.

Albert stirred. 'Yesterday, you said you were going fishing in the pond for a murder weapon. I can't imagine how I've forgotten to ask. Did you locate such an item?'

'I went and had a poke around and I did find something.'

'And?' he prompted.

'And I've been thinking about how it might fit our picture. If I'm right, and it is actual evidence from the crime, then it was an exceptionally elaborate murder.' Taking a moment to order her thoughts, she shuffled in her seat so she was angled towards her companion. 'I found a silver metal canister. It might have had a label originally, but there was nothing I could see on it. I know what it is though: it's a nitrous oxide canister.'

'Isn't that laughing gas?'

'It is.'

'After all the alcohol and chocolate I have felt obliged to consume this evening–' Albert winked '–I am a touch wamblecropt. I'll need you to explain the significance.'

She grinned. 'This is what I think happened. The murderer used the gas to kill Simon. They might have only meant to knock him out, but it's tricky stuff. People die when they're just trying to get high. And the thing with it is, as you're inhaling, you feel euphoric, so it's unlikely Simon knew what was happening. I'm not sure how he was persuaded to inhale it in the first place, but once he was dead, he was stabbed in the back. I'm almost positive he was dead from the gas first, because there was so little blood from the stab wound.'

'Forgive me, but isn't noz popular with teens these days? Might the canister belong to some experimenting youngster, like those I've seen hanging around by the pond?'

'Possibly, but Ben said there's never been much trouble with nitrous oxide around here. It could have nothing to do with the murder, but it would be a bit of a coincidence that I found it near the pond where the killer was seen by Hetty and Constance.'

'They saw the assassin?'

'Well, they saw someone there at around the right time. But they didn't get a good look,' she admitted. 'Noz would explain how come Simon was dead before he was stabbed, though.'

Albert interlaced his hands and touched his two index fingers to his lips, brows drawn down.

'It shakes up my previous suspect list a bit. It isn't that hard for anyone to get hold of the gas, but there are four people in this village alone who could have easy access to it by virtue of their profession.'

'Dentists?' Albert hazarded.

'I don't think there are four dentists in Elderwick. But there are four cooks or chefs who would use it for whipped cream: Hetty, Constance, Jo, and Elise.'

Chapter 35

Maggie

'That's the chocolate torte done. Are you ready for your next dessert?' Hetty's apron was dusted with flour and cocoa power, but the worktop was gleaming once more as she cleaned down between demonstrations.

Maggie's apron was spotless. She looked down at it, wondering if it made her less of a baker if she wasn't covered in ingredients. 'What are we tackling now?'

Constance navigated across the room to her lowered workstation. 'It's time for choux.'

'And this one is all Constance. Pastry, of every kind, is her speciality.' Hetty gave her hands a last wipe, popped the torte into a tin for Maggie to take home, and settled herself on a stool beside the door.

'You're staying to watch?' asked Maggie. She felt nervous enough with only one sister there, let alone one teaching and the other observing.

'Imagine I'm a student. I promise I won't heckle.'

Maggie laughed, although she wasn't entirely sure whether Hetty was joking.

Constance talked her through the steps of making choux

and said they would use the pastry for éclairs. 'We can pipe them with fresh cream, and I'll show you how to get the perfect chocolate for the top.'

Sensing an opportunity, Maggie pounced. 'Is it right you use noz for whipping the cream?'

In unison, Constance and Hetty gaped at her, then burst into gales of laughter. 'Oh my goodness. Noz?' spluttered Constance. 'Who do you think we are, a couple of glue sniffers?'

Maggie was perplexed, that's what Laurel had called it. She didn't know what had tickled the sisters so much.

Hetty gained control of herself first. 'It is referred to as noz, but usually by teenagers huffing it in the bus shelter. We prefer to refer to it as nitrous oxide, but yes, you're right, we use it for whipped cream. Not planning on picking up a bad habit, are you Maggie?'

Maggie felt the heat in her cheeks, but she grinned along with her friends as Hetty went to a cupboard and pulled out a small tank of the gas.

'This is what we use.' She showed it to Maggie.

'Would you know if you're missing one of those?'

'Missing? Why would we be missing one?'

Maggie hesitated. Laurel had been put out about things she'd shared with Hugh, but this was Hetty and Constance. 'You can't tell anyone, but Laurel's working on a theory about Simon's murder involving noz, nitrous oxide. I don't know the details, but you know how clever she is.'

'And she thinks it's connected?'

'Maybe.'

Constance wheeled back from the counter and swung round to face the room. 'Even if it's connected, nitrous oxide is pretty easy to get hold of. Though the kids tend to use small metal canisters of it, not a tank like ours. Either way, no one but us has access to our store, so it didn't come from here.'

'I heard Simon was stabbed,' said Hetty. 'Why would nitrous oxide be involved? I mean, it's a much nicer way to go, from what I understand. Dying laughing, yes, please. When my time comes, that is.'

'I'm not sure that bloke deserved to go laughing,' Constance muttered. 'Sorry, that's an awful thing to say, but he was an arse.'

'Did you know him?' Maggie hadn't heard any particular opinions about Simon. No one local seemed to have had more than fleeting contact with him. She caught Hetty and Constance sharing a look.

Hetty ran a hand through her hair, leaving a faint dusting of white flour. 'He came in here. I think it was the Saturday before he died. He was on the phone–'

'Which is rude to start with because I greeted him, and he did that thing where he held up one finger. Like I'm going to twiddle my thumbs while I wait for you, mate.'

'Anyway,' Hetty cut back in. 'Constance came back through to the kitchen where I was, but we could hear him talking. He was banging on about LGBTQ+ and how he had no problem with it *but*... you know, the usual crap bigots spout before they say something massively offensive.'

'Should we tell her what he said about *you know*?' Hetty asked Constance, who nodded in reply. 'Before he ended the call, he said, and I'm quoting, "Even the f-ing vicar is one." So, yeah, not a nice guy.'

'You should have let me give him a piece of my mind,' Constance said to her sister, sounding angry.

To Maggie, Hetty explained, 'We didn't bother going back out to serve him. He shouted a couple of times but eventually gave up and left. Good riddance.'

Maggie scowled. 'What a nasty piece of work. A proper... jerkface.'

'Woah, strong words.' Hetty chuckled. 'But you're not wrong.'

'We didn't kill him, though,' added Constance. 'In case you were wondering.'

Maggie laughed along with them; the image of them as killers was as ridiculous as sugar-free cake. Christopher, on the other hand... she didn't like the idea but she couldn't dismiss it out of hand.

Chapter 36

Laurel

'Her heart sank when his head appeared round her office door. 'Hugh, I told you, we can't meet anymore.' It was far too early for this nonsense. 'This isn't therapy and anyway, I've had your agent warning me off, accusing me of suspecting you over Simon's death.' The audacity still rankled. True, she did suspect Hugh, but neither Hugh nor Natalie was in a position to tell her who was above suspicion.

'Do you think I was involved?' He sounded amused. 'Wait a minute, what's Charlotte got to do with anything?' He invited himself in and settled into one of the low chairs. He couldn't take her desk chair this time since she was already sitting in it.

'Who's Charlotte?' she asked. The name felt familiar.

He peered at her, eyebrows drawn together, a vein pulsing in his temple. 'My agent.'

'Your agent?'

'Oh, good grief, we're getting nowhere here.' He scrubbed at his face. 'You said my agent, Charlotte, warned you off.'

'No, your agent, Natalie.' Self-doubt flashed through her thoughts. Had she got Natalie's name wrong? Oh! The memory resurfaced. The other week Hugh had talked about Natalie's boss, *Charlotte*.

He grimaced. 'Natalie is not my agent.' He wrinkled his nose and slumped back in the chair.

'Does Natalie know that?' Laurel looked him over while trying not to be obvious about it. His hair was dishevelled and there was an orange stain on the sleeve of his grey sweater. Marmalade? He looked worse than when she'd bumped into him outside The Pleasant Pheasant after he'd read Simon's journal.

'Charlotte Drake is my agent and the director of Greenleaves Literary Agency, but I am temporarily, having to make do with Natalie. She is fine, for the time being.'

'But...'

He held up a hand to stop her. 'If you have a problem with whatever Natalie has been saying to you, I suggest you take it up with her. Now, if we've quite cleared up the issue of who is and who isn't my agent, there's something we need to discuss.'

'Again, I'm not your therapist.' She fought to swallow her frustration. He was intent on his own agenda and her protests were falling on deaf ears. She'd find out what he was after then lock her office door as soon as she could get him out.

'If it helps, I will state right now, unequivocally, and for the record, I am not your patient, and this is not therapy. Happy now?'

'That's not the point.'

He ignored her. 'Good. Now, Christopher has refused once more to explain why he met with Simon, and the police weren't interested when I relayed this information to them. I can't understand why not, for the life of me. They bring me onboard for my expertise and then ignore my advice. Therefore, we need to work away at this ourselves. Your friend Albert, he's pally with the vicar, isn't he?'

She didn't like where this was going. 'Yes.'

'You need to get him to talk to Christopher, subtly of course, and find out once and for all what went on between him and Simon.'

'First, no. I'm not going to ask Albert to do that. Second, he wouldn't do it anyway. Third, why are you so convinced Christopher has anything to do with this? You've never given me any reason that makes the slightest sense.' Feeling uncomfortable behind her desk she moved to sit in the low seat next to Hugh's. 'What do you have against him?'

He shuffled his feet and pulled at his cuffs. Noticing the orange stain, he reached for a handkerchief and scrubbed at it, but it was stubborn and after a last vicious wipe he gave up and exhaled loudly. 'I don't trust the man,' he said eventually. 'Let's just say the church and I do not have a good relationship. A Catholic boarding school from age eleven to sixteen will do that for you. And yes, I know Christopher's not Catholic, but it's all the same when it comes down to it. Simon would have understood.'

This was her opening. 'You said you and Simon were at school together. Was that the boarding school?'

He looked away, shoulders tense, his posture stiff. 'It's the age-old story, okay. I'm not going over it with you; that's what my real therapist is for.'

Her initial reaction was to retort at his rudeness, but she caught the words before they left her mouth as the implication of what he'd said sank in. He was in pain, and while she wasn't his therapist, she could listen.

'You don't need to tell me anything you don't want to.' She let the silence grow.

Straightening up and catching her eye once more, Hugh heaved a great sigh. 'There's not much to tell really. I had a bloody dreadful time at school. Simon was... we used to be friends, but something happened and afterwards he was *troubled*. He thought I betrayed him over... well, it doesn't matter what it was. Suffice to say, we parted on bad terms.'

Myriad avenues opened up and she was tempted to explore, but as she'd so forcefully stated, she was no longer Hugh's therapist. One question though was still fair game. 'I'm confused: why did you agree to the article?'

He didn't answer immediately, and she thought he was about to shut down.

'I was naive. I believed his article, this piece he was writing about me, was a way of mending bridges.'

'I'm so sorry about what happened.' She imagined how jarring it must have been for Hugh to read Simon's journal. To have uncovered what Simon really thought, and to learn that in his notes he'd included the details regarding the death of Hugh's schoolmate.

'You don't even know what happened,' he snapped.

She'd slipped up. She had to keep her story straight. Hugh wasn't aware she'd read the journal. 'I'm sorry for you, and I'm sorry for Simon, that as children you had to deal with difficulties whose impact appears to have remained with you to this day.' She was certain he was referring to the death of Xavier Houghton.

She risked prodding him a little further. 'Simon's profile of you wasn't going to be flattering?'

'Far from it.' He shook his head. 'I wanted to believe he'd finally understood that I hadn't betrayed him. And I thought he did, I really did. He was excited about writing about me. Every time we met to talk about the profile it was like we were best friends again. Fooled me.'

There were tears in the corners of his eyes, but he wasn't letting them fall. 'I wanted to believe he was my friend again.' He took a shaky breath and blotted his eyes with a handkerchief. 'There's a memorial for him this afternoon at St Michael's in Chiswick. Perhaps it will help if I go and say my final goodbyes.'

Her feelings towards Hugh had softened, but he wasn't off her suspect list yet. As soon as he left, she grabbed her laptop. *How did Miss Marple ever manage without Google?* With the name of the church fresh in her mind, it was easy to find the details for Simon's memorial.

If she drove straight to Hull, there was a direct train she could get to King's Cross and if she grabbed a taxi from there, she could make it in time. She'd have to be careful not to be seen by Hugh, but it was too good an opportunity to miss; there could be other childhood friends of Simon's present. Who knows what she might uncover, whilst being diplomatic and sensitive, of course.

After shutting down her computer, she rushed back to Myrtle Cottage and up to her room to look for something suitable to wear for the service. As she explored the contents of her wardrobe, she was thinking about her confusion over the identity of Hugh's agent. It was curious. For such a big-shot author, she was surprised he wasn't managed by the head of the agency. She pulled out a smart black dress she used to wear when she worked at the hospital back in Somerset. It was frumpy but it would do. She checked her watch and saw she had a little time before she needed to set off for the station.

The literary agency website was easy to find. She scrolled through the advertisements for their new publications and was amused to see Hugh's latest, *Death Dances with Destiny*, was included, but with the shortest blurb and no photo of the book or the author. Clicking onto the list of staff it took her a moment to locate Natalie. Her title was given as junior agent.

Dubious as to how far it would get her, she decided to call the agency. If she could speak to Charlotte Drake, she might learn something useful. Thinking back to the first time he'd mentioned her, Hugh had called the director 'a piece of work'. What had he meant by that?

She jotted a few ideas of what to say to whoever answered the phone. Her goal was to make her call sound important, imperative even, without outright lying... not much, anyway.

Her strategy worked and she was put through to Charlotte herself.

'This is Ms Drake. My assistant tells me you've called to speak about Hugh Quintrell, and you're from a publisher? I'm not familiar with you. Are you a new?' She sounded harried and sceptical.

'Thank you for taking my call. I'm not a publisher, sorry, I think your assistant misheard.' She hoped she wasn't about to get the assistant into trouble.

'Can you get to the point? I'm a very busy woman. Who are you exactly?'

She crossed her fingers and hoped this was one of the rare occasions her title carried some weight. 'My name is Doctor Nightingale and I've been supporting Hugh – Mr Quintrell – since the death – the murder – of his colleague Simon Forster.'

'Let me stop you there,' Charlotte broke in. 'I can tell you Hugh is represented by this agency, but he is currently handled by Natalie Marwood. You'll need to contact her. However, she's on leave for a couple of weeks and I believe Mr Quintrell is abroad and will be for some time.'

'Actually, Natalie and Hugh are both here.' Her revelation was met with silence. She ploughed on. 'Given the traumatic nature of Mr Forster's death, and the relationship between him and your client, I'm concerned for Hugh. Did you know he's writing a book about the murder and–'

'He's writing a book?'

'Yes, about Simon's murder. He was killed here in Elderwick the other week.'

'And Natalie and Hugh are there? For God's sake.'

'Pardon?'

'Nothing. They're in– Where did you say you are?'

'Elderwick, East Yorkshire.'

'And they're there now?'

'Yes. He's staying at High Field House and–'

'Fine. I'll sort this out myself. Goodbye.'

The call ended leaving Laurel staring at the handset as though it could explain what had just happened.

Chapter 37

Laurel

The train had been delayed meaning she'd had to rush. She arrived at the church sweaty and dishevelled. The taxi she'd taken from the train station had dropped her off at the end of the road by one of the new low traffic neighbourhood planters that were always on the news – a large wooden box filled with earth and planted with weak and straggling greenery that effectively blocked the road to cars. She was certain the cabbie could have driven round another way to get her closer, but she hadn't argued and ended up hobbling along the depressingly long avenue on which the church was located. *I huve should have worn flats.*

She eased through the door and tiptoed to a row in the rear. The memorial had already begun, and someone was giving a reading from the lectern. There was no coffin of course; Simon's body hadn't yet been released for burial. The seats weren't full, but it was a good turn-out and a well-dressed one. She pulled the hem of her dress over her knees and tried to straighten the neckline feeling self-consciously gauche. London had that effect on her, and this crowd was her sartorial nightmare.

She scanned the backs of the heads in front of her but

couldn't see Hugh. She'd been worried she'd bump into him at Hull station or on the train, but perhaps he'd driven instead.

The mourners were a mix of ages, mostly older. She craned her neck to see the woman who must be Simon's wife, sitting at the front flanked by an older couple, almost certainly her parents. A second, older couple – Simon's parents in all likelihood – were across the aisle, heads bowed, her shoulders trembling, his rigid and still.

What am I doing here? In her haste to investigate further she had forgotten this was about a man who had died, and those who knew and loved him coming to pay their respects. She was ready to get up and sneak back out when a man halfway down the aisle caught her eye. He looked familiar but she couldn't immediately place him. He was shifting around in his seat, glancing towards the rear of the nave then back to the speaker. Perhaps if she could see him face on and not in profile... She shifted in her seat but drew a glare from a man nearby so subsided and went back to scanning the attendees.

She'd expected more from the church itself. Simon was an important person in the world of journalism and in her mind, she'd pictured a place of worship more akin to Westminster Abbey. Which she now realised was ridiculous. St Michael's was ugly on the outside and utilitarian inside. It might be in an upmarket part of Chiswick, but it had none of the charm of St Stephen's in Elderwick. There weren't even proper pews, only chairs in rows.

The memorial was over quickly, and she had learned nothing new from the words spoken in memory of the journalist. She lowered her head, pretending to study the order of service, as people filed out, paying their respects to Mrs Forster and Simon's parents at the door. The fidgeting man passed her, and she scrutinised him from under her lashes. He was alone, blond haired, Roman nose and a square jaw, rather attractive. Much as she was tempted to follow him, she dare not move until she was sure Hugh had left, though she still hadn't seen him.

As the last of the mourners shuffled past, she tagged onto the tail end, gave her condolences to the families, and shook the hand of the priest. Back outside, she was surprised to see the previously overcast sky had cleared to an unclouded blue. Whilst some of the attendees lingered, most were getting into cars or walking down the road. There'd been no opportunity to speak to anyone yet and no wake was planned. There would be one following the actual funeral, the vicar had announced, at the time when Simon's body could be properly laid to rest.

Fearing she'd wasted an afternoon, and gate-crashed in the most indelicate way, a lifeline presented itself via an overheard conversation. A small group of mourners were retiring to a local pub. She surmised they were mostly work colleagues who'd known Simon from the magazine and newspaper world. Her luck was in when an elegant brunette on the fringe of the group noticed her lingering.

'I'm Deborah Wentworth. Don't think we've met?' said the stranger, holding out her hand. 'How did you know Simon?' she asked, her voice a mix of RP with a dash of east coast US.

Laurel had always maintained her lack of style came from being so short; at only five foot four inches she found it a challenge to pull off fashionable sophistication. Deborah Wentworth, at barely five foot in her impeccable grey skirt and pristine white blouse teamed with neat kitten heels exposed the lie.

'Nice to meet you, I'm Laurel.' She omitted her surname in case word got back to Hugh. However, it occurred to her moments later how her unusual first name would give her away anyway. Her mum had named her after Lauren Bacall, but her dad had made a mistake on the birth certificate. Hence having been Laurel for forty-two years, she'd heard all the Laurel and Hardy jokes many times over.

'I only met him recently.' It was technically true, but she hoped Deborah wouldn't notice the flush in her cheeks. 'He was working on an article with a friend of mine. How about you?' She hoped her answer was enough to satisfy curiosity without inviting further scrutiny.

'I've known– I knew Simon for years. He went to school with my brother, and I used to have such a crush on him.' She giggled. Even her laugh was charming. Turning serious, she added, 'I can't believe he's gone, and in such a horrible way. Look, we're heading to a pub up the road, fancy joining us?'

As they made their way along the footpath, Laurel probed for further information. 'I hear the police haven't got much to go on?'

'I can't imagine who would want to kill Simon. I mean, he had a sharp wit, and he wrote some caustic articles, but that's journalism and everyone in the business understands how it is. It's not as though he were an investigative reporter working on exposing an evil empire or whatever.' She shook her head.

'You said your brother was at school with him. Is he here today?'

'James? Yes, he's the one with the stupid hat, up there with Roddy and Edward.' She pointed to the group of men ahead of them. 'They went to St Cuthbert's too. You'd think they were still schoolboys half the time, they're so childish.'

'Was James very close to Simon?'

Deborah shrugged. 'Close enough for Simon to spend a summer holiday with us once, but I don't think they were best friends or anything. It hit James hard though when we heard the news. We were back in the States visiting Mom and Dad at their house in Connecticut, when James got a call from his editor with the news.'

'He's a journalist too?'

'He's with *The Times*,' she said with pride.

They'd reached the pub and piled through the doors into a dimly lit but attractive bar area. 'Can I get you a drink?' Laurel offered.

'That's very sweet of you, but James will put his card behind the bar. Make the most of it: he's usually such a tight bugger.' She shouted her order to her brother and prodded Laurel towards him while she went to sit with the others at a table in the bay of a large window.

James was tall, dark haired and conventionally attractive, but there was nothing interesting about him, rendering him bland. He was leaning against the bar, dictating a list of drinks to a member of staff.

'What's your poison?' he asked her as she approached.

Asking for a Chardonnay might not give the right impression. What was a cosmopolitan drink? 'I'll have a Cosmo, please.'

He smirked at her. 'Not sure they do cocktails here. I'll get you a white wine.' He didn't wait for her agreement.

The blush reached the roots of her hair, but she couldn't let embarrassment scupper her plan. 'You're James, right? You went to school with Simon?'

He nodded not looking at her.

'So, you must know Hugh Quintrell?'

Now he regarded her with a flash of his perfect teeth and a predatory smile. 'Who are you? I don't think I caught your name.'

'I'm Laurel, I knew Simon and I'm a friend of Hugh's.' She was worried he was closing down before she'd had chance to ask anything pertinent. 'Confidentially, I'm helping the police with their investigation into Simon's murder.'

'Really?' He raked his eyes up and down her body making

her want to turn away or cover herself even though she was fully dressed. 'You're not from one of the London papers, I'd know if you were. If you're some hack from some no-mark local rag wanting to dig up gossip about Simon, you can show yourself out right now. This is his memorial and you're not welcome.' His voice was low enough that only she heard him.

'I'm not a journalist.' Maybe the partial truth would mollify him. 'I'm a doctor of clinical psychology.' She delved into her handbag and pulled out a business card. He didn't take it. Judging by his face, she only had one more shot at this. 'The police are concerned an event from Simon's school days could be linked to his death.'

James got right up in her face and hissed, 'This is a memorial and I'm not raking up crap again about Xavier's death! It was an accident. If the police want to ask me about it, or about Simon, they can speak to my lawyer. Now get lost.'

Deborah called after her as she fled from the bar and back out onto the street, but she didn't pause. James had scared her. She shoved her card back into her bag, thankful he hadn't taken it after all. She walked quickly away, not looking back, trying to bring her breathing under control. Too upset to pay attention to where she was going, she found herself back at the church, her heart pounding. She needed to get a taxi to the station, but there were none in sight.

'You were at the memorial.'

The voice from behind made her jump. It was the blond man who seemed familiar. Now she could see him better, the realisation hit. He was the author Zack Beech, and one of the people named in Simon's journal.

'I don't like funerals and all this death stuff,' he said.

'Hanging around graveyards though...'

He gave her a lopsided grin. 'I know, right. I'm waiting for my taxi. Zack Beech.' He held out his hand.

'Laurel.' Here we go again, she thought.

'What's your surname?' he asked.

This time she was honest. Zack struck her as interested rather than threatening. She spelled it out for him and he pulled out his phone and tapped away.

'Okay, you're legit.' He held up the screen showing her photo on her website. 'What brings you here?'

Desperate to get something concrete from her journey, she gave him the unfiltered highlights: how Simon had been in Elderwick with Hugh, the connection to the death at St Cuthbert's, and that Zack's name was in a list of people Simon had intended to contact.

'Simon never got in touch with me about Hugh, and I don't know what I could have told him if he did.' A car pulled up to the kerb. 'Ah, that's my taxi. Look, can I drop you somewhere? I'm also a St Cuthbert's boy, for my sins. I'll tell you what I can en route, and you can make of it what you will.'

Thanks to traffic, it took twenty minutes longer than the outward journey to get back to King's Cross. Which was fortuitous since Zack had proved very willing to talk about the death of Xavier, and what he'd had to say got her mind spinning with possible implications.

Chapter 38

Laurel

'Laurel.' Ben jogged down the lane towards her. 'Are you just getting in? I thought I'd come and take a look at those letters, if you still want me to? Sorry I couldn't get round sooner. I was working most of the weekend and it was a busy one.' He fell in beside her.

It was well after dinner time, and she was hungry and exhausted. She'd caught the train back to Hull with seconds to spare and had spent the journey mulling over her conversations with James and Zack.

'Hey, Ben,' she greeted him, wishing she didn't look so travel worn. 'No need to apologise. I appreciate your concern.' The familiar distress regarding the letters settled back into her stomach. She'd almost forgotten about them whilst away from the village.

She stole a glance at him, he was very attractive. Elise was a lucky woman. *Seriously, after what happened with the last police officer you fancied!*

'Speaking of concern, do you happen to know how Dorothy is doing, or if there have been any breakthroughs in the case?' She held her breath, afraid of what he might tell her.

He looked up and down the lane and reassured they were alone and said, 'I can't tell you officially, and you mustn't say anything, but Dorothy is doing better. She hasn't been able to answer our questions, but she's going to be okay.'

She gave a shaky laugh as a weight lifted. She hadn't realised how much responsibility she'd shouldered for Dorothy's attack. The letters had only added to what she'd quietly suspected, that she was bad for people's safety. 'That's a relief, I can tell you.'

He patted her on the shoulder. It was an awkward gesture, but she appreciated it.

They reached Myrtle Cottage, and he joined her walking up the short flagstone path through her neat front garden. It was no longer visible, but Laurel knew exactly where on her front door, the crossbow bolt had hit, millimetres from her head when she'd been shot at a few months before. She could have had a new door fitted, but she kept the original in defiance of the ordeal to which she'd been subjected. However, Albert had filled the hole and together they'd put on a fresh coat of paint.

Ben had been the first to come to her aid that dreadful night. He'd lifted her from the sodden ground and led her to the safety of his police car. He'd been her knight in navy blue. *It probably explains why I'm a little smitten*, she rationalised. *Who doesn't want a dashing defender?*

With a guilty thrill, she invited him in and through to her living room where momentarily she forgot why he was there.

'Are they in here?' he asked.

Jolted back into action, she opened the drawer of her writing desk and pointed to the letters. 'I touched the first one, but I used gloves for the second. I recognised the envelope, so I knew what it was.'

He pulled on a pair of blue nitrile gloves, a familiar sight from her days working on hospital wards in her previous life.

'I'll take them with me, if you don't mind?'

'Help yourself. I'll let you know if any more arrive.'

Ben put the letters into a plastic bag, sealed it and stowed it in a pocket. 'You've made this place really nice,' he said.

'Thank you.' Laurel could feel tension coming off him in waves. 'Can I get you a drink?' she offered.

'Thanks, but I'd better get going. I'm meeting Elise from work.' He ran a hand through his hair and took a step closer. 'Look, I was wondering–'

A knock at the door made them both jump. They moved apart.

'Laurel?' As was her habit, Maggie let herself in. She came to a halt on the threshold, her eyes moving between Laurel and Ben, and back again.

'I'll see you around.' Ben turned to leave, giving Maggie a brief smile on his way past.

They watched him go.

Why do I feel guilty?

'Have I interrupted?' asked Maggie, a smirk on her face.

'No.' It came out far sharper than she'd intended. 'No, he popped round to give me some home security advice. You know, after the attack on Dorothy and all that.'

'Sure. Well, *whatever* you two are up to, I have news and chocolate torte.' She bustled off to the kitchen and Laurel could hear her putting out plates. Coming back, she handed a slice of the dessert to Laurel, and established herself on the sofa.

As nonplussed as she was that Maggie had invited herself over again, Laurel couldn't resist devouring the torte. 'So?' she asked eventually. She could tell Maggie was desperate to share her news.

'So, I have it on good authority that Simon was a homophobe and a racist. Might that have been a motive for him getting bumped off?'

Laurel set down her plate. 'It could be,' she said. 'I'm not sure though. Exactly which *authority* informed you of this?'

Maggie recounted what Hetty and Constance had told her.

'So, I get that he was anti LGBQT+, but racist?'

'Hetty said he said, "even the eff-ing vicar is one." Which sounds horribly racist to me.'

Laurel turned the words over in her head, she had an idea Maggie was wrong. She didn't think Simon was racist. Well, he probably had been, but his turn of phrase made her think it wasn't race he'd been referring to in his phone conversation. Which would mean that Reverend Christopher Ibori was gay, and Simon had known about it. 'Or...'

'Oh... you think...?' Maggie put the pieces together.

'I do.' She'd lost her appetite. Damn Simon. 'If Christopher is gay and Simon knew about it, maybe he threatened to expose him. It could explain why they met and why Christopher doesn't want to talk about it. I don't think the church has as much of a prejudice towards gay clergy as they used to, thank goodness, but I bet some parishioners still do. For Christopher, being black in a parochial village is probably enough to deal with, without being involuntarily outed as homosexual.'

'Richard Coles, that guy who used to be in the Communards and is now a Church of England priest, he's openly gay. Why would Christopher have any difficulties?'

'Because sadly, we live in a world where there are too many intolerant people. Besides, it isn't anyone's business but Christopher's.' Non-discriminatory ideals aside, her stomach lurched. Maggie was right, Simon's bigotry could have been a motive, especially if Simon had tried blackmail. She was hesitant to go to the police though. As she'd said, it was no one's business but Christopher's, and they had no proof beyond an overheard phone call.

'We need to talk to Reverend Ibori.'

'The poor vicar.' Maggie clasped her hands. 'He's going to be at the hospice all evening; he mentioned it in church this morning. Shall we go to see him tomorrow morning?'

Laurel's annoyance towards Maggie lingered, but the pull of the case outweighed her reluctance to join forces again. 'I think we'd better.'

'Do you think he killed Simon?' whispered Maggie.

'No, I don't.' It was a gut response. She'd never bought into Hugh's baseless conviction of the vicar's guilt. 'Do you?'

'Not for a second.'

Laurel meant what she said, but nagging at the back of her mind was what Christopher had told her. When Christopher and Simon met, before the murder, Simon had commented on his missing journal. He'd told the vicar he thought Dorothy might have it. If Christopher believed his sexuality had been revealed within those pages, what might he have done to get it back?

Chapter 39

Laurel

'Is it too early?' Laurel pulled her scarf tighter around her neck, but it did little to protect her from the biting wind. She was bundled up in her thickest winter coat, had earmuffs on her head, and mittens on her hands. She hadn't been able to find her gloves so, even though they made her feel eight years old again, mittens were better than icicles for fingers.

'No, he'll be there.' Maggie's voice was muffled by the gold scarf looped around her neck. 'It's like open house on a Monday morning. Anyone who wants to see him can turn up.'

'I'd have thought he'd want the day off after a busy Sunday?'

'He said Sunday services stimulate the conscience of the flock, but it's not until Monday that people are ready to talk, and he likes to be there to catch them. He generally has his time off on a Tuesday.'

'Excuse me.' A tall woman, impeccable in all black and high heels, stepped out of a sleek navy Tesla and blocked their path. 'I'm looking for High Field House can you point me in the right direction?'

'GRNLEAF,' Maggie muttered, reading out the

personalised plate on the car. 'Greenleaves! Are you from Hugh's literary agency?'

'Who are you?' was the sharp response.

Maggie looked at Laurel, hurt showing on her face.

Laurel wasn't standing for that. 'Who are you?' she retorted in return. A sinking sensation in her stomach told her she might know exactly who this was. Self-conscious of her mittens, she shoved her hands into her pockets.

'I haven't got time for this.' With a roll of her eyes the woman turned back to her car, but before she got in, Maggie spoke up. 'If you're looking for Hugh, he isn't there. He and Natalie are at The Grange on Whirligig Lane.'

'What're you doing?' hissed Laurel, hoping the buffeting wind would disguise her words from the interloper.

Maggie leaned close to whisper, 'Hugh and Natalie are having some kind of conflab at mine, so if she wants to speak to Hugh, better she do it where we can listen in.'

Laurel smirked. 'You're devious.'

Laurel and Maggie were only moments behind the woman from the Greenleaves Literary Agency. Her car was slewed at an angle in the driveway, the engine ticking as it cooled. Maggie eased open the front door and they tiptoed across the entrance hall to listen at the sitting room door.

'Charlotte, how lovely to see you.' It was Natalie's voice, taut and brittle.

'Hugh, my favourite client. How are you doing?'

Maggie leaned closer to the gap in the door. Hugh was delivering a muffled reply. 'What did he say?'

'I don't know. But shush.'

'Why are you here?' Natalie again.

'Be a darling and run and make some tea, will you? Do you have camomile? Can you even get camomile here in the back of beyond?' Charlotte laughed, high and bright. 'I set off hours ago and I am exhausted. Off you go. Hugh and I have things to discuss.'

Laurel almost felt sorry for Natalie, and a touch guilty, especially as it was her phone call that had drawn Charlotte to Elderwick. She was certain Hugh's whereabouts had come as a surprise to the agency director. The mention of a new book had brought her running. Natalie was about to get pushed into second place.

Too late to hide, they heard Natalie's footsteps approach the door.

'Shush.' Laurel put a finger to her lips and Natalie managed to stifle her gasp.

Shamefaced, Laurel watched Natalie realise she and Maggie had been eavesdropping, but thankfully, she didn't speak up, instead she mimed that they should listen further.

'Hugh, I guarantee you, we can make this huge. You writing about Simon's murder is brilliant, but we need more. I need that family reconciliation you pitched. It will be the heart of the story. Father and daughter reunited in the face of a senseless death. Daughter forgives famous author. Maybe you could co-author a memoir piece as a follow-up. There are limitless opportunities here.'

'You're taking me back from Natalie then? Is that it?'

'Hugh, darling, you've always been my number one. I had to give Natalie some experience, but I oversaw all her work.'

'Bollocks,' Natalie hissed beside them.

'Well, you didn't do a very good job. She's a nice enough girl, but let's be honest, she's done nothing for me.'

Laurel was afraid the young agent would storm back into the room, but she crumpled in on herself, face pained in devastation. Maggie took one look at her and swept her up into a hug and led her away to the kitchen.

Laurel tuned back into the conversation between Hugh and Charlotte.

'You'll have to leave my daughter out of this. Things have changed so it's not happening publicly, no way.'

'We'll see.'

'No. That's final.'

'I could always approach her directly.' Charlotte's tone was soft and melodic, but the threat rang loudly. 'You're under contract with us. You can't take your series elsewhere. You need us, Hugh. Don't forget that.'

'You go near her and I'll...'

'You'll what?'

Silence.

'That's what I thought.'

Chapter 40

Maggie

When Laurel said she was taking Natalie back with her to Myrtle Cottage to get her away from Charlotte, Maggie, with a little trepidation, offered to talk to Christopher alone. She was anxious not to offend him, and to prove both her investigative skills and her discretion to Laurel.

'Maggie,' boomed a cheerful voice as she peered round the door and into the dim hollow of the church.

She clutched her chest. That wasn't the vicar's rich baritone. 'Who's there?' Her words floated away in echoing space. It wasn't especially bright outside, but her eyes were still adjusting to the gloom of the inner sanctum. She squinted, trying to locate the source of the greeting. The church was typical of those found in the villages scattered throughout the gentle hills of East Yorkshire. It had pews of warm, worn oak, a font by the entrance to the nave, sublime stained-glass windows, and a magnificent shining brass eagle lectern.

From behind the eagle Albert appeared.

'Oh, thank goodness. I didn't know who was here,' she said as she made her way down the aisle to meet him.

'You look quite on edge, my dear Maggie. If I didn't know better, I'd say you're engaged in some hugger-mugger?'

She loved Albert's quirky way with language, but she didn't have the faintest idea what he was calling her. 'I'm a what?'

'You're being secretive.'

She thought about what she should tell him. Laurel had already been cross at her for sharing information. This was Albert though. As she crafted a partial explanation in her head, she couldn't help but reach out a hand to caress the eagle's wing. If Dorothy were there, she'd be on her with a duster faster than she could say *look but don't touch!*

'I'm here to have a quick word with Christopher if he's free. Have you seen him?'

Albert glanced back at the door into the vestry before answering. 'He's not having the best day. I'm not sure he's up to visitors.'

'Albert, it's okay. You can bring Maggie through,' Christopher's voice called from the other room.

Maggie thought he sounded tired, but she wouldn't be put off. It was best she speak to him as soon as possible, even though it wasn't a conversation to which she was looking forward. 'Albert, it might be better if I see the vicar alone. Do you mind?' She didn't want to divulge information that wasn't hers to share.

Christopher had come to the doorway. 'Albert can hear what you have to say, Maggie. I don't mind. Come on in, both of you. Let's get the door closed.'

Ever the good host, Christopher fetched the tin of biscuits and set it down on the coffee table between the three of them. 'Something is on your mind, Maggie. How can I help?'

She felt their expectant eyes on her. To buy time, she unbuttoned and took off her heavy winter coat and stood to hang it on a hook on the back of the door. Sitting back down, she smoothed her hair and brushed a piece of lint off her rose-pink jumper.

'Shall I help you out here?' Christopher asked. 'This is to do with Simon, isn't it?'

'How do you know?' She was relieved he'd spoken first; it would make it easier to ask what she needed to ask.

The vicar rubbed his temples, mouth downturned. Albert reached over to lay a hand on the man's shoulder. 'It's going to be okay.'

'I appreciate that, Albert. Thank you. Let's get this over with then.' Addressing Maggie, he answered her unasked question. 'I always knew word would get around sooner or later in a village like this. I'm going to tell you the whole thing from the start so at least you have the truth and not some sordid gossip from a hack reporter.' He winced. 'Sorry, the man is dead, I shouldn't speak of him in that way. "Love your enemies and pray for those who persecute you, so that you may be sons of your Father who is in heaven".' He closed his eyes and mouthed, 'Amen.'

Maggie was mortified to see the distress on his face. This was a bad idea. Christopher couldn't have killed Simon. She simply didn't believe he had it in him.

Opening his eyes, he declared, 'I am a gay man. I am a homosexual Anglican priest.' He held his head high and spoke with strength. 'My sexuality is known by my superiors, but it's not something I chose to share with my congregation, and for what I believe is a good reason. In my last parish, a troubled young man came to speak with me about his own sexuality. I did not disclose to him that I am gay, but his father, who refused to accept his son's truth, found out I'd counselled the boy and accused me. I would not lie and so it became common knowledge. It is challenge enough being a black man of the cloth, but black and gay was too much for some. The bishop felt it best I move on.'

'I thought the situation was improving in the church?' asked Maggie. As she'd said to Laurel, wasn't the Reverend Richard Coles a famous example of increasing acceptance?

'Only to a point,' interjected Albert. 'And some people are relics who should–'

'Albert, I know how you feel.' Christopher smiled at his friend. 'But the church is what it is. Whilst change, I believe, will progress, it will not be rushed.'

Albert muttered under his breath; his fists clenched.

Christopher continued. 'Simon's mother lives in my previous parish. She was one of my most vocal detractors when the news broke. I can only assume that's how Simon knew. He came to see me, told me who he was, and we spoke of my position here. I won't say he threatened me with exposure, but–'

'He absolutely threatened you,' Albert burst in. 'It was horse-crap.'

Maggie looked from one to the other and back. 'Why did he threaten you? What did he want?'

'I don't know.'

She caught a sharp look from Christopher to Albert. There was something he wasn't saying, and he didn't want Albert revealing it.

'He was a homophobe, that was enough.' Albert's mouth puckered as though he was sucking on a lemon.

Christopher crunched on a Hobnob. He appeared more relaxed now. Brushing crumbs off his shirt he predicted, 'You're wondering if I killed Simon so he wouldn't disclose this information?'

Maggie's cheeks burned.

'After he left here that Monday evening, I admit, I followed him to Tulip Cottage. I don't know what I thought I could achieve, but I had to try and reason with him. I am not ashamed of my sexuality; I am as God made me. However, I have come to love it here in Elderwick.' He reached over and clasped Albert's hand. 'And I don't intend to be forced out by small-minded bigots.'

Maggie wanted to reassure him. It pained her to think he felt at risk from anyone in the village. 'If it were known, I wholeheartedly believe you would find support from all of us— most of us here.' She couldn't deny it, not everyone would come out in support.

'That's the thing, it would be *most* of you. Sadly, there are people who would not be supportive and who, I have no doubt would make their views perfectly, publicly clear. Nonetheless, I wouldn't harm anyone; I believe there is good in all of us, sometimes you just have to look a little deeper,' said the vicar.

'Mariana Trench deep,' muttered Albert, under his breath.

Feeling uncomfortable, but anxious to probe further, Maggie followed-up with another question. 'When you went round to the cottage, did you speak to him, to Simon?'

'No, I decided there was nothing to be gained. I came back here to the church to pray in the hope a solution would offer itself. Of course, his murder is not what I had in mind.'

'Of course not,' echoed Maggie.

Chapter 41

Laurel

Laurel installed Natalie in her living room with a pot of tea and the wifi code. Her original plan was to stay with the young agent until Maggie returned from seeing Christopher at the church. Unfortunately, waiting for her on the doormat, lurking like a bad smell, was another letter. She swept it up and stuffed it into her pocket.

'Make yourself at home,' she invited Natalie. 'I need to nip over to my office for a little while, but I'll be back soon. Do you need anything before I go?'

'No, honestly, I'm good. Thank you for getting me out of there. Charlotte can be a bit harsh, but she's my boss and I can't afford to lose my job.'

'She did seem to be a bit of a–'

'Yeah.'

'Hugh said she used to be his agent? Got to say, today it sounded like she was planning to take him back.' Laurel perched on the arm of the sofa, not wanting to get drawn into a long conversation, but curious to uncover exactly why a junior agent had been tasked with Hugh's career if it was quite as stellar as he – and Maggie – made out.

Natalie groaned and lifted her feet to rest them on the coffee table. Laurel bit her tongue.

'Honestly, it does feel a bit like she gets me to do all the hard work then she waltzes back in when there's the sniff of a new best-seller. Hugh's written loads of books, and most did really well, but the last few years, there's been a slump.'

'His books have become formulaic?'

'No, not at all.' Anger flashed in Natalie's expression. She brought her feet back to the floor with a thud and sat forward. 'The problem was Charlotte was bored with him and she wasn't pushing his books like she should have been. These days all anyone wants are *high concept, sweeping narrative, genre blending manuscripts.*' Natalie mimicked Charlotte's plummy tones. 'That or trope-laden romantasy, which isn't Hugh at all! Hugh tells stories, and people love them. Shouldn't that be enough?'

Laurel didn't know enough about the world of literary agents or publishing to give an informed opinion. 'I guess.'

Natalie was animated as she continued. 'Charlotte asked me to take care of him and while I resent her motivation, it's been the opportunity of a lifetime. He's an incredible man and a formidable writer.'

'He wasn't very complimentary about you. He said you've done nothing for him.' Laurel felt bad for repeating it, but thought Natalie was holding back and hoped with a push she would reveal her true feelings. If she were upset or dissatisfied with Hugh, she might let something slip about him. Until now, there'd been no shaking her commitment to being his staunch defender.

Natalie waved a hand. 'He wasn't serious, he was playing the game. Authors need their agents and Charlotte's as prestigious as they come. In all fairness, she can do more for his career than I can. If she wants him back, well, I can't stop her, but I'll still get to work with him. She's good for my career too.'

It sounded as though Natalie had justified it all in her head. Laurel knew if it were her boss who'd swooped in and insulted her to boot, she'd be furious.

Making her apologies again, she hurried off to her office. It was interesting to know Hugh hadn't been doing well in recent times. You wouldn't know it to hear him talk.

It was a chilly dash up the lane and across the green to her office building. She couldn't resist touching the discreet plaque bearing her name by the entrance. It never failed to thrill her to have her own practice after so many years with the NHS. She missed the hospital and her old colleagues, but the autonomy of working for herself was liberating.

Settled behind her desk, door locked, she regarded the latest envelope. *May as well see what this one says.* She opened her bottom drawer and pulled out a pair of the same blue gloves Ben had worn to take the other letters from her. She always had some lying around the office, she never knew when she might have to pick up snotty tissues after a client had left a session. As she eased them onto her hands, she thought about calling Ben and handing this latest delivery straight over as he'd advised, but curiosity was nibbling away at her sense of logic.

She ran a finger under the poorly gummed flap of the envelope and teased out the single sheet of paper from inside. Once unfolded, she laid it on the desk in front of her.

What if it's one of your friends whose next. You're putting them in danger. This is your last warning, you don't belong here. LEAVE!

With the first letter, she'd almost been able to dismiss it as a silly prank, but each subsequent envelope dripped more anxiety into her veins. Since the attack on Dorothy, the words of the anonymous writer cut closer to the bone. Running away from trouble, from confrontation, from her emotions had always been her go-to coping strategy – that and eating her feelings – and once again, the seductive voice was calling. Whoever was sending these messages wanted her to leave and in truth, the evidence was mounting that she *was* a liability to her neighbours. What if one of her friends was the next person to be hurt?

No! She shook her head. This was what the coward behind the poison pen wanted. Whoever he or she was, Laurel wasn't going to give them the satisfaction. Instead, she was going to expose them and to do so, she needed to know the true motivation behind the letters. Sure as hens laid eggs, they weren't being sent out of concern for the Elderwick residents.

At first glance, the messages were all about the safety of others, but why be coy about such worries? There was no reason to be. It wasn't shameful or likely to bring trouble in response. Could it be Simon's murderer behind the notes? Were they trying to scare her away or divide her focus? Was her digging and investigating getting too close for comfort? She couldn't see how; she learned very little about the journalist's death so far.

She read the letter again, one word at a time. Something was bothering her, other than the obvious. She'd taken photos of the first two letters on her phone. She pulled them up now and it leapt out at her. In the first letter, the writer had used 'your' when it should have been 'you're'. In this new letter though, they'd correctly used 'your' and 'you're'. This time, they'd misused 'whose' instead of 'who's'. *Interesting.* Were these just mistakes or was the author deliberately, if inconsistently, making spelling errors?

Once more she read the note, willing it to give up another clue:

What if it's one of your friends whose next.

Her breath caught in her throat. There was no question mark. What if the words she'd taken as a warning were actually meant as a threat?

———

'Maggie, we need to talk.'

'Laurel, you need to hear this.'

They spoke in unison, the words spilling out as they rushed towards each other across the green, Maggie coming from the church and Laurel from her office.

'You go first,' said Maggie, flapping her hand at Laurel. 'I'll catch my breath.' She looked extraordinarily red in the face.

Although tempted to ignore the possible threat, Laurel knew she had to tell Maggie and Albert about the danger they could be in. Then she would go and see Ben and get his help.

'I've been getting letters, and the third one arrived today. I think someone is threatening you and Albert. It could be Simon's killer, but I'm not sure. Where's Albert right now? We all have to be careful from now on.'

Maggie goggled at her. 'Oh Laurel, you must be beside yourself with worry. Why didn't you tell me sooner? Why would the murderer target us? Why send letters? What shall we do?' Her voice rose with each question.

Laurel sensed imminent panic in her friend. Fighting the adrenaline coursing through her own body, she spoke slow and soft, 'Let's find Albert, and together we'll go and talk to Ben. He knows all about this and he'll tell us the best thing to do. It's going to be okay.'

'Albert's with the vicar; he was there when I arrived.'

'Okay, let's get back to the church, and you can tell me your news on the way.'

Maggie relayed her conversation with Christopher then summarised. 'So, now we know that our vicar is gay, and that Simon was aware of this and tried to blackmail him. But I don't like what that suggests.'

'It does give Christopher the perfect motive for silencing Simon.' Laurel hated to say it. 'He's already been hounded out of one parish; who'd want to go through the same upset again? And it answers the question of the figure in a dress seen near Tulip Cottage the night of the murder.' As uncomfortable as it made her, Laurel felt compelled to add, 'I think we have to consider him a suspect.'

'But he's such a lovely man, and besides, Albert vouches for him.'

It *was* hard to imagine Albert being wrong about anything or anyone. Thinking about Albert, from Maggie's account it sounded as though her warm-hearted neighbour had been taken into the vicar's confidence. 'Neither of them would tell you why Simon was threatening to expose Christopher's sexuality?' she asked. The reporter must have had an angle, something he wanted in return for keeping quiet. Had Christopher made a deal? If he had, there would have been no reason for him to kill Simon. Unless he didn't trust the other man to stick to his side of the bargain. Judging by her own meeting with the vicar, he struck her as a man of principle, and not someone to be bullied or easily intimidated.

'The two of them shared a look, I saw it,' Maggie insisted. 'There's absolutely something they weren't willing to share with me.'

Much as Laurel would have appreciated a chance to whittle away at the vicar's and Albert's obfuscation, the opportunity wasn't to be. Albert was coming down the lane towards them and the issue of the letters, and her friends' safety, felt more pressing.

The moment she'd told him about the letters, his face paled, and he hurried them round to Ben's.

Chapter 42

Laurel

Ben had done his best to reassure them that the chances of imminent danger were low, but Laurel double-checked all her doors and windows when Maggie, Natalie, and Albert finally left her house that evening. Maggie and Albert had each offered to stay with her or for her to stay with them, but if an arrow shot at her head a few months earlier hadn't made her leave, a coward writing letters wasn't going to force her out.

Huddled in the living room, fire blazing away, curtains tightly closed, Laurel once more sat with her notebook open, pencil in hand, and considered the case so far. Albert had given nothing away but had reaffirmed his faith in the vicar. Christopher was staying on Laurel's suspect list though, alongside Hugh and Elise.

Whilst every day brought new information, the identity of the killer, the motive for Simon's murder and for the attack on Dorothy, were as obscure as ever. She was making no progress, merely turning in circles.

Maybe wine will help. She was never a big drinker, but there was still a bottle of Chardonnay in the fridge and that evening she was pleased to see there was a decent amount left. She poured herself a generous glass, admiring the buttery yellow of the liquid as it sloshed from the bottle. Standing at the kitchen counter, she took a sip and almost choked as there was a knock at the door.

The glass teetered as she set it down, clattering loudly enough to be heard by whoever was outside. Over the sound of her racing heart, Laurel strained to listen. Had the letter writer come to threaten her in person? She wouldn't answer the door, that was the best course of action.

The knock came again, then a shout. 'Laurel? It's Ben.'

For a second, she doubted her ears and entertained the idea the caller was only pretending to be Ben. 'Ben?'

'Yes. Can I come in? It's freezing out here.'

Her heart rate continued apace, but for a different reason. She smoothed her hair and checked her reflection in the microwave door. She was wearing an unflattering but comfortable dress and mismatched socks. Hoping to play off her sartorial choices as charming and quirky, she turned the key and slid back the bolts.

Blowing on his gloveless fingers, Ben hurried inside, away from the frigid night air. 'Sorry to call round unannounced.'

'I only saw you a couple of hours ago.' She was afraid he was the bearer of bad news. 'Is everything okay?' She went on into the living room, assuming he'd follow, delaying the inevitable.

'Oh, I'm not here about the letters. Yes, everything's fine. Sorry, I didn't mean to worry you. I, er–' He stopped on the threshold of the room and shuffled his feet. 'Sorry.'

'I'm not sure why you keep apologising and you're making me anxious hovering in the doorway. Come and sit down.' She pointed him to the space next to her on the sofa.

He lowered his tall frame and perched about as far from her as he could. 'Thanks.'

The silence expanded between them.

He smelled pleasantly of fresh soap and cold air. Trying not to stare, she took in his polished black boots, indigo jeans, grey sweater under a black peacoat. Each item fit, snug, but not tight. The light from the fire caught his silver hair turning it to gold as the flames danced. *Stop it, he has a girlfriend.*

'This is completely inappropriate,' he began, looking at the floor, 'but can I ask you something?'

Now he'd spoken, she didn't want him to continue. If he had come round to make some kind of romantic overture, she couldn't reciprocate. She wouldn't do that to another woman. It would sour her opinion of him too. However, her ego was hanging on his every word, hoping he'd... what, declare his undying love? She stifled a laugh. Better to make fun of her dangerous thoughts than indulge them.

Oblivious to her dilemma, Ben finally looked up and explained his presence. 'I don't know if you can help. Elise is lying to me. I know you're a psychologist and not a relationship counsellor, but I'm hoping you could give me some pointers on how to talk to her?'

Laurel felt deflated and relieved all at once, but before she could answer, he stood.

'I'm sorry, I shouldn't have come round.' His face was a picture of misery as he shifted his weight from foot to foot.

'No, sit, sit back down.' It was ingrained, she couldn't turn a person away when she might be able to help. Although she was single herself, she knew most problems in relationships could be resolved, or ameliorated at least, through improved communication. 'Look, I can't give you specific advice, but I can tell you about some techniques I recommend to couples.' Since this wasn't a formal session, and Ben wasn't her client, she indulged her curiosity and asked, 'Why do you think Elise is lying to you?'

'This is going to sound bad, but it's not what you think.' His eyes latched onto hers. 'The day before Simon Forster was killed, Elise met him in The Pleasant Pheasant. It was a Monday morning when she doesn't usually work, but she specifically told me she needed to go in for an extra shift that day. I found out she lied when Maggie and that Natalie showed up at our door and asked her about her conversation with Simon.'

It was the same conversation with Simon that Laurel was sure Elise had lied to her about when they met for coffee in Beverley. 'So, it's not a suspicion; you know she lied to you?'

'Yes, but I don't know why, and she won't talk to me about it. Why would she lie?'

'Why do you think she lied?' Another habit. As a psychologist she didn't have the all the answers, her skill lay in helping people to uncover their own solutions to problems. *Does Ben suspect Elise of being involved in Simon's death?*

'I don't know. So far in our relationship, she's been completely open about all aspects of her life, including some really difficult, traumatic stuff even, from when she was younger. At least I thought she'd been honest, but now I don't know. What could she need to keep from me about talking to Simon? And it gets really messy because as a police officer I should be talking to the investigating team about her meeting with him, but how can I tell them? She'd hate me forever.' His forehead furrowed and small lines worried at the corners of his eyes.

'You asked her about why she lied?'

'I did, straight after Maggie and Natalie left. All she would say is she got mixed up with her days and she told me some nonsense about Simon wanting to know about the church and the vicar.'

'But you didn't believe her?'

'No.' He slumped back into the cushions, inadvertently coming closer to Laurel.

She pulled at the neck of her dress. The heat from the fire had become stifling and her head was pounding. Had Simon tried to get information from Elise about the vicar? Could Elise know Christopher's secret? Was she protecting him? It was a possibility. She may have felt it wasn't her information to share, even with Ben.

Ben cleared his throat. Laurel realised she had drifted. Refocusing, she stumbled over what to suggest he try when approaching Elise about his concerns. He was watching her with an intense gaze.

'I got the impression Maggie and Natalie didn't believe her either,' he revealed. 'Did Maggie say anything about it to you?'

A trill interrupted them before she could answer.

Ben looked at the screen on his phone. 'Damn. Sorry, it's an urgent message and I've got no signal to call back. Can I use your landline?'

'Sure.' She lifted the handset and passed it to him. He went out into the hall as he was dialling.

She slipped her socks off in an attempt to cool down and half listened to his side of the conversation. Her mind turned back to the mystery of Elise's lies and the reason for Ben's presence in her house. Then five words commanded all her attention.

'A fire at The Grange?'

Chapter 43

Laurel

Ben had advised Laurel to stay home, but there was no chance when Maggie might be injured, or worse. She grabbed a coat from the rack by the door and hurried after him. Sirens echoed and against the night sky she could see the billows of smoke rising from the burning building. A sickly orange glow lit their way.

'Where's Maggie?' she demanded of the first person she saw as they strode up Whirligig Lane. The stranger shrugged and turned away. Laurel pushed into the small crowd gathered like rubberneckers at an accident on the motorway. Smoke was blowing away from her, but the smell was all around, sticking to her clothes, her hair, the back of her throat. She could feel the ferocity of the fire in the heat radiating from the blaze. Flames poured from the lower floor and licked at the windows upstairs.

Two fire engines blocked the road, hoses unrolled through the gates of The Grange, fat and full of water, the torrent directed into the burning building. The pulsing lights of the vehicles were a heartbeat against the dark and blood thundered in her ears. She spotted an ambulance and everything and everyone else faded into the background as her attention, and fear, were focused on the figure being tended by green-clad paramedics.

'Maggie?' She willed it to be Maggie, needed it to be her friend safely out of the burning building. The closer she moved the less sure she was. 'Natalie?' Dismay and panic hit her in the gut. 'Natalie, where's Maggie?'

Natalie turned blank eyes towards Laurel's voice but didn't seem to register she was being asked a question. An oxygen mask was being held over her nose and mouth and a blanket draped over her shoulders. Natalie's hands, black with soot, lay limp in her lap. It didn't look as though she'd suffered any burns but Laurel couldn't be sure and in that moment didn't care.

'Natalie, please, where is she?' Desperation cracked in her voice.

'I'm sorry,' said the paramedic crouched in front of the literary agent as he turned to face, and block Laurel. 'She can't talk now. She needs medical care. I need you to give her some room.'

'The owner. Maggie Wright, do you know... is she okay?' Laurel begged.

'There was another woman, an older lady. They took her to hospital that's all I can tell you.'

The words were ash in her mouth as she rasped, 'Thank you.' Hospital could mean anything: dead or dying. Her legs trembled and she would have collapsed there in the road if Hetty hadn't caught her and steered her towards Constance who held out a flask and insisted she take a drink.

'Finally, my hip flask proves its worth. It's brandy, for your nerves.'

Laurel took a swig and coughed as the alcohol hit the back of her throat, but it felt good going down.

'Maggie is okay.' Hetty was looking her in the eyes and rubbing her hands to warm them. Laurel hadn't noticed that her fingers were like ice. 'They've taken her for observation because of the smoke inhalation, but she's basically fine.'

'Oh, thank goodness.' The fear lost its hold and fatigue hit her. 'I'm going to sit down for a moment,' she said as she slumped onto the kerb by Constance's wheelchair. Around them the circus swarmed until at last it looked as though the hoses were winning against the flames.

'What happened?' She almost missed the look between the sisters. 'What is it? What haven't you told me?'

Hetty broke the news. 'They think the fire was set deliberately.'

'I overheard the fire chief–'

'Chief fire officer,' Hetty corrected her sibling whilst casting admiring looks at a striking firefighter who'd removed her helmet to mop her face.

Constance rolled her eyes. 'I heard her saying she thinks it was set deliberately, but they won't know until there's been an investigation. Poor Maggie. To lose her beautiful house after everything she's been through with Nicholas.' Constance swiped a tissue under her nose. 'Why would someone do this to her?' She lowered her voice and asked, 'Or could it have been Natalie who was the target? You know, because of this thing with Simon and Hugh. I saw her with the ambulance guys, I don't know if she's okay?'

'I just saw her. She looks like she might be in shock, but they're treating her here so it can't be serious.' Laurel's mind was racing. Who could have done such a thing?

'Thank goodness. I suppose we need to focus on the positive that no one's been badly hurt,' said Hetty. 'At least, I hope no one else was in there?'

'The whole village must be here by now,' observed Constance. 'Is there anyone not accounted for?'

'Albert?' Dread leapt back into Laurel's chest. 'He was at

mine with Maggie and Natalie earlier, maybe he walked them home and stayed for a while?'

'No, I saw him with Hugh a minute ago.' Hetty pointed off down the lane where other small groups had formed. 'And Christopher is with Maggie's next-door neighbours; Sam and half the pub are behind that fire engine; Jo and Elise were with Albert. Ben! What about Ben, I haven't seen him?'

Laurel blushed and hoped they couldn't see as her cheeks were already washed crimson by the flames. 'Ben was at mine. He got a call, and we came straight over.' She fancied Hetty gave her a quizzical look, but she might have imagined it.

Constance gave her a wink, then asked, 'So, who set the fire, and have they come back to watch it?'

Laurel's first instinct had been to go directly to the hospital, but reason won out; there was no way she'd be allowed to see Maggie in the middle of the night. Instead, she was at the nurses' station the moment visiting hours began the next morning.

It was a challenge to convince the nurse to let her in to see Maggie. One of the healthcare assistants took down Laurel's name and was dispatched to check if the patient felt up to visitors. Laurel waited with bad grace. She couldn't help but picture the burns victims she'd worked with in her previous role as a clinical psychologist in a busy acute hospital. Hetty had told her it was only smoke inhalation, but what if...

Her worrying was interrupted with the return of the young HCA who told her she could enter the ward. 'Bay three, bed two, by the window.'

The ward buzzed with staff, but Laurel stepped quietly into the bay searching for the familiar face. There were four beds, only one was occupied. Maggie looked small nestled in the sheets. Her eyes were closed, and her hands rested like two broken birds on top of the covers. Laurel felt tears spring into her eyes. She hated seeing her friend like this. Maggie would hate the ugly gown they had her in too.

Maggie's eyelids fluttered. 'Laurel?'

'I'm here. You're okay, everything's going to be okay.'

Opening her eyes fully and shuffling herself upright in the bed, Maggie coughed. 'Thank you,' she rasped as Laurel held a straw to her mouth so she could sip from a cup of water that had been left for her on the bedside cabinet.

'Don't try to talk. You should be resting, getting some sleep.'

Maggie lifted a hand to her mouth and made a strangled noise, which become a bout of coughing, before shifting into laughter. Laurel looked on confused.

'Rest? I don't need rest, I'm perfectly fine. I was just resting my eyes. Apart from this husky new voice and damned cough, I'm fit as a fiddle.'

Evidently the patient wasn't as frail as Laurel had feared. Slightly glassy eyes and a gravelly voice appeared to be the extent of her injuries. If it weren't for the blankets and a drip, Laurel would have grabbed her and hugged until her arms ached. The prickle behind her eyes eased as the tears released and flowed down her cheeks. She smiled.

Feeling lighter than she had in weeks, an apology spilled from her lips. 'Maggie, listen, I'm sorry, I've been awful. I've been jealous of the time you've been spending with Hetty and then with Natalie. It's selfish of me. Can we go back to how things were? I've been so obsessed with showing Hugh I'm more capable than he is of solving the murder that I've neglected us and...'

Maggie took her hands and shushed her. 'You have nothing to apologise for. We're friends, and all friends have their ups and downs. Know this, no matter how much time I spend with other friends, I always have time for you.'

As genuinely sorry as she was, there was one more thing she needed to say. She released her hands from Maggie's grip and sat in the chair by the bed. 'I was hurt you complained about me to Hugh and Natalie. Natalie told me all about it. I understand you were worried about how I was coping after finding Simon and then Dorothy, but I wish you'd come to me about it instead of speaking to them.' She held her breath, not sure how Maggie would take the rebuke.

Maggie shook her head, frowning. 'Oh Laurel, I'm sorry, but it was Hugh and Natalie who were worried. I don't know what Natalie was doing speaking to you because they'd said it'd be better coming from me? Either way, I shouldn't have let myself be influenced.' She rolled her eyes. 'You know what I'm like around Hugh, I'm such a fan girl! Is that right, fan girl? Looking back, I suspect Hugh was more afraid of you accusing him than he was worried for your wellbeing. It's obvious now. I know you're no delicate flower. You're Elderwick's very own middle-aged Nancy Drew.'

Laurel's throat was tight with more tears. 'It might be my fault your house was burned down,' she blurted.

Maggie didn't miss a beat. 'Nonsense! How could it be your fault?' She waggled the line of her drip as she tried to free herself to rearrange her covers. 'Wait, is this about those letters?'

'Not just the letters. You've got to admit, bad things seem to happen to people who know me.' The truth of it, in light of Maggie's close escape from the fire threatened to overwhelm her. She clamped down on the rising tide of despair and plastered a smile back onto her face. Now was not the time. Ben had promised to speak to his boss about the potential risk. She just hoped the police would take it seriously and advise her, Maggie, and Albert on how to keep themselves safe. Until then, she was banking on Maggie being a patient in hospital to keep her out of harm's way.

Having finally finished fidgeting, Maggie said, 'You could say the same of Albert or me. The people you know are the people we know. So, put that idea right out of your head and listen to this: I've been sleuthing whilst detained here at the hospital. They won't let me leave until the consultant has seen me, and goodness knows when that will be. Anyway, I thought I'd use my time wisely, so I had a poke around up on the tenth floor, which happens to be where Dorothy is. They're keeping her in for further tests. Nothing to do with the attack; poor woman, they've found a problem with her heart.'

'Isn't your throat sore?' interrupted Laurel. She was happy for the conversation to move away from the fire, but doubt remained lodged in the tension of her neck.

'Probably, but they've got me on some lovely painkillers,' Maggie replied with a smile. 'Where was I? Oh yes. So, Dorothy is all but recovered from her brush with death. After she got over the surprise of seeing me here – and telling me to bugger off – I think she was pleased to have a visitor. You know, I don't think anyone except Christopher has been to see her the whole time she's been here. She had two brothers, but they both passed away some time ago.'

Laurel wondered exactly which drugs had been prescribed. Whatever they were, Maggie was in excellent, chatty form. 'What did Dorothy say?'

'I'm getting off track, aren't I? Yes. Well, Dorothy opened up a bit. They must have her on some strong medications!' Maggie giggled. 'She doesn't remember much of what happened that night and she doesn't know who attacked her. But here's the interesting thing, she wanted me to check her bank account on her app – she doesn't really know how to use it – to see if she'd still been paid the full amount for Simon's stay. Can you believe it? The poor man's dead and she wants to know if she's been paid.' She lapsed into silence, shaking her head, lips turned down in a disapproving frown.

'And?'

'Oh, and she had been paid. And do you know who paid for his stay?'

'No.'

'The Greenleaves Literary Agency.'

Chapter 44

Laurel

Maggie's revelation should have had her diving back into the mystery of Simon Forster's murder, but Laurel's heart was no longer in it. The anonymous letters loomed ever larger in her thoughts as she drove back to Elderwick from the hospital. The journey took her through some of the most beautiful scenery the East Riding of Yorkshire had to offer: neat hamlets with manicured village greens; rolling fields spotted with the tiny white clouds of early lambs; wooded lanes frosted with snowdrops. Laurel registered none of it.

Ben hadn't called her back and she was afraid the letters alone weren't enough to convince the police there was a credible threat. She was certain the fire at her best friend's house would be passed off as an unfortunate coincidence, but she didn't believe in coincidences.

LEAVE ELDERWICK NOW

The words of the latest letter loomed large in her mind. Maybe she should leave. It was all very well for Maggie to dismiss the messages, but the fact was the letters had been sent to Laurel, making them her responsibility.

In the short months since she'd arrived in Elderwick, Laurel had made wonderful friends and felt fortunate every single day to have been taken into their hearts. Her fledgling private practice was finding its feet and word of mouth was bringing her new clients every month. She loved her consulting room, and the work was endlessly rewarding.

After her mum died, Laurel had thrown herself into work. Having lost her father as a child, and having no siblings, there was no one to tell her she was taking work too far and impacting her own health and wellbeing. It was only after a distressing incident in her last place of employment, and her subsequent flight – avoidance – that she was finally able to see she achieved nothing by running away. Maggie and Albert had helped her to change. It had meant becoming vulnerable, opening herself to the possibility of being hurt, but it also meant beginning to *live* her life for the first time in over twenty years.

How was she repaying those kindnesses? By acting as a lightning rod for harm. What if Maggie had been seriously injured or even killed by the fire? Even if it meant running away again, this would be different, she'd be doing it for a good reason. The best reason, to protect those she loved.

She could let out Myrtle Cottage and move back when – if – it became safe again. It wouldn't be hard to find a good tenant; house prices had become ridiculous in recent months, and she knew many of the younger people from the village had to travel as far as Hull before properties were within their reach. Her home was one of the smaller houses but had stretched even her budget and she was a forty-something who'd been earning a generous wage.

She remembered the estate agent telling her another buyer had made a higher offer on Myrtle Cottage after Laurel's initial bid had already been accepted. It had been made by a man, not a local, looking to acquire another property for his rental portfolio. She'd been relieved and grateful when the vendor insisted on honouring her original offer.

The more she thought, the more it made sense for her to leave Elderwick for a while. Even if it meant leaving her beautiful house, even if it meant running away again. It was the right thing to do.

Her phone was in her pocket, and she felt the buzz of a text come through. Not many people sent her texts: there was no signal to speak of in Elderwick and no one from her old life had her new number. Her palms started to sweat against the steering wheel. She was still a couple of miles out from the village as she pulled into a convenient lay-by on the crest of a hill.

Through the windscreen she could just make out East Street winding its way towards North Street and the pond. The new houses being built on the edge of the village stood out in their fresh orange brick. She could see the small figures of the workmen scrambling around the scaffolding. She stepped out of her car and fancied she could hear the faintest strains of music from the radio that played constantly on the building site, but it was probably her imagination.

She swiped in her passcode and opened her messages. On first reading, the words refused to make sense. The text was from Hugh.

> Can we schedule a session

> The body they found at The Grange in the early hours of this morning was Charlotte

Two lines.

Two lines to break her apart. The fire *had* killed. The threat was not idle. Charlotte had only been in Elderwick because

Laurel had phoned her. Her call had led to this woman's death. It wasn't just her friends who were in danger, it was anyone with whom she came into contact!

She sank into a crouch, hot tears blurring her vision as, once more, guilt ignited in her chest. The blood pounded in her temples and her face felt hot and swollen. Her vision narrowed and sound receded. She was going to pass out.

As best as she could, Laurel brought her head lower and tried to regulate her breathing. Her temperature flipped from hot to cold and saliva filled her mouth. The vomit splattered her shoes and the dirt between her feet. She'd skipped breakfast so there wasn't a lot to bring up, but her stomach contracted again and again until her muscles ached and her throat burned.

Now there was no question about her leaving or not. It was only a question of how quickly she could be gone.

Chapter 45

Maggie

'Hugh, Natalie, what a surprise.' Maggie clutched her gown to her neck, anxious not to flash the famous author. 'Do you want to sit down?' She was torn, any time spent with Hugh was thrilling, but it was still early morning, and she wasn't feeling up to more company yet.

Hugh sighed as he threw himself into the only chair. Natalie disappeared out of the room, probably in search of another.

Hospitals seem to go out of their way these days to discourage visitors, Maggie thought as they waited in silence.

Head now in his hands, Hugh remained mute until Natalie was back and sitting beside him on an ugly orange plastic thing with wobbly legs.

'How are you, Natalie?' asked Maggie. She'd been worried about the young woman having only glimpsed her being tended by a paramedic as she herself was wheeled into an ambulance and rushed to the emergency department. 'They told me you tried to get into the house before the fire brigade arrived.'

'I thought you might be trapped in there.' Natalie shrugged and looked at her feet.

'She's a hero,' declared Hugh.

'She is. I'm just so sorry you got hurt trying to save me.'

Natalie looked flustered. 'I'm okay, a bit of smoke inhalation, but nothing serious.'

'Thank goodness you were out when the fire started.'

'And you... Are *you* all right? I'm so sorry about your house.' Natalie leaned forward and grasped Maggie's hand.

'I'm on the mend, no major harm done. I'm devastated about The Grange, but it's only a house. I'm just thankful no one was hurt badly. Things can always be replaced.'

Hugh looked up and Natalie took a sharp intake of breath.

'What is it?' Maggie's voice wavered.

'Haven't the police been to see you?' asked Hugh, eyes wide, darting looks between Natalie and Maggie.

'The police? What on earth for? They don't think it was an insurance job, do they?' Maggie laughed at her own joke but sobered quickly as she looked again at their faces. 'What's going on?' A cold hand inched its fingers around her heart.

'It's Charlotte,' Hugh blurted. 'She's dead.'

Maggie thought she must have misheard. 'Charlotte? Your agent? The agent from Greenleaves? How?'

'We don't know,' said Natalie, sniffing. 'All we've been told is that a body was found in the pantry at The Grange. Hugh managed to speak to one of his contacts at the police station who told him there was a handbag recovered at the scene and it had Charlotte's ID in it. There doesn't seem to be any doubt it was her.' She snatched a tissue from a box on the bedside table and held it to her pink-tipped nose.

Maggie was dumbfounded. How could Charlotte have died in the fire? She had a million questions, but before she could ask them the door swept open and a man and a woman stalked in. They didn't look like doctors.

Natalie jumped to her feet. 'Honestly, you can't barge in

like that. Come back later. We're breaking some upsetting news to our friend and it's not a good time.'

The woman spoke. 'I'm DI Coral and this is DS Hill. You two need to leave now.' The officers crowded into the small area round the bed, faces impassive.

Natalie looked ready to argue, but she was forestalled by Maggie. Stunned by the revelation about the body, she said she wanted to hear what the police had to say.

Hugh didn't speak as he rose and left the room. Natalie paused by the door but only long enough to scowl at the officers.

Once they were gone, DS Hill perched on the end of the bed. 'I'm truly sorry we weren't able to be here earlier to break the news. I take it from what we overheard as we arrived Mr Quintrell and Ms Marwood have told you?'

'About Charlotte?' The quiver in her voice betrayed her feelings. 'Yes, they told me.'

'I'm sorry we have to do this whilst you're still here and meant to be resting and getting better, but we need to ask you some questions.'

'I'm certain Mrs Wright appreciates the seriousness and urgency of the matter.' DI Coral didn't sound as though she gave two hoots how Maggie was feeling.

Maggie's mind was whirling as they quizzed her on why Charlotte had been at her house, how the fire might have started, and how she and Natalie had made it out to safety, but Charlotte hadn't.

She answered them as best she could, but she was as much in the dark as they were. She talked them through her movements, how after getting back from Laurel's, she'd had a quick cup of instant hot chocolate, before taking herself off to bed for an early night. It must have been about fifteen minutes later she'd received a call from Natalie to tell her she'd be out late, then she'd fallen asleep.

She didn't know exactly when the smoke detectors had burst into life, only that she woke terrified and disoriented. The flight from her bedroom to safety was a blur of a smoke-filled hallway. Natalie's bedroom was closest to the staircase, and she thought she remembered checking the room and finding it empty as she fled, but she couldn't be sure.

'At what point did you call the fire brigade?' asked Hill.

'I didn't, or if I did, I don't remember doing it.' The questions were feeling more akin to a grilling now and she was impatient for the interlopers to leave. 'I don't have a mobile phone, and I don't think I stopped to use the landline.'

Hill made a note in a little black notebook and Coral studied her face. 'So,' she asked, 'who did call them?'

'I don't know.'

'Hmm.'

Maggie moved her hand slowly, slowly to her right, on the opposite side of the bed to the officers. The call bell was almost in reach.

'You're friends with Laurel Nightingale, isn't that correct?'

Maggie pushed the button hoping it wouldn't sound in the room but would summon a nurse. It was soundless and she breathed a relieved sigh.

Coral misinterpreted the sigh. 'Why does that question bother you?'

'It doesn't bother me. Laurel is one of my best friends. Why are you asking about her? She wasn't there.'

'Maggie?' A nurse bustled in. 'How are we doing? Not long now until we can get you home, as soon as the consultant has seen you, we can let you go.' She turned to Hill and Coral. 'Visiting time was over ten minutes ago. I have to ask you to leave.'

'We're here on police business.' Hill showed his ID, but the nurse was having none of it.

'My patient needs her rest. Are you getting tired, Maggie?'

In a tremulous murmur, Maggie said, 'I am a bit. I think I need to have a break now.'

Coral glowered, but the two stood to leave.

The nurse waited until they'd gone.

Maggie squinted at her name badge. 'Thank you, Susan, you're a life saver.'

'My pleasure.' Susan beamed and left Maggie alone.

But rest was the last thing she was able to do. There were far too many questions needing answers, and most pressing was what had Charlotte been doing in her home?

Chapter 46

Laurel

Laurel hoped to slip back to Myrtle Cottage, pack some essentials, and disappear without being noticed. She owed Albert and Maggie an explanation, but she would call them later. She left her car on Manor Road instead of parking outside her home and kept as close to the hedge line as possible as she crept up Birch Lane. With one wary eye on Albert's door, she reached her garden gate. Knowing it would squeak as she opened it, she opted to inelegantly scramble over her low garden wall instead. Under other circumstances her evasive manoeuvres would have been funny, but the faces of all those hurt or injured since she'd moved into the village were lodged in her brain. All those who knew her were in peril for as long as she stayed.

Inside she rummaged in the back of her wardrobe for a compact suitcase and began stuffing it with the basics she would need. With a selection of clothes packed, she bumped back down the stairs and into the living room. She dithered over taking her notebook and felt again the heavy weight of guilt. She should have followed her own advice from the very beginning and kept her nose out of the whole murder business. Though it was hardly her fault she'd been there when Simon's body was discovered.

The police, she was aware, believed otherwise. When DI Coral had listed all the people with whose death or injury Laurel was in some way connected, she made it very clear she thought Laurel was directly involved. What would the police make now of Charlotte's death? Would they find out it was Laurel's call that brought her to Elderwick? A new and nasty idea raised its head. The detectives already had her on their radar. Was it possible this latest death and the circumstances surrounding it might convince them to come after her in a very real and criminal sense? Wouldn't that be perfect: a poison pen letter writer and the police, all out to blame her. Even more reason, should she need one, to leave.

When the shrill ring of the landline sounded, she froze. Who was trying to contact her now? Hugh didn't have her home number, so it couldn't be him again. Maggie or Albert perhaps? She reached towards the phone. *It might be the police.* She snatched her hand away and held it to her chest as though she were afraid it had a mind of its own and would pick up the handset unbidden.

The ringing stopped and she shuddered. The repeated spikes of anxiety were surely taking years off her life. She'd decided to leave but she didn't have anywhere to go and didn't know what she'd do when she got there.

The tapping at the French windows was the final straw. She let out a yelp and staggered away, searching for a face beyond the glass. There was no one there, no one human at least. The wild beating of her heart only slowed when she spotted her visitor. A cackle escaped her lips. She was thankful no other person was there to hear it, she sounded hysterical. *Maybe I am.*

Aroon eyeballed her from the terrace, his beady stare following her progress across the room. A light breeze ruffled his rich ginger plumage. Laurel would swear he thought himself a most handsome bird. What he didn't realise was how endangered he was because at that moment she could cheerfully have throttled the cocky trespasser. If he'd been after her chickens again– She stopped; who would look after her hens? They were new and still getting used to their home. Her previous flock had all turned out to be cockerels – a fact Albert had pointed out with great mirth – so had been re-homed. Her replacement, and definitely female, brood were only now settling down. No eggs yet though.

The obvious solution to her chicken care problem was Albert. He would be sure to take care of her girls, but it raised the problem of how to ask him. She didn't want to see him in person because he would want to know why she was going away and would try to talk her out of it. She could drop a note through his letterbox, but again, he might see her. She supposed she could post a letter in the box on her way out of the village.

Aroon was back, tap-tap-tapping with his beak on the window. An idea struck.

Unfortunately, her desperate plan to attach a letter to his leg was not a success. By the time she'd scribbled a note, he had wandered away to the hen coop and was more interested in preening in front of the girls than he was in anything Laurel wanted of him. She had one final attempt at catching him, but he was too wily and fast.

'Fine,' she said. 'You win. I don't have time for this. You know, I've only ever tried to do the right thing. Why does this village hate me?' Aroon launched himself up to the top of the coop. It wasn't a graceful flight. 'Okay, no, you're right, the village doesn't hate me, but it's not good for me and I'm not good for the village. Albert will understand, won't he?'

The cockerel looked as though he was listening.

She'd followed him to the far end of her garden, from where

she could see into Albert's plot. She could see his barren summer vegetable beds, waiting for the last frost before they'd be planted with broccoli, beetroot, leeks, and later on, courgette and pumpkins.

Aroon, evidently tired of showing off to the hens, threw himself back to the ground and set off to the hedge where he squeezed himself through a hole linking the two gardens.

'I bet you'll be glad when I'm gone,' she called after him. 'You come over here, tapping on my windows, but you don't want to be friends. You've only ever been interested in my chickens.'

Chapter 47

Laurel

Back inside, a knock at the door threw her off balance. *Seriously! What now?* She didn't have time for visitors.

'Ms Nightingale? It's the police. I need you to come with me please.' She could see navy and fluorescent yellow through the wavy window.

The urge to laugh again bubbled inside her but she tamped it down. She didn't need a psych assessment foisted on her too. She hadn't heard him pull up outside, no lights or sirens to alert the neighbours. Not that the residents of Elderwick would need such obvious signs, they would all know about this within moments, such was the efficiency of the local grapevine.

Without opening the door, she called back. 'Why?' It was the best she could think to ask as she scrambled through her memory for any advice she'd gleaned from old episodes of *Law and Order* or even *The Bill*.

'DI Coral needs to have a word. Can you open the door, please.'

With reluctance, she did as asked. There was no sense in risking having it broken down; it would be another delay to her escape plan if she had to wait to get it fixed. *Would they do that, she wondered, break down the door if I refuse to go quietly?*

The baby-faced officer on her doorstep looked relieved. 'If you could come with me.' He gestured to his car.

'Am I under arrest?' It felt like the kind of question she should be asking.

'No, DI Coral would simply like to speak with you. You don't have to come to the station but...'

He let the sentence hang.

It looked like the same room she'd been in the last time. It certainly smelt the same; sour sweat and vomit overlaid with stale coffee. The institutional green paint on the walls was peeling and in one corner black mould crept across the ceiling. Once the formalities were out of the way, DI Coral and DS Hill didn't waste any time before getting stuck in, leaving Laurel reeling over what they were implying, even though she'd expected the worst.

'No, I had no idea Charlotte was at Maggie's last night.'

Hill was asking the questions, whilst Coral watched her like a snake. 'But you saw her earlier in the day?'

'Yes, in the morning, but–'

'And where was she when you saw her last?'

'She was at Maggie's–'

'That's The Grange on Whirligig Lane, Elderwick, correct?'

'Yes.'

'So, it's reasonable to assume you did know Ms Charlotte Drake was at The Grange yesterday?'

'Well, yes, but that was in the morning. I didn't know she was there last night.' Thinking about it, when she'd visited her in hospital, Maggie hadn't said anything about Charlotte. If she had known Charlotte was at her home when the fire started, wouldn't she have mentioned it? Why had Charlotte still been there?

Hill waited as Coral wrote something on a notepad and showed it to him. Resuming the interrogation, he asked, 'Do you know why Ms Drake was in Elderwick?'

'No.' Short answers seemed safest because this was dangerous ground. How could she explain why she'd contacted the Greenleaves Literary Agency without divulging her attempts to poke around into Hugh's professional life? Since he was so chummy with the SIO on Simon's murder, it might not go down well in the station.

'Did you telephone Ms Drake on Monday of this week?'

Her strategy was shot to pieces. She couldn't keep the wariness from her voice as she answered, 'Yes.'

'Why did you call her?'

'I'm thinking of writing a book.' It was a lame explanation, but she was banking on them not being able to disprove it even if they didn't believe her, and the looks they gave her said they didn't buy her excuse for a minute.

'Did you ask her to come to Elderwick?'

'No, why would I? Besides, why would she come here even if I had asked her?' Answering a question with a question was a tactic she used often in session with a client, and she was good at it.

The probing continued and it was clear to Laurel that the two detectives were convinced she was connected to, if not directly responsible for, Charlotte's death. It was exactly as she had predicted, and in their shoes, she would probably have thought the same thing.

She tried to show she understood their job and dilemma. 'I can see you want justice for Charlotte, but I didn't have anything to do with it. I didn't even know about the fire until Ben – PC Templeton – got a call about it.'

Coral whispered to Hill then spoke. 'Why were you with PC Templeton?'

Laurel felt her cheeks flush. 'He called round to talk about something.'

'He called round to your home?'

'Yes.'

'What did you speak about?'

She didn't want to air Ben's personal issues with his work colleagues. Her hesitation was noticed.

'We can ask PC Templeton directly, but it would be easier for all concerned if you could be truthful with us.'

She bristled at the thinly veiled accusation. 'I've had some anonymous letters and Ben was helping me with them.'

'You reported them to him?'

'I guess.'

'You guess?' Coral wasn't hiding her disdain.

'Yes, I reported them, and he brought them to the station. They upset me and I was concerned.'

Once more, Coral muttered to Hill, who left the room. Laurel and the other woman sat in silence. Alas, Coral was on form. She was stock-still, not fidgeting, not looking at her papers, nothing. Laurel felt an unbearable temptation to laugh. A silence competition, how ridiculous. Instead of giving in to the urge, she clamped her lips together and counted the ceiling tiles until Hill returned ten minutes later.

'There's no record of any letters,' reported Hill.

The confusion must have shown on Laurel's face.

'You seem surprised?'

The time counting tiles had given her the opportunity to remember one other thing from the TV cop dramas she'd seen.

Her voice shook, and she had to repeat herself to be heard. 'I want to leave now.'

Chapter 48

Laurel

His car was outside his house so there was every chance he was at home. After her ordeal at the police station, Laurel was wrung out and in no mood to be messed around. Her mouth was dry as she raised her hand to knock. She wanted the truth.

Ben looked wary when he opened the door. 'Hi. Is everything okay? I'm a bit busy at the moment.'

She wasn't going to be fobbed off and cut over him. 'We need to talk, and I suggest we do it here and now if you don't want me speaking to your boss.'

The colour drained from his face. He stood back and ushered her inside.

She went ahead of him into the living room, and as his tall frame filled the doorway behind her she experienced a shiver of trepidation. The house was quiet; she was certain he was home alone, which she'd thought she'd wanted. She surveyed the room and tried to take the chair nearest the door, but he got there first. She berated herself: she should know better; she'd been fooled by a police officer before.

Ignoring her racing pulse, she squared her shoulders and lifted her chin. 'Ben.' She perched on the edge of her seat, ready to defend herself if she had to. 'It's about the letters. I've already told Albert about this, and he knows I'm here,' she lied. 'Now, I need you to explain yourself.'

He looked everywhere but at her. 'What do you mean? I'm sorry we've not been able to do anything about the letters, but no crime has been committed.' He licked his lips.

Laurel hardened her stare. 'I was hauled into the station today by DI Coral and DS Hill and when I mentioned the letters, they didn't know anything about them.' She held up a hand, cutting off whatever excuse he was about to make. 'They asked around; no one has heard anything about them.' She tried to slow her breathing, hoping he couldn't see how scared she was. 'And that's when I realised who'd sent them.'

The seconds ticked by, and she didn't think he was going to confess until his face crumpled. 'I'm sorry. I'm so, so sorry. I had no choice.'

It was a bit rich of him to be throwing excuses around so quickly. 'I'm not happy to be right about this. At first, I thought I must have got it wrong, but the only possible reason you would fail to report them would be if you were involved.' Her blood was heating up as the worry she'd felt since the first letter arrived was replaced with anger.

'I'm sorry, I never meant for you to be scared.'

She had to lean forwards to hear him. 'Seriously? How did you think I'd react? Why did you send them? I don't understand, if you wanted a reason to spend time with me, why couldn't you have been up front about it? I mean, I would have said no because of Elise, but what could you ever achieve with anonymous letters?' She was shouting now.

When he didn't respond she glared at him, but instead of looking ashamed, he was frowning.

'Hold on, you think *I* sent them? I thought– oh Laurel, no.'

Panic ratcheted up her heart rate. This wasn't going how she'd planned. Why was he denying it now?

He came off his chair and knelt in front of her. She reared back, alarmed by his proximity.

'Sorry.' He backed off an inch or two. 'Please, let me explain.' He sighed and hung his head before explaining, 'It was Elise who sent the letters.'

Now it was her turn to be confused. 'Elise? Why?' she spluttered.

Ben sat back on his heels and ran a hand through his hair. 'Look, don't judge her on this. I realise that's asking a lot, but she's not had an easy life, and she has trouble with insecurity.'

Laurel remembered her chat with the chef in the Beverley coffee shop, she'd enjoyed Elise's company, and Elise hadn't given any indication she harboured the feelings expressed in the letters, nor that she was troubled, as Ben was suggesting. Should she have seen the signs?

'It can be tough on a relationship, I can tell you, and I haven't always been as understanding as I should have been.'

'All very touching. What a self-aware boyfriend you are,' she snapped.

'I'm not trying to minimise what she's done, or my covering it up. I just want you to have some background.' He was trying to keep eye contact now. 'I made the mistake of telling her about you and how we'd bumped into each other at Dorothy's when the body was found. Then when we saw you in the café Elise got herself all wound up about how pretty you are and–'

The snort came out without Laurel intending it. 'Elise is gorgeous! Why would she ever be concerned about me?' She cringed as she spoke. The self-deprecation sounded needy.

'You're a beautiful woman, Laurel, and intelligent, successful. You shouldn't need me to tell you.'

To her annoyance, heat bloomed in her cheeks.

'She got herself into a state and I didn't know what she'd done until you showed me the letters. I recognised her handwriting even though she'd tried to disguise it. I confronted her and she admitted it. I didn't know she'd sent another one. She promised she wouldn't.' He returned to his seat and picked up a photo of Elise from the coffee table beside him. 'She's an incredible woman, but she has problems. The funny thing is – sorry, I know none of this is funny – but the thing is, she really likes you.'

Laurel was lost for words. She'd liked Elise too but was furious with her now. Complicating everything was her attraction to Ben, which persisted, underneath the current of her outrage.

'I hope you understand why I couldn't report the letters? When I got home after the fire, after you'd told me about the third letter, I sat Elise down and gave her a choice, either she stops with the letters and gets help, or I was going to tell you.'

'You probably shouldn't have been round at mine before the fire, and you shouldn't have been asking my advice about Elise.' After his revelations, she was recalling their meetings and conversations in a whole new light.

'No, I shouldn't, but I wanted to know if you suspected Elise. I was wrong. I know I've said it already, but I'm sorry.' He put the photo back down and stood to pace to the window and back. 'I need to ask you a question,' he said, coming to a halt by the fireplace. 'What are you going to do now that you know?'

She could see the plea in his eyes, and she wanted to reassure him, but she was seething. She'd been prepared to leave the village. She'd thrown up she was so upset about the horrendous idea she was to blame for the fire and Charlotte. She'd scared Maggie and involved Albert. Goodness knows what the police had made of her claim to have received threatening letters. What's more, she no longer had any proof: she'd given them all to Ben, and no one else had seen them. She needed time to think things through.

Eventually she said, 'I don't know, Ben. I don't know.'

Chapter 49

Laurel

'Are you sure you're feeling up to a walk?' Laurel was being overly cautious, but Maggie had only been out of the hospital for a couple of hours.

'I'm fine. My goodness, you're a fusspot. It's a beautiful afternoon, after all this death and sadness let's make the most of it.'

Lost in thought, and chewing over Ben and Elise's deceit, Laurel had spotted Maggie parking her cute little car outside The Snooty Fox. After Laurel had helped her to move her meagre belongings into a pretty room overlooking the village green, Maggie had talked her into taking a stroll.

'I know I've been a pain lately, but my spare room is very cosy. Why don't you stay with me instead of at the pub?' Laurel offered.

'My insurance is paying for it, and I quite fancy the idea of having someone else clean my room and cook me breakfast every day for a few days. I know you'd be happy to do the same, but I'd feel I was imposing on you. Hetty and Constance, and Albert too, you've all offered and you're all wonderful, but this way I have my own space and Sam gets the extra business; March isn't a busy time for the B&B.'

Mollified, Laurel let it go. 'Where's Natalie going to stay, or has she gone back to London?'

'No, Hugh's allowing her to stay with him at High Field House, the place he's rented. Goodness knows, it's big enough, but from what Natalie tells me, he wasn't particularly gracious, she practically had to beg him.'

Was Maggie finally seeing beyond Hugh's facade?

'I understand him though, a writer needs his own space.'

Maybe not.

They turned onto Church Lane and waved to Christopher who was sitting on a sunny bench in the graveyard.

'Poor man,' said Maggie. 'Having to hide who he is because of some small-minded bigots! I've a good mind to have a word with Dorothy once she's home. Or I would if it wouldn't risk betraying the vicar. She's coming out tomorrow you know. I snuck up to see her again as soon as they discharged me. She's on a new medication for her heart and doesn't think they'll need to do surgery, thank heavens. Her head is all healed, and there's no sign of any lasting damage. I may disagree with some of her views and beliefs, but I'm glad she's recovered.'

'Still no recollection of who attacked her?'

'None.'

From Church Lane they could turn onto School Lane or continue straight ahead past the meadow where the metalled surface became a dirt track. They chose the track. In the hedgerows and grassy verges signs of spring were thrusting through the mud and detritus of the previous year. The daffodils would bloom within a week or so and the snowdrops already in flower nodded in the soft breeze. The sun finally had some heat in it and Laurel closed her eyes and turned her face to enjoy the warmth.

'There's a bench up here; shall we pause a while?' Maggie suggested.

They crested a gentle rise and took their place on the worn wooden seat. A plaque attached to the backrest set forth the exhortation: *Don't let anything stand in the way of your dreams. Anon.* Laurel thought about the words as she sat. Her dream was clear to her now; it was no longer about work, professional or academic success; it was to live a happy life amongst her friends.

'Right,' said Maggie, settling herself. 'I think it's time you gave me a proper update on all that's been going on, including those dreadful letters. Have you heard anything from the police?'

Laurel hesitated to share what she'd learned from Ben but couldn't keep it from her friend. It was time they worked together again, as they had when they'd solved the murders the year before. She wasn't going to hold back any longer.

After listening in silence, shock evident in her expression, Maggie was characteristically generous in her reaction. 'The poor girl! But I'm glad you know now and can stop worrying you're putting us all in some kind of danger. How awful for her to shoulder such self-doubt. I can't imagine what she's gone through in life to come to this. Have you decided what you're going to do?'

It was the same question Ben had asked. Scared as she had been by the letters, Laurel had no desire for revenge or retribution. Whatever demons drove Elise, it was help and support she needed.

'I'm going to leave it. Nothing good can come of getting Elise in any kind of trouble, but I will follow up with Ben to ensure she gets professional help.'

Maggie patted her hand and smiled. 'It's the right thing to do.' She had a small bag on her shoulder which she pulled onto her lap to delve into its depths. 'Here, have a toffee and then we need to talk about Charlotte. I can't for the life of me work out why the poor woman was back at The Grange, or how she got in when the doors were all locked.'

There was a different question Laurel wanted to tackle first. 'These last couple of years, the deaths, and now this fire, have they changed the way you feel about Elderwick?' She gestured to the landscape rolling away in front of them. Across the fields they could see the spire of St Stephen's and the rooftops of the cottages on Church Lane. From the direction of the school came the faint sounds of children laughing. If she didn't know better, she could imagine it was the perfect English village.

Maggie chewed determinedly on her sweet before offering an answer. 'Yes and no. It's been my home for so long now I can't picture myself living anywhere else, even after all this horrible business, plus the unpleasantness with Nicholas. The people who live here are my friends, my neighbours, and despite their faults, I love every one of them. I don't know of anywhere more beautiful. So, no, my fondness for my home hasn't altered.'

She paused but looked like she had more to add. 'I know you'll think I'm ridiculous, but for a short time I wondered if this Carter-Bell person who wants to buy Elderwick Hall could have killed Simon to... I don't know, sully the village? Put Dandelions off wanting to build a centre here. Since the fire and Charlotte... well, now it seems a little far-fetched.'

Laurel considered Maggie's words. Elderwick Hall hadn't occurred to her as a potential motive for the murders. 'I think it's unlikely,' she said, carefully. 'But we should be open to all possible explanations. Albert mentioned doing a bit of digging into Mr Carter-Bell. We should ask him.'

'Good idea,' said Maggie.

'But back to my original question,' Laurel prompted. 'You said yes and no. So, *something* has shifted?'

Maggie's hand stalled in the process of transporting a second toffee to her mouth. Placing it on her lap and rolling the sugary confection in her fingers she adjusted her position on the seat, so she was facing Laurel.

'I take more time now to value my life and the people in it. I recognise my fortune and privilege.' There were tears in her eyes which she blinked away before popping the toffee onto her tongue.

Laurel smiled and reached for Maggie's hand. 'Ew, it's all sticky.'

'We do need to talk about Charlotte.'

'I know.' Despite all her experiences: the loss of her parents; her professional career in palliative care; the Elderwick murders, she would never fail to be shaken by the finality of death and the ferocity of grief. She gathered herself. 'What happened yesterday after I left with Natalie?'

Maggie stowed the remaining toffees in her bag and drew out a packet of wipes to clean her hands. 'Nothing much. It would only have been a couple of minutes after you'd gone, and I heard Charlotte gathering her things and saw her flounce out. Then Hugh came into the kitchen. By his face I'd say he was surprised I was there and not Natalie. He made a joke about highly-strung agents before he left too. I think he went back to High Field House, but I haven't the foggiest where Charlotte disappeared to. I assumed she'd head back to London and her car wasn't anywhere in sight when I set off for the church to find Christopher.'

'What did you make of Charlotte and Hugh's conversation about his daughter?'

'She had a nerve to threaten exposing his daughter. I don't blame Hugh for being upset.'

'Even though he's estranged from her? Even if he exploited and exposed his daughter for the sake of his books?' She raised her hands. 'I haven't got it in for him, I'm merely playing devil's advocate.'

'She's still his daughter. As a parent, I'd do anything to protect my kids.' Fire flashed in Maggie's eyes.

'But would you go as far as arson and murder?'

Chapter 50

Laurel

'Hugh.' She puffed up the stairs to find him sitting in the waiting room, tapping his foot. His text, which had arrived via an unexpected moment of mobile network coverage, had pulled her away from the bench with Maggie but they'd both agreed Laurel should meet with him and capitalise on the opening to ask about Charlotte.

'I've been trying to reach you all day.' He pouted. 'You know about–'

'The first I heard of it was your message this morning–'

'Oh, you got it then? I assumed, since I didn't hear back from you, that the vagaries of the mobile signal around here had thwarted my efforts to contact you.'

'I had a few things I needed to attend to, and I'm here now, not as your therapist,' she added. She couldn't risk this being thought a confidential conversation. She didn't want ethical constraints to navigate if she needed to report anything Hugh said to the police.

She unlocked the door to her consulting room and led him inside. This time, she pointed him towards the chairs to the side of the desk. She wasn't going to play any status games today. He sat and leaned forward in his seat, radiating agitation.

She knew he was there to talk about Charlotte, but his absence from Simon's memorial was still bugging her. 'I hope you don't mind my asking, how was the memorial?' The more she'd thought about it, the more certain she was Hugh hadn't attended despite him telling her he was planning to go.

He cleared his throat and turned to the window to watch a noisy group of workmen filing into The Pleasant Pheasant.

'Hugh?'

'It was depressing. How else would it be?' he muttered as he continued to stare out at the village green.

She wanted to push him on his answer but couldn't think how to challenge him without admitting she'd been there herself.

Seizing the gap left by her hesitation he expelled his distress. 'The police suspect me in Charlotte's death, and I've been shut out of the investigation into Simon's murder. They're grasping at straws. Why would *I* hurt Charlotte?' He pushed his glasses onto his head and rubbed his eyes which were bloodshot and bagged.

Fed up with the recent weeks of stepping gently around the case – cases now – Laurel didn't sugarcoat her reply. 'She threatened to expose your daughter and, what was it you said? "You go near her and I'll..." You'll what, Hugh?'

A vein pulsed in his temple and his hands clenched into fists. Laurel braced, ready to run or defend herself. The tension in the room swallowed her thoughts and muted the sounds from outside the window. She caught his eyes and held them, daring him to lie.

'You heard that did you? And I suppose you told the police?'

I'm so stupid! It hadn't occurred to her at the time, she'd been too concerned with keeping her own head off the chopping block. She should have told them, of course she should, and she would, as soon as she was safe to do so. 'I had to tell them.' Would he spot her lie? It was becoming a habit, telling untruths.

He twisted his lips. His shoes today, usually spotless, were scuffed and muddy, his glasses were smeared, and his hair was dishevelled. He was rattled but was he guilty?

'Did you set the fire?'

'Wow!' His head snapped up. 'Don't beat about the bush, will you. No, I bloody didn't.'

'He has an alibi.'

Startled, they swung round to see Natalie in the doorway. 'Hugh couldn't have started the fire; I was with him all evening. Come on,' she said to him. 'We're leaving.'

Laurel could only watch as Hugh got to his feet and Natalie hustled him out of the office.

Chapter 51

Laurel

'The dream team back together,' said Laurel to Maggie as they warmed themselves by the fire in Albert's front room. Outside, the day was already fading to dusk.

'And Albert too,' he said as he came in hefting a tray laden with scones, a pot of jam and three mugs of hot chocolate.

'Albert, you were always a part of the team,' Maggie corrected him.

He placed the tray onto a side table and handed round the refreshments. 'I am humbled to be considered a member of your crime-busting squad. Laurel, I've got a couple of plain scones for you, I know you don't like cooked fruit.'

She grinned. 'Thank you.' Back with her friends, and with the cloud of the anonymous letters lifted, she was beginning to feel steady once more. 'Right, let's get to it. I've faffed about too long trying to get one up on Hugh. This can't continue, we need to protect our village and I need to show the disagreeable DI Coral and DS Hill I am not some crazed killer.'

Maggie gasped. 'The police suspect you?'

'Oh definitely. You have to admit, since I've arrived in Elderwick, there have been three murders, one attack, and a possible arson resulting in a death, it does look a bit sus. Much as I dislike them, I suppose they wouldn't be doing their job if they didn't question me. Actually, can I ask...' She wasn't sure she wanted to hear the answer but had to know. 'Do you think I'm a bad luck charm or whatever? A lot of horrible events have occurred since I moved here. Is it me, somehow?' She searched first Albert's face then Maggie's.

'Collyweston and cow-slaver.'

Maggie giggled.

'You're a smart young woman, you know perfectly well you're no Jonah,' Albert admonished. 'Now, let's get on with solving this case, shall we. Take your pews and grab your pens. From the beginning. Laurel, you start.'

She acquiesced to his demand and allowed herself a small smile over his compliment. 'Okay, so we start with Simon's murder. This is what we know about him and his death: he was a journalist; he was here to write about Hugh; Hugh thought it was going to be a flattering piece, but it turns out Simon was raking up all sorts of muck. Simon and Hugh were at school together and there was an incident when a classmate died: the boy was locked outside and died of hypothermia. Simon had a copy of the police report in his journal. It was ruled accidental death, but I'm not so sure.'

Maggie nodded at her to go on.

'Simon met with the vicar, which we now know was because he knew about Christopher's sexuality and was threatening to expose him. He also met with Elise, but we haven't had a satisfactory answer as to why. She lied about it to Ben, to you, Maggie, when you and Natalie saw her, and to me. What else?'

'Hold on, can we back up,' said Albert. 'Hugh and Simon knew each other from school and one of their contemporaries died? This was in the journal? I don't recall you mentioning it before.'

Laurel squirmed. 'As you know, I wasn't meant to have the journal, let alone read it, so...'

'Yes, I see,' said Albert.

'...and I didn't know the whole story until I went to a small memorial they held for Simon in London.'

Maggie gasped.

Laurel felt grubby thinking about how she'd gone off to Simon's memorial with the intention of interrogating grieving friends. She ploughed on before Maggie or Albert could pepper her with more questions. 'I met someone mentioned in the journal, someone Simon was going to interview for his piece on Hugh, an author called Zack Beech. He was a pupil at the same school and was very open about the incident.' She broke off, anxious to recall the details correctly before sharing the story.

'Zack, Hugh and Simon knew the boy who died, Xavier Houghton. I looked him up online and I couldn't find anything different to what was recorded in the police report Simon had. I can understand why Hugh wouldn't want the event brought up, but as far as Zack is concerned, Hugh had nothing to do with the boy's death.'

'The report did say it was an accident,' said Maggie. 'But there's more?'

'There was another old pupil at the memorial, a journalist at *The Times*, James Wentworth.' She shuddered at the memory of his breath in her face and the sneer on his lips. 'He was quite unpleasant. Simon didn't know this, but Zack and Hugh always believed James goaded, no, bullied Xavier into going outside that night, that freezing night in the middle of winter. They have no proof, but they suspect James of locking the door so Xavier couldn't get back in. Whether it constitutes murder I don't know, and as Zack told me, they never had any proof.'

'But Simon didn't know,' Maggie pointed out. 'So, James – if he was mixed up in Xavier's death – had no motive to harm Simon.'

'No.'

'Ah, not so hasty, Maggie,' exclaimed Albert. 'Permit me if you will. I believe a motive may be hiding here. Correct me if I'm wrong, but Hugh suspected James' involvement, correct?'

Laurel murmured agreement.

'Therefore, if James should have come to know of Simon's plan to interview Hugh – and as they moved in the same circles, it's reasonable to expect he did – could James have worried the story would get out?'

'Um, I should have said. James was in the US with his family when Simon was killed so it couldn't have been him.'

Albert groaned and threw up his hands. 'You could have mentioned his alibi sooner.'

'It was a good theory though.'

He chuckled. 'You don't have to humour an old man.' He reached for a scone and sliced it carefully in half with his knife and spread it with a thick layer of jam. 'Shame, revenge for an historic crime would have made a neat rationale. What else do we have?'

'Do we know for certain how Simon was killed?' Maggie asked.

Laurel shook her head. 'He'd been stabbed, but judging by the lack of blood I'm sure he was dead *before* he was stabbed. Which brings us to the nitrous oxide canister from the pond.'

'I spoke to Hetty and Constance about that,' said Maggie. 'Apparently, the gas induces a feeling of euphoria as it suffocates you. What if someone persuaded him to inhale some and then they made him keep going? He maybe couldn't put up a fight because of the effects of the gas.'

Laurel gave a grim smile. 'I think that's what happened and

if it did, it gives us at least three more questions: why use the gas and then stab him; how did the killer get him to inhale the gas; how did the killer get hold of the nitrous oxide?'

Maggie relayed the opinion of the sisters. 'It's not especially hard to come by, but the people who would have particularly easy access include cooks, chefs, bakers and so on. It's used a lot for whipped cream.'

Albert put down his empty plate and picked up a pen to jot notes as they talked. 'And we know a number of people who fall into those categories who also came into contact with Simon: Hetty and Constance; Jo at the café; and Elise. I bet they use it in her fancy restaurant.' He listed their names next to the words 'nitrous oxide'.

'But remember, we have no proof the canister was anything to do with the murder. Ben never told me what happened when he took it in.' Laurel picked up her mug and blew on the steaming liquid. She sipped, relishing the warm, velvety drink. 'Pass me the jam could you, Maggie?' She swapped the mug for her scone which she slathered in the raspberry conserve.

An idea occurred and she spoke through a mouthful of crumbs. 'It's quite theatrical... sorry.' She swallowed. 'The way he was killed is theatrical. Stabbed in a locked room, very Agatha Christie. You weren't here to see my masterful demonstration of how the locked door bit was done, Maggie, but it's not an easy thing to stage and whoever did it would have needed to plan in advance.'

'Could you show me?' Maggie asked.

'No!' exclaimed Albert. 'I'm not risking my woodwork or wallpaper again.'

Maggie huffed and Laurel said she'd talk her through it later, then added, 'To use my method, the killer had to have had tools with them, and they had to know the type of doors in Tulip Cottage, whether they had hinges you could unhook.'

'Dorothy is the only person who'd know,' Maggie stated.

'Actually, I thought so too, but I did an online search, and the Tulip Cottage website has a video walkthrough. Anyone watching it can see the doors, and the hinges, clearly.'

Albert frowned.

'Oh my goodness!'

'Exactly,' said Laurel, enjoying Maggie's realisation.

'We know from Dorothy's bank statement that Greenleaves booked the cottage for Simon.'

Albert grunted in surprise. 'A significant clue!'

Encouraged, Maggie pushed on. 'If Charlotte booked the cottage for Simon, she could have done all the planning you mentioned, Laurel. Perhaps, like Hugh, she was under the impression Simon would be writing a complimentary article and somehow, she found out otherwise, so she killed him.' She stretched towards the coffee table to place her empty mug onto the tea tray.

'When I spoke to her on the phone, she pretended she didn't already know Hugh was here in Elderwick.'

Maggie's head whipped round. 'When did you speak to Charlotte?'

She explained her phone call to the agent's offices. The more she said, the more she realised how much she'd been keeping from Maggie and Albert. She should have done this far sooner. Together they might have already solved Simon's murder and could have prevented the fire and Charlotte's death. 'The police think I lured her to Elderwick to kill her.'

'Really?' asked Albert.

'Well, not quite, but it's only added to their conviction I'm some kind of magnet for death.'

Albert chuckled. 'Well, with your work history...'

She delivered a gentle thump to his shoulder.

Maggie rolled her eyes at them. 'Getting back on topic, if Charlotte killed Simon, who killed her?'

Albert doodled a picture of a door on a blank page. Midway through sketching a key in a lock, he cleared his throat and said, 'We're assuming too much. Maggie, my dear, I don't say this to in any way alarm you, but what if Charlotte wasn't the intended victim of the fire?'

Like Laurel, he must have seen the fear spring into Maggie's eyes because he hurried to reassure. 'Or perchance, our firebug didn't intend for anyone to be hurt?'

Laurel dabbed her finger in the final crumbs from her scone. 'Let's go back again,' she said. 'Who had a motive for Simon's murder?'

Albert reeled off two names, 'Hugh and Charlotte.'

'I don't think Hugh should be included,' huffed Maggie.

'I do,' said Laurel. And Albert, I think we need to add Christopher to the list too. I know he's your friend, but we can't pretend he didn't have reason to shut Simon up. Plus, we should keep Elise in mind. She has access to nitrous oxide, and she met and lied about her meeting with Simon. She's clearly troubled, what with sending those letters and everything.' Laurel had given him a quick rundown of her conversation with Ben and his admission regarding Elise's poison pen letters.

He didn't look happy about it, but Albert added Christopher's name.

'Are we any closer to a solution?'

Laurel and Albert each shook their head.

'If Charlotte was killed deliberately, it muddies the waters further still.' Albert turned his notebook so they could see a diagram he'd drawn. 'See, if Charlotte killed Simon, that means there are two killers.'

'It's the same if Hugh killed Simon. I saw Natalie earlier today, and she alibis him for the night of the fire.'

'Does she? That's interesting.' He tapped the pen against his teeth. 'Do we trust her? From what I know of her, she is devoted to Hugh. Might she lie to protect him?'

'Natalie lying is more likely than there being two killers running around our small village.' Laurel was tempted to bang her head on the table. 'Everyone is lying and we're no nearer the truth.'

Maggie cleared her throat and said, 'I have two suggestions, but they're both silly.'

'Every theory is valid,' said Albert.

Maggie recounted her speculation over Mr Carter-Bell's determination to purchase Elderwick Hall. 'Laurel said you know a bit about him?'

'He's an unpleasant piece of work,' Albert confirmed. 'From what I have read, he doesn't like to lose and doesn't believe in charity. If nothing more, that alone may be fuelling his persistence. But I don't believe Elderwick Hall is worth killing for. What was your other suggestion?'

'I don't like to think it could be so, but what about Hugh's daughter?' Maggie blushed but continued. 'She would have ample motive for wanting to keep Simon from writing his article because we know he intended to include her story. Then Charlotte wanted to expose her too.'

Laurel wanted to cheer. Finally, a piece which fit the puzzle. 'That's brilliant. She has the perfect motive and Hugh could be covering for her. You said it yourself, Maggie, a parent will go to extraordinary lengths for their child.' She felt re-energised. There was more investigating to be done, and she knew exactly where to start. 'I think I have a phone number for her.' She looked at the clock on the mantlepiece. 'It's a work number so it's probably too late to call now, but we can sketch out our approach and I'll try calling tomorrow. Let's bring her into the light and see what she can tell us.'

Chapter 52

Laurel

She waited for as long as she could bear it the next morning, but it was still only 7am when she sprang from her bed and went to retrieve the notes she'd made when reading Simon's journal. The phone number she'd copied was right there. All she had to do was dial and ask for Holly Quintrell.

Simon hadn't been able to get a home or mobile number, only one for Holly's place of work. It was unlikely anyone would be answering the phones so early.

She dialled anyway. *You never know.* It rang, once, twice, three times. On the fourth ring it connected. She clamped the phone hard against her ear.

'Thank you for your call. We're closed right now...'

Damn it. She was ready to hang up when the next few words set her heart racing. She could have kicked herself it was so obvious.

The restaurant was small but elegant, the few tables spaced for comfort and placed to foster intimacy. Empty of customers,

Laurel could hear the staff working behind the closed kitchen doors. Elise tried, and failed, to hide her discomfiture when she spotted her visitor. Laurel didn't know if Ben had told his girlfriend that he'd confessed to what she'd done, but she wasn't there about the poison pen letters.

'We need to talk,' she said.

Without question, Elise guided her to a table in an alcove, away from the picture windows.

Once they'd sat down, Laurel placed a book on the table between them, *Murder of Innocents*. She watched Elise blanch, her eyes darting around the room. 'I understand Hugh used his daughter's life as the basis for this story. It must have been awful for her. I don't know what I'd do if my dad had exploited my life in the same way he did with Holly.'

Elise went still, head down, hands gripping the edge of the table. 'You know, don't you?' She spoke so quietly Laurel had to lean forward to catch her words.

Gratified as she was to have uncovered the identity of Hugh's daughter, it didn't feel good to bring more distress to the woman's doorstep.

When Elise looked up again, her face was pinched and her eyes haunted. 'Yes, Hugh is my father. I've done everything I can to cut that man out of my life, but he won't leave me alone. That's why he's in Elderwick, you know. He's hired private detectives more than once to track me down. I finally thought I'd found somewhere safe, somewhere for me, but lo and behold, dear old Dad rocks up. Again.'

Now she'd started, her words came fast. 'His book, it's quite a piece of work, isn't it?' She smacked the cover of the hardback. 'He took my whole life and laid it out there for any stranger to consume. He said it's fiction, but it didn't take people long to connect it to me.'

'It sounds like it's been dreadful for you.' Laurel

sympathised but had to press her further. 'You're Polly in the book, the victim?'

'He barely even changed the name. My birth name is Holly for God's sake,' she growled.

'He wants to reconnect with you?'

Elise scoffed. 'Yeah, he wants to be in my life, but on his terms. Here I am, putting myself together, I've got a job I love, a great partner, a life I'm proud of. It took a lot of therapy, and you'll understand how gruelling that was. I had to take apart everything I'd experienced before I could build a better me. He doesn't get any of that. He thinks he can say sorry, and all is forgotten. How dare he! How dare he come into what's mine, my home, and what's more, he brought that hack to my door!' Her pretty mouth curdled into a snarl.

'Simon Forster?'

'Yes. He knew too. He knew who I was, and he was determined to write about me, to use me in his pathetic little magazine piece. Hugh did that, he brought that man into my world, and he was going to blow it apart. I'm Elise now, I'm not Holly and I don't want anyone knowing who I used to be.' Her raised voice brought a face peeking round the kitchen door. Elise noticed and waved them away. 'See, it's already started.' Her breath hitched. 'They'll all want to know what this was about once you're gone.'

Laurel grimaced; in her impatience she'd behaved no better than Simon. On the other hand, Elise could be a killer. 'How did you know what Simon was going to write?'

'He told me. Oh, he was completely upfront with me. I think he wanted to use me against Hugh. He said he wanted to hear my side of the story, but I'm not stupid, I learned the hard way never to trust journalists.'

'That's what you were talking about with him in The Pleasant Pheasant?'

'Yes. I could hardly tell you the truth, could I. I knew he'd be there in the café for his breakfast, and I needed to tell him to leave me alone. I didn't want to speak to him in public, but I was afraid to meet him in private.'

'How did you feel when you heard about his death?' Laurel wished she could take notes as they spoke but resisted the urge.

'I'm not going to lie, once he was gone, I thought everything would go back to normal. Fat chance! But I'm not sorry he's dead. You might think I'm horrible for saying it.' She shrugged.

'And then Charlotte showed up.'

'Who?'

Laurel studied the woman's face. There was no evidence of her tell; she wasn't touching her face or covering her mouth like she had the last time she'd lied.

'Your dad's literary agent. You didn't know?'

'I don't concern myself with any part of Hugh's life, especially his *work*.'

'She turned up in Elderwick the day before the fire. Maggie and I overheard her telling Hugh she was going to write about you. It sounded as though she was picking up exactly where Simon left off. You didn't know any of this?'

'Wait, she's the woman who was killed in the fire, wasn't she?'

'I'm afraid so.'

'I see.' The realisation was drawn on her face. 'You think I had something to do with these deaths, is that it? Seriously?'

Laurel let the ensuing silence spin out.

'Look, I like you and I understand why you're asking. Ben's told me you solved those murders last year.'

Laurel thought she caught a moue of antipathy on Elise's face at the idea of her speaking with Ben, but that could be her own guilty conscience jumping to conclusions.

'I can promise you I had nothing to do with Simon or the agent woman.'

Again, there was no obvious evidence of a lie.

'I need to ask you something. Are you going to tell the police that Hugh's my father?'

As with the letters, Laurel wasn't immediately sure what to do for the best. 'Does Ben know about Hugh?'

Elise gave her a searching look then said, 'Yes. I broke down the first day I saw Hugh in the village. Ben's been great. Even offered to have some of the blokes from work *encourage* Hugh to go elsewhere.' She laughed, but there was no humour in it.

Simon's article and Charlotte's threat to Hugh gave Elise motive for the murders but with a start, Laurel realised Elise had given Ben a viable motive too. If Elise were innocent, could the culprit be Ben? His devotion was evident in his cover-up of the letters. How much further might he have gone to protect his girlfriend?

Chapter 53

Laurel

This time they were meeting in the bar of The Snooty Fox. It wasn't open yet for the evening, but Sam was happy for them to set up shop in a secluded corner and work their way through snacks and drinks. Laurel had updated Maggie and Albert on her conversation with Elise and they were trying to fit the new information into their emerging understanding of events.

'I can't believe Elise is Hugh's daughter!' Maggie exclaimed for the third time. 'And what does that mean for our investigation?'

Laurel rubbed her temples. 'Why would Hugh meet Simon in Elderwick if his daughter was here? When we overheard what he said to Charlotte, it sounded like he was trying to protect her. So, it doesn't make sense he'd want a journalist here, does it?'

'Here's a question: until Simon was killed, and his journal found, or finally handed in by Laurel at any rate, how did anyone know he was a quidnunc?' Albert sipped his pint of cider. 'Oh, that's hit the spot.' Laurel and Maggie stared at him.

He chuckled. 'Quidnunc, it means a busybody, wanting to know everyone's business.'

'Sounds like most of Elderwick,' Laurel remarked. 'As far as I know, only Elise could have known ahead of time because Simon told her outright.'

'What about Christopher? Could Elise have confided in Christopher and Christopher told Hugh?'

Albert was shaking his head at Maggie's suggestion. 'Christopher wouldn't betray a confidence like that.'

'But it's possible,' Laurel argued. 'Which leaves us, in terms of possible culprits for Simon's murder, with Hugh, Christopher, Elise, and Charlotte.'

'Correct me if I'm mistaken, but aren't we meant to be narrowing down the suspect pool?' Albert sighed and finished off his drink. 'Does anyone desire a further libation?'

'And now Ben too,' Maggie reminded them.

'I may move on to the hard liquor,' grumbled Albert, as he wandered off in search of the bar manager.

Out of sight, they heard Albert utter a greeting and moments later Hetty appeared wide-eyed and pink cheeked.

'I thought I might find you lot here. I already tried your place, Laurel and Albert's, then the café. Been running all over the village.' She brushed a stray hair off her forehead and squashed onto the bench seat next to Maggie. 'You've got to hear this.'

Albert came back without any drinks. 'Sam's going to bring them over, I didn't want to miss this young lady's urgent news.' He winked at Hetty who beamed at him in return.

All eyes turned to the baker.

'I had a lunch date today with Florence, the chief fire officer from the other night, and this needs to stay between us, I'm sworn to secrecy, but you know.' She shrugged and grinned.

'She was back at The Grange today with the police who told her, and she told me: that Charlotte Drake woman who died in the fire didn't die in the fire.'

Laurel didn't know if it was cynicism or fatigue, but she wasn't surprised by the news. 'How did she die?' She hoped she would never become inured to the violence visited on people in the village, but in her current state, she had precious little left in her emotional reserves.

'She was already dead when the fire started. There was no smoke damage in her throat or lungs. She'd been bashed over the head. At first, they thought she'd been overcome by the smoke and stumbled or fallen, but now they know the head wound was the cause of death.'

Maggie put a hand to her mouth. 'Just like Dorothy. Only she didn't die of course. Oh, my goodness.'

'Did they speculate per chance, on whether the fire might have been started to hide the evidence of this murder?' Albert queried.

'I don't know, she didn't say, but I wouldn't be surprised. Promise you won't tell anyone I told you? I really like Flo and I'm rather hoping for a second date.'

'We won't utter a word, my dear,' Albert reassured her along with nods from Laurel and Maggie.

'So, it was murder then,' whispered Maggie.

'Another one.' Laurel felt the defeat settle in her stomach. It was one step forwards and six steps back.

'I think the moment we learned of her death we suspected it wasn't accidental. Don't you agree, Laurel?'

'I know, but it sucks now it's been confirmed.'

'I'm so mad!' Maggie banged her fist on the table making the others jump. 'How dare this person, whoever they are, kill that poor woman, leave her in my house, and start a fire to cover it up? They could have hurt who knows how many other people. I could have... it could... I don't feel so well.' Her colour drained.

'Looks like I've arrived in the nick of,' said Sam, approaching the table with their drinks. 'In fact, let me nip back behind the bar and get you something stronger, Maggie. Brandy should do the job. You're white as a ghost.'

He returned with a double measure which Maggie accepted with a wobbly smile. 'Thank you,' she managed. She had a couple of sips then set down the glass.

Hetty took her hands and rubbed them and from her other side, Laurel placed her arm around Maggie's shoulders, hugged tightly and said, 'You're safe, we won't let anything happen to you. I promise.'

Maggie's colour began to return but she stayed quiet as the other three debated the latest revelation. They bombarded Hetty with questions about the possible murder weapon, how the door came to be unlocked, and the location of Charlotte's distinctive car, which none of them had seen since the fire. Hetty had to admit she had no other answers for them, but grudgingly agreed to see if she could wheedle more out of Florence if she saw her again.

'At this rate, she'll think I'm only interested in one thing, her job,' she groaned. 'Speaking of jobs, I've left Constance alone in the bakery. I'd better get back to her or she'll kill me.' She clapped her hands across her mouth. 'Damn it, sorry, poor choice of words.'

'Maggie,' said Laurel when Hetty had left, 'does Natalie have keys to The Grange?'

'She only had one for the front door while she was staying with me. I can't imagine her bashing someone over the head and setting a fire though, can you? And she must be about a hundred pounds soaking wet. I doubt she'd have the strength. Besides, she was with Hugh.'

'Regardless of Natalie giving him an alibi, to my mind, he is our best suspect for both of the murders and the attack on Dorothy,' said Albert.

'I think we need to speak to the police.' Laurel scowled as she said it. It wasn't top of her list of fun things to do. In fact, perhaps she shouldn't be the one to approach them. They'd probably accuse her diverting attention from herself by accusing innocent parties. 'That is, when I say *we*, I think it should be one of you two. Both of you would be better still.'

Maggie fiddled with her empty glass and pulled a face. 'Could we speak to Ben first?'

'No, I'm not convinced it would be good to go to him. He lied about the letters; he lied about reporting the letters; and he has a motive.'

'Fiddlesticks, I'd forgotten, and he's such a nice man.'

'So was Nathan,' Laurel shot back, remembering the previous village policeman with whom they'd been friends. 'I think I'm going off the police altogether.'

'Right, plan of action.' Albert finished his second drink, pulled a notebook and pencil out of a pocket, licked the tip and began to write. 'Maggie and I will speak to the police this afternoon if we can. I'll check with my contact at the station who's best to approach and we'll go in person so it's harder to fob us off. Hetty is going to see if she can winkle more information out of Florence. Laurel, you see if you can't hook up with Natalie and put Hugh's alibi to the test.'

'I want to speak to Elise again too,' Laurel insisted. 'I don't see her as a killer, but now we know she's Hugh's daughter, we can't ignore her as a person of interest. Albert, would you tackle Ben?'

'Of course, and once we've completed our allocated missions, we shall regroup and review.'

'And Christopher?' Laurel prodded.

Albert pressed his lips together. 'It wasn't Chris.'

Laurel saw something in his eyes and chose not to push the issue. 'Okay,' she said. She had faith in Albert, but she wouldn't write the vicar off completely, not yet.

Chapter 54

Laurel

On the off chance she would catch Natalie alone, Laurel left The Snooty Fox and headed out of the village to High Field House, the accommodation Hugh had rented for his stay. It wasn't far but it got her wondering how Hugh and Natalie had come to be at The Grange before the fire engines on Tuesday night. What or who had alerted them?

An explanation of sorts presented itself as she reached the gates to the imposing, red brick double-fronted property tucked away up Long Lane. Turning her back on the house, she saw she'd been walking up a gentle hill, one gentle enough to be almost unnoticeable, but which provided a clear view down to the village. The fire at The Grange would have been easily visible once the flames had taken hold. Being a rural village, the fire station was some miles away, so it was reasonable to accept Natalie and Hugh had seen the fire and reached Maggie's before the fire brigade.

Natalie's lemon-yellow car was parked in the driveway, a conspicuous vehicle amongst the mud splattered drab green, grey, and black cars and farm vehicles more common to the area.

There was no sign of life, but High Field House was a large building no doubt containing many rooms.

Laurel picked her way along the edge of the lawn, avoiding the gravel which offered no chance of a quiet approach, and stepped up to the door. Raising her hand to ring the bell she hesitated at the sound of raised voices. She shuffled closer, pressing her ear against the wood, bending low so she wouldn't be seen through the stained-glass insert.

'I can't believe you're doing this to me again. When the police find out who I am they're going to start asking all kinds of questions I don't want to answer. You did this. You are responsible.'

'I won't let them. I'd never do anything to hurt you, you know that.'

'It's too late for that, *Dad*.'

She recognised the voice. It was Elise. Holly.

'Everything is ruined. Laurel knows, but I think you already know that being the one who told her in your *therapy*. God knows why *you* think you need therapy.'

'I didn't tell her.'

'I don't care what you have to say,' she shouted. 'Now I have to leave and start all over again somewhere else. Don't ever look for me again!'

'Holly, please!'

A door slammed and footsteps pounded down the hallway. Laurel leapt back and hurried for the corner of the house, hoping she wouldn't be seen through the window. She ducked out of sight just as Elise flew out of the door, ran down the driveway, and out of the gate.

'Honestly, you shouldn't eavesdrop, you know,' said a voice behind her.

She yelped. 'Natalie! Bloody hell.'

Natalie had a lit cigarette in her hand. She took a drag and blew the smoke away in a long stream. 'You know then?'

Laurel nodded, still recovering from the shock, and feeling like a child caught being naughty. 'You knew already?'

'I did. Hugh insisted on coming here for his *period of seclusion* and I couldn't understand it. So far from civilisation.' She waved her cigarette in the air. 'Eventually, he got mad and told me it had to be Elderwick because of her.' She pointed to the gate.

'Did you hear what they said?'

'Just now? No. I let her in, and I could see she was steaming so I got out of the way. I don't listen to other people's conversations.'

Laurel's cheeks flushed. 'You've got a good view of the village from here, is this where you were the night of the fire?'

Natalie gave her an appraising look and took another deep drag. 'Yes, we were working. Hugh wanted to sell Charlotte on his true crime book and convince her he could do it without exposing his daughter.'

They were standing between the wall of the house and a high hedge of leylandii and it was a funnel for the wind. Laurel shivered, wishing she'd gone home to get her long coat before walking up to Hugh's from the pub. Natalie didn't take the hint and didn't invite her to go inside.

'Would he have been successful? Charlotte seemed pretty set on her plan.'

'I guess we'll never know.'

'Hugh was with you the whole time on Tuesday evening?'

Natalie laughed. 'You're not very subtle, you know. Yes, he was with me the whole time. No, he didn't have time to go down to the village and set the fire.'

'Do you know what Charlotte was doing, why she was still in the village that evening?'

Natalie glanced to the side, took a final puff on her cigarette, then dropped it and ground it under the toe of her shoe. 'No, after you and I left Maggie's together, I didn't see her again. I assumed she'd gone back to London. Any more questions?' She raised a perfectly shaped eyebrow.

'Not that I can think of.' It hadn't gone quite the way she'd hoped, and Natalie was right, her cross-examination hadn't been subtle, but it hadn't been a wasted visit.

'Laurel? What the hell are you doing here?' Hugh came round the corner and fixed angry eyes upon her.

She felt, rather than saw, Natalie melt away behind her.

'Come inside.' He didn't wait but stalked ahead leaving the door swinging behind him.

She caught up with him in a large room off to the left of the entrance hall. Books on built-in wooden shelving covered two walls, there was a writing desk, two armchairs and a fireplace. Clearly in working order, it was empty other than for a drift of grey ashes.

'Sit.'

Their roles were reversed. She sat.

Hugh paced in front of her. 'Holly tells me you know she's my daughter?'

'Yes.'

'Why does she think I told you?'

'I don't know. I've never spoken to her about you attending sessions with me, or the unofficial meetings we've had since.'

'And how *do* you know about Holly? Natalie wouldn't have told you'

'No, no one told me, I worked it out.' She wasn't sure how to explain it further without admitting she'd found Holly/Elise's number whilst reading Simon's journal. If Hugh knew she'd read the journal he'd know she knew about the death of his classmate and she didn't think he'd be pleased about that.

Considering she suspected him of being a violent murderer, she had to avoid angering him further. Natalie had disappeared and Laurel wouldn't bet on her to come to the rescue if Hugh snapped.

Hugh simply nodded, seemingly taking her at her word. 'I need your help.'

'Pardon?'

'Are you hard of hearing? I need your help. I told you I've been cut off from Simon's murder case by the police, and now they've spoken to me about Charlotte's murder. Of course, I have an alibi, that is, Natalie and I were here all Tuesday evening, but I'm worried about Holly.'

'Elise,' she corrected. Elise was her chosen name and Laurel would continue to use it. It was no longer Hugh's place to choose his daughter's name. 'Why are you worried about Elise?'

'Yes, yes, Elise. Why? Because the police already know she's my daughter and there's some information they've read in Simon's journal – I don't want to say what – and I believe they're looking at her in connection with the murders.'

'They must have good reason.'

'No, they don't. Come on, you know that. They've had you in their sights too which is ridiculous.'

Not sure if she should be grateful for his belief in her innocence, she asked the obvious question, forgetting what was meant to be her cautious approach. 'You don't believe Elise could–'

'Elise had nothing to do with either of the deaths!' A fleck of spittle landed on her cheek. 'She's my daughter for heaven's sake. I know her and she is not a murderer.' He stopped pacing and glared down at her. 'I need you to find a way to clear her. I can't lose her again.' His voice cracked.

Marginally reassured he wasn't about to attack her, Laurel eased back from the edge of the chair and asked, 'Do they suspect her for any reason other than the journal?' It would be useful to know what the police had shared with him.

He chewed on his thumbnail, a frown creasing his face. He subsided into the second chair and closed his eyes. Eventually, he looked back at her and nodded to himself. 'This goes no further?'

'Of course.'

'Simon was killed with nitrous oxide. It was made to look as though he was stabbed, but he was already dead by then. Elise uses nitrous oxide in the restaurant. If the police haven't figured it out and gone round there already, they will soon.'

'Hugh, when she was here just now, did you warn her?'

His silence was her answer.

Chapter 55

Laurel

The light was fading as she hurried back to the village. Though the year had slipped into March, the trees remained bare, weeks away from being in leaf, and offering no protection from the insistent winds chasing across the fields. Laurel buried her hands in her pockets and hunched her shoulders. The weather matched her mood.

Approaching Myrtle Cottage, she could see the windows at Albert's were dark. He and Maggie must not be back from seeing the police. She was still weighing up what Hugh had, or rather hadn't, told her about his warning to Elise. Did he suspect his daughter of being guilty despite his denial? If he did, then logically it meant he couldn't be the killer.

She tried to put herself in his shoes as a parent estranged from his daughter. There was an argument to be made that he would warn her about the nitrous oxide even if he were convinced of her innocence. Should the police find it, they were guaranteed to think it significant. It didn't take much, just being present when a body was found was enough to make them suspect a person, as Laurel could attest.

Hugh was many things, but he wasn't stupid. He would

understand that Elise had a motive to kill both Simon and Charlotte. Goodness knows she, Maggie, and Albert had reached that exact conclusion.

But was there one killer or two? That question again. It made more sense for there to be only one, one who had ended the lives of both Simon and Charlotte. The odds of there being two active murderers in a tiny East Yorkshire village were exceedingly slim.

Laurel winced, the trouble was, Elderwick had already proven itself to be exceptional with two other murders occurring within days of her moving to the village. Begging the question, why was she discounting the far-fetched?

She looked at her watch. Elise would have had to head straight to Beverley from Hugh's to get back to the restaurant in time for the dinner service. It was a Thursday so it wasn't her day off, but would she be in work with everything going on? If she was there, was she destroying evidence? If she wasn't there, could Laurel salvage evidence before she could get rid of it? Whether the nitrous oxide used by the restaurant would prove Elise's innocence or guilt, it would be a bad idea to interfere with it, but if she got a look at it, she would know if it matched the canister she'd found in the pond.

Her car keys were in her bag, and she was back on Birch Lane. There was nothing else she could achieve until Albert and Maggie returned from the police station. Mind made up, Laurel got in her car, started the engine, and pulled away from the kerb and headed for town. How she'd get into the restaurant kitchen was a puzzle she'd tackle when she got there.

Despite the weather there was a lot of foot traffic in Beverley for early on a Thursday evening and the parking spaces near Aroma, the restaurant where Elise worked, were all taken. A silver BMW fifty metres ahead was sitting, engine running, lights on and Laurel slowed hoping they were about to leave, but luck was not with her. A beep from behind made her move on. There was more parking further up, slanted cobbled bays. She spied a space and approached with a grim expression. Wedged between a large flower planter and a low stone wall, it was small. She indicated and pulled over, letting the few cars behind pass her before she lined up and attempted to fit into the gap. She made it, but it was a tight squeeze.

Exiting her car, a sudden gust of icy wind caused her to gasp and shudder. Eager to get out of the cold, she hurried along the pavement to the restaurant. It wasn't open yet, but lights were on, and staff were buzzing around inside behind a polished copper bar. There was a narrow passageway off the main road running down the side of the business. She guessed there would be rear access to the kitchen so slipped into the lengthening shadows of the alley to try her luck with a back door.

What am I doing?

She'd been right: the restaurant had a sheltered yard that opened onto the passage. Staying mostly concealed behind the wall, she craned her neck to see it contained large waste bins, a pile of cardboard and a chair next to a damp collection of cigarette butts. She whipped her head back when the rear door opened, and Elise appeared, framed in a light from behind. Her long blonde hair was scraped off her forehead and tied in a sleek knot. She wore spotless chef whites and navy clogs on her feet.

Laurel shuffled further back trusting the shadows to keep the woman from noticing she wasn't alone.

Elise threw a bag of rubbish into one of the bins calling over her shoulder, 'One second. Are we going over tonight's menu? Okay, I'll be through in a sec.' She wiped her hands on her trousers and pushed a stray strand of hair back into place.

Through a grimy window, Laurel watched three staff move from the kitchen and disappear out of sight. Elise turned and retreated inside, following the others. The door snicked shut behind her.

It was the only chance she was going to get. She left the safety of the gloom and trod lightly into the yard. She peered through the window; the kitchen remained empty. Taking hold of the door handle she took a deep breath and turned. She felt disappointment and relief when it refused to budge. It was locked.

Stepping away, her gaze landed on the large metal container into which Elise had thrown the black sack. A noisy black sack. It was too much to hope. Would Elise have risked throwing the gas containers into the Aroma's own refuse? She might if she planned to retrieve them later and dispose of them at a safer location.

Wrinkling her nose at the mix of disgusting smells, Laurel nudged the lid up and squinted at the contents. It was full and there was a bag sitting on top that had to be the one Elise had deposited. With her free hand she snagged it and lifted it clear as quietly as possible. She stole a glance at the buildings and the alley behind her, but no one was there to observe. Now she had to decide whether it was best to remove potential evidence or to look through it and replace it so Elise wouldn't realise it had been disturbed. She had her phone, she could take a photo of anything relevant and if necessary, if she found damning evidence, she could call the police and wait right there for them to arrive.

The knot in the bag resisted her efforts and in her haste, she ended up tearing a hole. 'Sod it,' she hissed, and ripped the hole bigger.

'What are you expecting to find exactly?'

Laurel screamed and dropped the bag. Food tins and a chicken carcass spilled out making her gag.

'Looking for gas canisters?'

There was no point in denying it, but she didn't want to have been caught in such a ridiculous task.

'I should call the police.' Elise stood with her arms folded, a scowl on her face. She was wearing her coat over her whites and had a handbag with her. She'd swapped her clogs for regular shoes. 'I thought we were friends.'

Laurel didn't mean to say it, but the words spilled out. 'That's a laugh, when you sent me those letters! You had me worried sick.' She snapped her mouth shut, but it was too late.

Elise's delicate face crumpled. She pulled the door closed behind her and ran past Laurel, bolting towards a red Audi parked where the alley widened out. As she neared the car, Laurel heard a phone ring and watched as Elise pulled her mobile out of her bag. Hoping to overhear the conversation, Laurel was disappointed when the chef beeped the locks and climbed into the vehicle. Seconds later, she peeled away in a cloud of dust.

Laurel toed the rubbish on the ground, but she'd lost any real expectation of finding canisters. Movement again behind the window made up her mind and she retreated, slinking back the way she'd come.

In the cosy bubble of her car, she slammed her palms against the steering wheel.

Chapter 56

Laurel

Two police cars and a fire engine raced past her, lights and sirens making a confusion of the road. She slowed and blinked hard to restore her night vision. It was full dark, and rain was streaking the windscreen. The shadowy trees lining the road were whipping back and forth, toyed with by the wind.

'What on earth has happened now?' she spoke aloud.

She passed the *Elderwick* sign and her headlights picked out figures moving towards the village centre. She gripped the steering wheel more firmly and drove on with increasing caution. As she neared the village green, a figure stepped into the road waving their arms. The shape resolved itself into Maggie.

She rolled down the window but a squall whipped away Maggie's words and Laurel had to ask her to repeat them. 'What? What's going on?'

'Oh, thank goodness, we didn't know where you were. You're not going to believe this: there's been a bomb threat.'

'What?' It had finally happened, she'd snapped and lost touch with reality, it was the only explanation.

'Leave your car here. Quick, we've all got to get to the village hall.'

Unable to form a coherent thought of her own, she did as Maggie instructed and pulled the car off the main road into one of the parking spots by the green. She had to concentrate to put on the handbrake, take the car out of gear, and kill the engine. Her hands were shaking.

Albert loomed by the window. 'Laurel my dear, come along, quickly now. To quote George, "One wants to live, of course, but one only stays alive by virtue of the fear of death".'

She stepped out into the madness and joined him and Maggie, following the other villagers as they streamed into the village hall.

Finding her voice, she risked asking once more. 'What's going on?'

Maggie linked arms with her and spoke close to her ear to be heard over the clamour of the crowd and the strengthening wind. 'The police started knocking on doors telling us we all need to get to the village hall. I'm surprised you got back; I heard they're setting up roadblocks.'

None of what Maggie said was making any sense. 'I thought you said there was a bomb threat? I must have misheard?' Maggie was shaking her head at her. 'Why? Why would anyone bomb Elderwick?'

'Oh no, no one's trying to bomb us. It was Ben told us, someone called up the police from the phone box and said they'd uncovered a bomb while gardening, but they didn't give the address, only said it was somewhere off the main street. I suppose the authorities thought it safest to move us all to one place, and since there are no residential gardens adjoining the village hall, and it's large enough for us all to squash into, it's the obvious location.'

Laurel let herself be swept along into the bright florescent lights of the musty hall. Usually an echoing, chilly space it had been transformed into a heaving mass of warm bodies and excited chatter. Already the tea urn was doing business and people lined up ready for a cuppa enjoying the novelty of the unprecedented situation.

'Let's stake out a space and in a minute I'll see what I can do about procuring us a spot of refreshment,' Albert suggested. 'First though, you'll want to hear the truly shocking news we have.' He guided them up onto the stage where it was less congested than the main floor of the hall. They sat awkwardly on the wooden boards off to one side by the curtains.

'I don't know what could be more shocking than a bomb.'

'Just you wait.' Maggie grinned. 'Can I tell her?'

'Be my guest.'

Maggie arranged her skirts around her and smoothed her cashmere jumper. She'd removed her coat and was using it as a cushion. 'Albert and I went to the police station, and they saw us immediately. Albert impressed on them how crucial it was we speak with them. Anyway, we told them everything and I have to say they didn't strike me as being in the least bit surprised.'

'Okay.' She was waiting for the punchline.

'Then, as we were leaving, Albert spotted Hugh. He was at the desk of one of the officers. Quick as a fox, Albert fakes an episode of frailty and has to sit down. We were behind Hugh so he couldn't see us. He was all flustered and upset–'

'My goodness, Maggie, Laurel looks fit to burst, please get to the denouement.'

Maggie pouted at him. 'Hugh has confessed to the murders.'

It could have been a literal punchline. The air left her lungs, and she groped for understanding. 'He confessed?'

'We heard it all.' Albert assumed charge of the tale. 'He admitted he killed Simon and Charlotte to stop them exposing his daughter. He said he set the fire, attacked Dorothy, everything.'

'But Natalie gave him an alibi for Tuesday night.'

'Exactly, I mentioned that to the officer taking Hugh's statement.'

'Which is why we were asked to leave. If you'd held your lovely tongue, my dear Maggie, we could have heard more. They hadn't noticed us listening until then. Of course, we were escorted out, but I did catch Hugh explaining how Natalie would do anything for him and she shouldn't be blamed for trying to protect him.'

Laurel shook her head; it was too much to take in and rather than feel elated at having her theory – okay, one of her theories – substantiated, the tightness in her chest persisted and unease swirled in her stomach. She drummed her fingers on the floor and tried to think.

'So, it's all over.' Maggie beamed.

'I'm not sure it is,' countered Laurel.

Chapter 57

Laurel

'I'm convinced Hugh has only confessed to save Elise.'

Albert and Maggie looked at Laurel with blank faces.

'He seemed quite sure he did it,' Maggie said.

The tension was messing with her head, she had to restrain herself from snapping a reply. Instead, she told them about her trip to Hugh's rental house and what she'd overheard. 'Hugh was worried enough about Elise being involved to warn her to get rid of any evidence. I've just got back from her restaurant and while I didn't see any gas canisters, she knew what I was looking for.'

'Where were you searching? In the restaurant?'

She squirmed. 'In the bins.'

'Oh Laurel.' Maggie wrinkled her nose.

'Natalie is devoted to Hugh, I can totally believe she would lie for him if she thought there was a chance he'd be accused of the murders. Maybe the police can get the truth from her. I wonder if they've spoken to her already?' She searched the faces in the hall around them but couldn't locate the young agent. 'Does anyone see her?'

'She was coming out of The Pleasant Pheasant with Jo

when we flagged you down. She must be in here somewhere.' Maggie joined her in scanning the crowd. 'Poor thing, I wonder if she knows yet?'

'If she admits to the police she lied,' said Albert, 'Hugh will have no alibi and with his confession, they'll stop looking for anyone else in connection with the crimes.'

'Meaning if Elise is guilty, she'll get away with it.' Laurel was putting pieces together and didn't like the picture that was emerging. 'But on the other hand, if Natalie sticks to her story of being Hugh's alibi, and I think she's dedicated to him enough to keep lying...'

Albert finished her thought. 'They'll wonder why Hugh confessed and the obvious conclusion would be he did so to protect his only daughter, putting Elise very much in the spotlight. Exactly what Hugh is afraid of.'

'And I wonder what Elise might do to prevent that from happening?' She stood and studied the faces spread out below them. 'Where is Natalie?' she asked again. 'Everything hangs on her.' A sliver of dread iced its way through her veins. She stripped off her coat, feeling constrained by the fabric.

'Elise wouldn't hurt Natalie. Would she?' Maggie's voice died away.

'If Elise has already killed two people, I doubt she'd hesitate to add another victim.' Albert too worked his way to his feet, taking his time in straightening up, a grimace betraying pain in doing so. 'Though how she'd cover it up this time, I don't know.'

'She's at the restaurant, isn't she? You saw her there.'

'I did, Maggie, and then I saw her leave, ahead of me.'

'Right, I see Ben, I'll go and see if he knows where Elise is. Maggie, is there a PA system in here? Can we use it to find Natalie?'

'Good idea.' Maggie picked herself up, blew out a breath and vanished into the wings.

'I'll go through the herd and ask around,' said Laurel.

The first people she approached didn't know who Natalie was. Hetty and Constance, taking illicit sips from Constance's hip flask by the fire exit, said they hadn't seen her. Next, she saw the vicar and made a beeline for him, he was reassuring two elderly ladies that they were unlikely to be blown to smithereens at any moment.

'Sorry to interrupt, Christopher, but it's urgent.'

He broke off and moved away with Laurel.

'Have you seen Natalie or Elise?'

'I saw Natalie a short while back, but I'm afraid I don't know where she is now. I haven't seen Elise. You look dreadful. Are you okay?'

As desperate as she was to continue the search, and forgetting the confidential nature of what she was saying, she blurted out her fear to the vicar. 'Hugh Quintrell has confessed to the murders, but I think he's doing it to protect Elise.'

'Elise? Why?'

She bit her tongue.

'Oh, you know, don't you?' He angled further away from the people around them and lowered his voice.

'You know?' she echoed.

'Elise told me, and Hugh also came to me about it. He knew she attended my church and wanted me to facilitate a reconciliation. I declined, naturally. It wasn't what Elise wished for.'

'She told me he tracked her down here. I suppose he was desperate, but that's low, trying to involve you.'

'I agree, his methods and ethics are dubious, but you're mistaken, he didn't know she was here before he arrived. He came to me the day he first saw her. He was in shock, I believe. Not to mention terrified she'd think just that, that he had, I don't know, hunted her down, you might say.'

'Laurel?' It was Albert calling her from over by the tea urn.

Torn between what Christopher had just told her and what Albert had discovered, she decided her immediate concern was to find Natalie.

'You go.' The vicar waved her on. 'I'll look for them both.'

'Laurel, quickly now. This fine fellow thinks he might have seen our missing agent, but he's not sure. Do you have a photo of her?'

Albert was standing with a man of about twenty years of age clad in heavy-duty work boots, durable trousers and shirt, and a high-vis vest.

'All right?' he drawled. 'I saw someone coming out of here as I came in, sounds like she might be who you're looking for. Skinny, youngish, but proper wrapped up in a huge coat.'

'I hope you're minding your manners, young man?' said a voice at Laurel's elbow. Jo appeared carrying a tin of biscuits. 'This *gentleman*,' she explained, 'is the unsavoury character I had to evict from the café a few weeks back, after he was effing and jeffing in front of my other customers. She waved the biscuits at the workman, and he swiped a chocolate Hobnob as they passed under his nose.

'You said you'd forgave me,' he said, grinning through a mouthful of crumbs.

Laurel couldn't maintain her patience much longer. 'Just let me show you the photo.' Desperation made her rude.

He ignored her. 'I'd had a bad couple of days. My girlfriend had just dumped me and then the next morning I've got a bangin' hangover and I'm getting harassed by the police who'd just found that body. Typical their first stop is the local building site. Just cos me and my mates are manual labourers it somehow means we're all dodgy. The boss sent 'em packing, but I was proper annoyed by time I come into yours that afternoon,' he said to Jo.

Trying to hold down her frustration, Laurel had already pulled up the Greenleaves Literary Agency website and navigated to the headshot of Natalie. She held it up so he could see.

He barked out a laugh. 'F– Bloody Nora, that stupid cow nearly run me over.'

'What? When?' Laurel wanted to shake him.

'Calm down. It weren't tonight. It was the same day my ex kicked me out, insult to bloody injury like. I was coming off site after work. Came out of nowhere, she did. She slammed on the brakes, and I got a pretty good look at her. Looked like she'd seen a ghost. Might have been her I saw tonight. Probably 'ave 'ad a word if I'd known.'

Her eyes narrowed as she willed him to get to the point. 'So, you have seen her?' She felt time, and Natalie's safety, slipping away.

'Maybe, but I don't know where she was off to.' He grabbed another handful of biscuits and merged into the throng.

'Sorry, love, I can't help either,' said Jo. 'She was in the café having a black coffee – never eats, that girl – when we got the order to come here. I had to lock up and she was gone when I came out.'

As Jo turned away to hand out more biscuits, Maggie's voice sounded over the public address system. 'Could Natalie Marwood please make herself known to Maggie Wright by the stage. It's urgent. If you've seen her, please inform Laurel Nightingale, Albert, or myself. Thank you.'

Albert shrugged and followed Jo, asking each person he passed about Natalie.

'Laurel, hey, wait up a sec.'

It was Sam, calling from a few feet away. He ducked his way around the people between them. 'You're looking for Natalie? We were all headed over from the pub and I can't guarantee it, but I saw someone who might have been her heading off up the road. I think she went up Church Lane.'

'Was she alone?'

'Far as I could see. Probably shouldn't have been heading up there, but like I say, it might not have been her. Is everything all right?'

'No, I really don't think it is.' Something the sweary lad had said was bothering her, but she didn't have time to figure it out. What she needed to do was to speak with whoever was in charge. If the police were coordinating the evacuation to the village hall, there must be a senior officer around. She couldn't risk speaking to Ben though, who was over by the tea urn and out of uniform.

She battled her way through the crowd to the front entrance where a flash of navy told her she was in luck.

'I might have known you'd be around somewhere,' DI Coral complained.

Laurel smothered a groan. Of all the officers why did it have to be Coral? Pessimistic as she was, she had no choice but to appeal to the woman. 'There's someone still out there.' She waved at the rain-soaked streets. 'Can you send one of your team to find her?'

'Much as you might like to believe we're here at your beck and call, no, I can't. My team are going street to street, they won't have missed anyone. I assume this person is an adult?'

'She is, but–'

'Then I'm sure she'll find her way back here. This whole circus is ridiculous as it is, but our new chief constable has a house in the village, so here we are, asking how high to jump for what will probably turn out to be a load of scrap metal dug up in a veg patch and–' She stopped abruptly, perhaps realising her indiscretion.

'You don't understand, I think she might be in danger from

whoever murdered Simon Forster and Charlotte Drake. Please.'
She'd beg if she had to.

'Not that I need to tell you, but we are confident the
perpetrator of those crimes is not running round Elderwick this
evening.'

Of course, Hugh had confessed. They thought they had
their killer. She weighed her options. Trying to explain her
theory about Elise would gain her short shrift. Maybe with
anyone other than Coral she might have had a chance, but Coral
was a lost cause; she could see it in the jut of her jaw. 'If you're
not going to help, I'll go and find her myself.'

'You will not. I'm not having another person running
around out there when we're trying to do our job.'

'Are you going to stop me?'

Coral didn't reply but turned to a hulking uniform coming
in the door. He shook rain off his jacket and mopped dripping
hair from his forehead. 'Constable, don't let anyone leave,
particularly her.' She pointed at Laurel and stalked off.

Chapter 58

Laurel

Taking advantage of the crowds and staying well away from the guard at the front, Laurel was banking on no one else paying her any attention as she ducked into the storeroom. She closed the door softly behind her and waited for her eyes to adjust to the gloom, the only light being a weak glow through a dirty window. She knew the emergency exit wasn't alarmed despite what the warning stickers claimed. If the police weren't going to do anything, it was up to her. She couldn't stand back and risk another innocent person being hurt. She slipped out into the night.

The wind grabbed her the moment she was clear of the steps, whipping her hair across her eyes and throwing stinging rain into her face. It wasn't so much the cold as it was fear chilling her bones as she pulled her thin jacket back on and cinched the belt. The only cheerful thought she could muster was that a least the dreadful weather and the dark would make it easier for her to move around unnoticed.

With the beam of the torch on her phone she managed to find the narrow snicket which took her past the small car park, away from the main road, and towards Whirligig Lane. From there she could head for St Stephen's, and at the far side of the graveyard, she'd cross Church Lane, dash up to the next junction, pass the school and the far side of the pond, coming out at the top of West Street close to Manor Road. Apart from a quick sprint across the main road, she would be able to check most of the village without being in view of the sentries outside the village hall.

On Whirligig Lane, opposite the burnt-out ruin of The Grange, her steps faltered, and she stared, astounded at the extent of the damage. The windows had all been boarded up but the black streaks stretching up the brickwork showed where the fire had raged. Part of the roof had fallen in, and the tidy front garden was a muddy swamp.

She thought of Maggie's homely, colourful kitchen and the long hours they'd enjoyed there together over cake. She hadn't even thought to ask Maggie what she would do now, rebuild or perhaps move to a new house in the village? Once again, she resolved to be a better friend. Once this was all over.

She shook herself. She didn't have time to gawp when someone was in danger. She had to keep her wits about her too. The next bit was going to be tricky. She had to cross the main road. It was a risk because South Street was well lit by attractive lamps at this, the well-heeled, end of the village. She could hear raised voices and radio transmissions, but the only figures in sight were swarming round the hall. Taking a chance, and a deep breath, she crouched low and moved slowly across the street. It meant she was visible for longer than if she ran, but quick movements were more likely to attract attention.

Expecting to hear a shout at any moment, it was a surprise when she reached the trailhead unmolested. She faded into the dark of the overgrown pathway. There was no need to step softly here, the noise from the tossing trees would cover a marching band. Branches grabbed at her clothing and roots reached for her feet, but she pushed on, running her hand along the low wall enclosing the church grounds, not daring to use the torch again.

Reaching the gap in the wall, she stepped into the long, wet grass of the church yard. She was halfway to the lych-gate before she registered the warm light spilling from the side door of the church. The door was ajar. Christopher would never have left it open. Had she found Natalie?

'Natalie?' The name died on her lips. A red Audi, Elise's car, was parked out on the lane.

She approached with caution and placed her hand on the door feeling the weathered wood under her palm. Peering inside, she could see no one was waiting to rush her. Cautious of squealing hinges, she opened the door enough to allow her to slip through. From her position, she could see that the vestry, ahead on the left, was in darkness.

She fumbled with her phone, hands clumsy from the cold. She should call for help, but of course she had no signal. Was there a phone on Christopher's desk? She couldn't remember. She strained to listen for any noises but struggled over the rushing of her blood.

The further she moved into the building the more the wildness outside faded replaced with the beating of her heart and the rasp of her breath. The cold from the stones soaked through her shoes into her bones. She drew level with the open doorway of the vestry, but looking inside, she couldn't see a phone.

Reaching the next doorway, she nudged a gap wide enough to peek through. The lighting was feeble and the pews to the right dwindled into blackness. There was no one there. No one she could see.

She stepped into the nave and stopped dead. Over by the organ there was a puddle of liquid. In the gloom she couldn't see the colour, but she knew it was red. 'No!' The word burst from her lips.

'Help.'

Laurel spun and saw a figure struggling on the ground in the aisle.

'Natalie?'

'Laurel, help, please, help me. She's tied me up. She's going to kill me.' Natalie's panicked voice echoed in the vast space.

'Hold on, I'm here,' she reassured in a half whisper. As she started towards her, the hairs on the back of her neck stood on end. Where was Elise?

'Get me out, please,' Natalie sobbed.

Self-preservation meant she had to neutralise any threat first. Hardening her resolve, Laurel moved away from the agent towards the church organ and the pool of blood. It flowed from behind an ornate carved screen above which rose the imposing instrument. There was no sign of movement, no sound, but inching forward, Laurel saw a foot, then a leg. A leg clad in trousers that used to be white.

Elise!

Laurel crept closer to the body, ready to rear back in case of an ambush.

'She attacked me,' cried Natalie. 'I tried to escape, and I think she fell and hit her head.' Her voice was frantic. 'Don't let her hurt you. Please, we have to go!'

Elise wasn't moving, not a twitch, maybe not even a breath. 'She might be unconscious. I need to check for a pulse.' Laurel's training demanded it, even for a murderer. She edged behind the screen and with a shaking hand reached for Elise's bloody neck.

It was faint, but there was a pulse beating under her fingers. 'She's alive.' Nausea rolled through her stomach when she glimpsed the deep wound on the chef's head. Elise was no threat to her in that condition. 'Natalie, hold on. I'm going to come and untie you and then we need to call an ambulance for both of you.'

She fumbled for her phone, praying once more for a signal she knew wouldn't be there.

On rubbery legs she rushed back to the aisle, but Natalie was gone.

Chapter 59

Laurel

'Natalie?'

A loose coil of rope lay on the aged diamond tiles.

Laurel shot a look back at the unmoving form of Elise. Torn between leaving to get help and locating Natalie, she felt she had no choice but to find Natalie first.

Placing her feet softly, she inched up the aisle, checking each row of pews. Had Natalie run off in fear? Wherever she was, Laurel needed to call an ambulance as soon as possible.

A whisper of air on the back of her neck made her turn and the blow caught her across the temple. She fell, hitting the back of her head against a pew. Through tears she made out Natalie's boot as it crashed into her ribs. She tried to curl inwards, hands over her head but Natalie landed another kick, this time to her kidneys.

Natalie stood back, her face made grotesque by light and shadow.

'Natalie? What?' Despite her confusion, Laurel's instinct for self-preservation kicked in. She shot out her hand and grabbed Natalie around the ankle and pulled with everything she had. Natalie stumbled, off balance, taken by surprise.

Ignoring the agony of her ribs, Laurel lurched to her feet and charged. They went down together. Natalie's head struck the floor with a meaty thud.

The agent wasn't knocked out only dazed, but it was enough for Laurel to roll away and crawl for the safety of the nearest pew. Hunched by pain, she shuffled to the far end where it opened into a side aisle. She didn't know if the north door was unlocked, but any attempt to return to the vestry would mean getting past Natalie. The main door was her only chance.

'You just couldn't leave it alone, could you?' The mocking tone echoed around the high ceiling, bouncing off the stonework, obscuring Natalie's location.

Staying low, Laurel whirled around, searching for the voice.

'I didn't want to hurt you. You've been useful to me.'

A shadow to her right drew her eye, but when she looked, it was gone.

'I heard Hugh's confessed. I leave him alone for two minutes and he risks ruining everything. They were meant to arrest Elise.'

Now the voice sounded as though it was behind her, but that couldn't be right. Laurel scurried up the aisle trusting the rows of pews to keep her hidden. Natalie must be using them as cover too.

'I'm the one who's been there for Hugh, when everyone else wanted to throw him on the scrapheap, I stood by him.' Natalie's voice rose to a shriek.

So, it had been Hugh, after all, not Elise? Laurel shook her head; whoever it had been, she had to focus on escaping from the church first and she'd deal with the rest later. The door was on the far side of the nave, to reach it would mean crossing the central aisle and Laurel still wasn't sure where Natalie was. She needed to hear her speak again. 'If Hugh killed Simon and

Charlotte, he needs to face justice. You can't go on protecting him.'

The laughter echoed, bouncing back from all sides. 'You think Hugh did this? Hugh didn't do this. I did!'

Natalie's the killer? Laurel was shaky and nauseated. She had to get out. Head spinning, ever so slowly, she crawled to the last pew in the row and along behind it, finally easing her head out to look towards the chancel. The aisle was empty. The door was so close now. Pulling back, she breathed through the pain and called, 'Why, Natalie?' She had to know how close the woman was before she made a run for the door.

'He's a genius, but he needed the right project and that's exactly what I've given him. True crime is hot right now. What better than a classic locked room murder and an estranged daughter turned multiple murderer? Hugh, the tortured father bringing her to justice because it's the right thing to do. And look at him, you saw, Hugh came here unable to write anything and now... now...'

Now she understood. 'Charlotte was going to swoop in and take all your credit.' Laurel shifted and winced. A sharp pain in her side could be a broken rib but if she didn't escape, Natalie was going to kill her.

'It was a pleasure to bash her brains in. I would never have let Maggie get hurt, though. I made sure I was there to get her out.'

'How heroic,' muttered Laurel. *Keep her talking.* 'I suppose you didn't mean to attack Dorothy either?'

'Stupid old bat was going to destroy Simon's journal, but I needed it to be found; it gave Elise a motive. If Dorothy hadn't caught me in the kitchen that night, she wouldn't have been hurt. It's not my fault she fell, I barely touched her.'

Laurel heard a footstep to her right.

'Lucky for me,' Natalie crowed, 'she couldn't remember what happened. Or should I say, lucky for her?' She tittered.

Laurel snarled, as much from pain as outrage. 'The bomb threat is ridiculous,' she goaded.

'It's dramatic. It'll be an incredible ending for the book.'

She no longer sounded close-by. Laurel flitted across the top of the aisle from one set of pews to those on the far side. Her heart was beating so hard she was certain it would give away her position. She could see the door. She was so close but would be exposed when she made a run for it. The temptation to hide instead was overwhelming. The only thought keeping her focused on escape was Elise. She'd been alive when Laurel had felt her pulse, but how long could she last?

'It's locked,' said Natalie, stepping into view.

With a cry, Laurel surged to her feet, but with the door locked she was out of options. In desperation, she cast around, panic making her miss it on the first pass. The tower! The door was closed, but if she could get inside, she might be able to lock Natalie out or even climb upwards and signal for help.

Keeping her eyes on Natalie, Laurel edged backwards.

'There's nowhere for you to go,' Natalie taunted.

She eased up onto her toes, feeling her muscles tense. When she moved, she had to be fast. There was a split second when Natalie blinked, and Laurel broke for the tower. She hauled on the door handle and flew inside, turning to close it, but too late. Natalie's body knocked the door into Laurel's face with such force she was thrown onto her back. She heard rather than felt the crack of her skull on the floor, registered with detachment the grating in her chest, the difficulty she was having in pulling air in to breathe, the roaring in her ears, her narrowing vision.

She must have blacked out because when she came too, Natalie had knotted rope tightly around her wrists and was tying it to an old cast-iron radiator. Her head throbbed and even moving her eyes increased the pain. The rope chaffed her skin, cutting into her soft flesh.

'I need to deal with Elise, but don't worry, I'll be back,' Natalie promised.

Laurel fought for breath. Pain and fear had stolen the air from her lungs. She couldn't run, she couldn't fight, playing for time was the only strategy she had left. Gasping, she sneered, 'Hugh doesn't even rate you as his agent.'

Natalie whipped round and slapped her face.

Tears poured down her cheeks and Laurel gulped, afraid the pain would overwhelm her.

'Hugh needs me. He may never know the level of my devotion to him, but he knows he'd be nothing without me.'

'Really?' Laurel had to speak through gritted teeth. 'Simon's the only journalist who's shown any interest in Hugh in years, and his article was going to be an evisceration.' She braced for another blow.

'Which is only one of the reasons why he deserved to die.'

'You knew it would be a negative profile of Hugh?'

Natalie slow clapped. 'Oh well done. Of course I did, I hired him and who do you think told him about Elise? I told him I was a disgruntled employee out to stick it to my boss. I know all about Hugh's past, how he and Simon went to school together and why Simon hated Hugh. It was too easy. I barely had to persuade the old hack. The fact he made a pass at me in one of our early meetings made it all the more satisfying to kill him.' She laughed.

Laurel shuddered in revulsion.

'I bet you think you're clever getting me to chat on. Honestly, I'm so far ahead of you it's embarrassing. No one is coming to save you. The police checked the church before the vicar left. I should know, I was hiding in here the whole time.

They won't be back and everyone will have to stay in the village hall until they find the bomb.'

A sob caught in Laurel's throat. 'Which they won't, because there isn't one.' Natalie was right, she had it all planned out. 'How did you get Elise here?' Blood trickled from her nose, but with her hands tied she couldn't properly wipe it away.

'That was easy, I called her and told her Daddy dearest had confessed to her crimes, but that I had evidence to exonerate them both. I told her to meet me here, and to make sure she was alone. Whether she came to save her own skin, or Hugh's doesn't really matter, I just needed her here.'

It must have been the call Elise received after she'd caught Laurel poking through the bins at the restaurant.

'Do you want to know how I killed Simon?' Natalie had her head on one side, smiling down at her. 'It'll be good to tell someone, someone who won't be around long enough to do anything with the information.' Her eyes were glassy, and she was giggling.

She's proud of herself. The realisation disgusted Laurel. A moment later, a second realisation dawned on her. The young lad joking with Jo in the village hall. Now she knew why something he'd said had been nagging at her. He'd claimed Natalie had nearly run him over outside his building site the night Simon had been killed. Which contradicted Natalie's claim she'd only just arrived when Laurel and Maggie had seen her and her yellow car by the green the day *after* his body had been discovered.

Undeterred by Laurel's silence, Natalie carried on. 'He thought I was meeting him for a bit of fun, if you know what I mean?' She leered. 'Sad old loser. He was well known for not being able to keep it in his pants. I met him at the cottage and told him I got a thrill from using nitrous oxide while having sex. He didn't hesitate, didn't so much as question why I'd brought some with me. He got so high and so happy, I'm not sure he even noticed when I put the bag over his head. He died laughing. It was more than he deserved.'

'And the dagger?'

'Theatre. All the better for Hugh's book.'

Laurel spotted an opportunity to take some of the wind out of Natalie's sails. It would be a small victory before death. 'The locked door, I know how you did it.'

'Good for you.'

To her shock, Natalie leaned over and kissed her on the forehead. 'So, this is how it'll go: Elise attacked me, and when you came to save me, she attacked you too. You pushed her and she hit her head and died. It was too late for you, but thank goodness, I was fortunate enough to survive. I think that'll work, don't you?'

Laurel trembled on the freezing floor as Natalie's footsteps receded, back towards the church organ and a defenceless Elise. She coughed and spat blood.

Elise probably had moments left to live. She needed to get help. She squinted into the shadows. She didn't know the church well, but she knew it had bells and even with a broken rib, if she could somehow reach them, she could haul on a bell pull. The bells would peel loudly over the storm. People would hear, they had to.

She tested the knots at her wrists. They held tight, but she was able to ease to a crouching position. The radiator was loose, but not loose enough for her to wriggle free. It clanged horribly as she pulled at it. Natalie was sure to have heard, and if she was coming back, Laurel had seconds at most to sever her bonds and reach the bells. Her hope was fading. Was the ringing chamber even on the ground floor? 'No, no, no, no,' she wailed in despair. There were no ropes in sight, not even tied back against the wall.

Natalie was back, her silhouette filling the doorway. 'What are you doing?'

Laurel braced herself against the wall determined to meet her killer face to face.

Natalie's eyes shifted to the left and back. Her mouth twitched. 'Back on the floor. Don't make me hurt you any more than I have to.'

Laurel saw her eyes flit again. What had she seen?

She began to turn.

Natalie lurched forward but she was too slow.

Laurel saw the switch.

She saw the label.

BELLS.

They were bloody automated!

Chapter 60

Laurel

The fluorescent lights were making her eyes itch. She gripped the kidney bowl the nurse had thrust into her hands and rocked slightly back and forth until the nausea passed.

'We caught up with her, thought you'd like to know.' A head appeared round the door and the smiling face of an impossibly young police constable grinned at her. 'That yellow hire car of hers was hard to miss.'

Laurel threw up. The face fell and withdrew at speed.

'You are an angel and a credit to your profession.' It was Albert's voice. 'I know it's late, we'll be gone before you know it. I promise.'

She wiped her mouth just as he and Maggie swept in.

'Laurel, my dear! I had to sweet-talk the nurses, but we were not to be kept from your bedside.' Albert was laughing but his pallor was off. His eyes searched her face before he finally relaxed, and the relief showed in his eyes.

Maggie pushed past him and fearing a crushing hug, Laurel held up a hand. 'Please, I would hug you, but my ribs are bruised and I'm not convinced the drugs have kicked in yet.'

'You poor thing! You nearly died! How could I be so dense, I never so much as suspected Natalie. I made her breakfast for heaven's sake!' She collapsed into the visitor's chair by the side of the bed. Her usually immaculate hair was skew-whiff, and she had black tracks where her mascara had run.

'None of us suspected her,' said Laurel. The puzzle pieces of the previous weeks finally made sense. 'Until this evening, when I spoke to a young lad from the building site, I didn't even know she was here in Elderwick *before* Simon's death. I took her at her word when she pretended she'd only just arrived the day *after*. Her conspicuous car; making a song and dance about breaking the news to Hugh; she played us from the beginning.'

'How did she know where Simon was staying though, and that Elise was here?'

'Maggie, perhaps we should let Laurel rest,' suggested Albert.

'It's okay, I can talk. Natalie must have tracked down Elise first, then she was the one who arranged the entire trip to Elderwick. I bet she booked and paid for Simon's accommodation which probably helped to convince him to come up here. She couldn't do it in her own name, but it wouldn't have been hard for Natalie to make the booking using the literary agency's account. We were led to believe that Hugh came to Elderwick and Simon followed, but that wasn't the case. Natalie engineered it all. Hugh probably still thinks Elderwick was his idea, but I'm certain Natalie planted the seed.'

'It wasn't Charlotte who booked Tulip Cottage then?' Maggie asked.

Laurel shifted her position in the bed. 'No, and when I spoke to her on the phone and she said she didn't know Hugh was here, I should have realised. I should have suspected Natalie.' It hurt more than the pain in her ribs to know that had she put it together sooner, Charlotte would still be alive.

'Don't be so hard on yourself,' Albert told her. 'In a company like that, there would be no reason for the boss to know the whereabouts of all her authors. Natalie was devious; even if you'd smelled a rat, she would have had an explanation to throw you off track.' He rubbed his chin. 'It never did make sense for Hugh to agree to meet Simon here if he was so concerned about Elise being exposed.'

'Christopher said Hugh was surprised to discover his daughter here. He didn't know. You're right, it was all engineered by Natalie. She admitted it.'

'Why did she do it?' Maggie asked.

'She claims it was all for Hugh's career. She wanted some dramatic, traumatic, true crime for him to write about. I mean she wasn't wrong; famous author reunites with estranged daughter who turns out to be multiple murderer, and it's dear old Dad who solves the case.'

'But it would have been a lie.' Maggie tutted.

'If I may quote Oscar Wilde again,' remarked Albert, '"The truth is rarely pure, and never simple".'

Epilogue

ONE MONTH LATER

'You would be credited in the book, perhaps as a consultant. I haven't worked out the details yet.' Hugh adjusted the crease in his grey wool trousers and brushed a lock of hair from his forehead. A lock of artfully styled hair. Hair now suspiciously lacking in any grey. 'We'll need to set up a series of interviews and there'll be the book launch and various promotional events. I'll need you to attend the odd gathering, but not all of them. I assume my new agent has been in touch with the details?'

'He has.' Laurel had been floored by what the agent had to say, but she shouldn't have been surprised. 'He said my role in the book would be "*portrayed differently*".'

Hugh looked uncomfortable. 'I'm sure you understand. It makes more narrative sense for it to have been I who tracked Natalie down to the church that night and saved my daughter's life.'

'Sure, narrative sense. Well, thank you, but I'd rather not be involved, I'm too busy here.' Laurel waved her hand around her office eager for the latest not-therapy session with the author to be over so she could meet Maggie, Albert and the others in the pub. She didn't want any publicity, or a credit in the book, preferring to move on and put the distressing events behind her. That said, having her actions appropriated by Hugh did grate.

'I can see I'm not going to be able to convince you.' He sounded relieved. 'At least allow me to send you a signed copy, and one for Maggie of course?'

'Thank you, that would be lovely, and I know Maggie will be thrilled.' *The book might make a good doorstop*, she mused while smiling at him.

Eager to change the subject, she said, 'I saw you talking to Dorothy yesterday. She looked upset?'

He wrinkled his nose and harrumphed. 'She hasn't changed. She still doesn't like me and actually blames me for everything Natalie did. She said it was my fault Natalie was here at all. I tried to explain, but there's no talking to some people. She said the only good thing to come out of all this, is that the charity, Dandelions, don't want to buy Elderwick Hall any longer because of the murders. How can someone take pleasure in a thing like that?'

'Maybe every village has to have a resident like Dorothy so we can appreciate how wonderful the other locals are.'

He gave a wry laugh. 'As good a way as looking at it as any, I suppose.'

Though anxious for him to leave, she needed to know. 'Before you go, how is Elise doing?'

Hugh's eyes lost some of their sparkle. He sat forward, elbows on his knees and the lock of hair flopped out of place again. 'She's much better. She's working with Doctor Barton again and we're going to try family therapy. We've got a long way to go, but I have to believe we'll get there. I've got a lifetime I need to make-up for. Physically, she's doing well; no lasting effects.'

Laurel appreciated that Elise had been dealt a rotten hand

in the past, so, despite the letters, she still liked her and wished her the best. It was a shame she'd broken up with Ben, but she could understand Elise's need to move away from Elderwick and take some time for herself.

'I had a meeting with Natalie yesterday,' Hugh continued.

'Oh.'

'She's in a secure hospital. I suppose you're aware they don't know whether she is mentally competent to stand trial.'

'The police told me. I'm surprised they allowed you in to speak to her.'

'She asked to see me, and I won't lie, it'll be good for the book. You know, the first thing she said when I saw her was "Have you started the book yet?"'

'You're her North Star.'

'For my sins.'

'Finally. Here she is, Miss Marple.'

'Very funny, Albert, but Inspector Clouseau might be more accurate.' Laurel nudged Maggie to move up and perched on the edge of the bench seat. Everyone was looking at her. 'What?'

'We did it, they've given their approval. We've got the Dandelions centre!' Maggie clapped her hands and Hetty whooped. 'It was Hugh, he pulled some strings and has agreed to donate some of the proceeds of his new book to the centre. The board ate it up and couldn't wait to sign on the dotted line.'

'We got you a large Chardonnay to celebrate,' said Constance, sliding an overfull glass towards her. 'Even the Rev is celebrating today.' She nodded to Christopher who was squashed in between Albert and Florence.

Florence, the chief fire officer had a bemused smile on her face. It was the first time she'd been exposed to the whole gang.

Hetty was gazing at her with a soppy, happy grin. They made an attractive couple.

'Now, Laurel, tell us again how you were going to keep out of the detective business.' Albert's grin transformed his face into a map of wrinkles and laughter lines. 'How did that work out for you?'

'I for one am thankful you did get involved,' said Maggie. 'Who knows what might have happened if you hadn't.' She shuddered. 'It doesn't bear thinking about.'

Laurel focused on her drink. They were being altogether too generous.

'I'd love to hear all the stories sometime.' Florence leaned forward eyes bright with interest. 'How did you discover it was Natalie who killed Simon and Charlotte?'

Laurel fiddled with her wine glass then grabbed a napkin to blot the liquid she'd accidentally sloshed onto the table. Around her, everyone was waiting. She was going to have to come clean. 'To be honest, until Natalie clobbered me over the head, I was convinced it was Elise.'

Albert threw his head back and laughed. 'You could say you're so good at this you get it right even when you get it wrong.'

'You could say that,' Laurel mumbled. 'I certainly went off down the wrong track... again.' She let a smile creep onto her face. 'But I got there in the end.'

'Yes, and you saved Elise and goodness knows who else.' Maggie would always be her champion.

'You have to admit, I did solve the biggest mystery of the case though, the locked room.' Laurel was pleased with how she'd unravelled the conundrum. As far as she knew, the police hadn't worked it out until she'd explained it to them from her hospital bed. Her only disappointment being that it hadn't been Coral or Hill who'd come to see her. It would be a long wait before she got any kind of apology or acknowledgement from them.

'I couldn't believe it when you told me how it was done. You were incredible to work it out,' gushed Maggie. 'How that slip of a Natalie managed to lift the doors on and off though, I'll never know.'

Albert was looking pained.

'Albert, are you doing okay?' asked Constance.

'Ah, yes, fine. I was mulling... ah...'

Sudden doubt pricked her pride, and Laurel felt her stomach sink. 'Really? Come on!'

Maggie looked back and forth between Albert and Laurel. 'What? What is it?'

Laurel sighed and answered since Albert was maintaining a gallant silence. 'Apparently I didn't solve the locked door mystery, but Albert has.'

He looked at her with a hangdog expression, but she knew him better than that; he wanted to spill the beans. 'Go ahead, it's okay. My pride can take the hit.'

'Your theory was excellent, and you proved it was possible. However, after you left my house following your demonstration, I got to thinking. Your point, Maggie, is a good one, Natalie is not built for shifting heavy doors, and I had been ruminating on how else one might achieve the desired outcome.

'As countless mystery writers have shown us, there are many ingenious ways one can create a *locked room* scenario. Unfortunately, after a chat with Dorothy and a visit to Tulip Cottage I am convinced a rather prosaic, but nonetheless, effective method was employed in this instance.' He paused to take a drink.

'Don't make us wait,' cried Florence.

With a maddening lack of urgency, he put down his glass, wiped his mouth and grinned. 'There was a second key.'

'No!' Christopher looked rapt.

'Quite so. It's possible to lock the door from outside the room, without pushing out the original key on the inside. When Laurel, Dorothy, and I were first at the scene, I looked through the keyhole from the outside and saw the key in the lock on the inside, but I didn't notice it wasn't all the way in. To be fair to myself, I don't think anyone would have noticed such a small detail. Then, by time the police arrived, we'd already dislodged the key and opened the door.'

'But Dorothy said there was only one key,' said Laurel, put out at such a simple explanation.

'There was, but Dorothy had a young woman stay at the cottage shortly after New Year, for one night only. The booking was made in the name of D. Steerforth.'

'D. Steerforth,' Maggie repeated. 'My goodness, it's DCI Steerforth! He's the main character in Hugh's first book,' she proclaimed.

'Natalie thought it was funny,' Albert rolled his eyes.

'So, the young woman was Natalie? Gosh, that's sneaky.'

Laurel wanted to pin down the details. 'Natalie made a copy of the key then?'

'It seems likely,' he confirmed.

'Didn't Dorothy recognise her when she came back to the village?' Christopher asked Albert.

'I enquired when I saw her, but she doesn't remember. She hasn't regained her memories for the days leading up to the attack.'

Desperate to claw back some mystery-solving kudos, not to mention, dignity, Laurel suggested, 'Maybe she did recognise Natalie and it's why Natalie tried to kill her. What's more, Dorothy had stolen Simon's journal and for Natalie's plan to work, the police really had to find the journal.' She swallowed and shot a look around the table. 'Which they didn't at first because I had it.' She groaned. 'Albert, I think you and I rather complicated the crime scenes.'

Albert looked bashful.

'But very clever, well done for working it out and besting me.' Laurel had to admit he had a knack for this kind of thing, and she wasn't going to be a baby about it.

'Brilliant.' Maggie and the others heaped admiration onto the blushing man.

He hushed them and motioned to Laurel. 'However it came about, Laurel here is responsible for bringing to light Natalie's evil scheme and she has undoubtedly saved lives.'

'Here, here,' they chorused.

'You know what though, if anyone else gets themselves murdered in Elderwick, the police are on their own. I am not getting involved. Never again.'

'Famous last words, my dear. Famous last words.'

<hr />

THREE MONTHS LATER

On seeing the envelope with unfamiliar handwriting on her doormat, Laurel's heart rate went up a notch. Since the anonymous letters from Elise, she'd developed an aversion to suspicious post.

Donning her Marigolds, just in case, she slit the envelope and shook out a newspaper cutting and a note:

> *Dear Laurel,*
>
> *I thought you might be interested in seeing this newspaper article – my old 'pal' James Wentworth has been arrested and questioned on suspicion of manslaughter.*
>
> *After spending time with you and your fellow*

Elderwickians, I decided writing a true crime book was disingenuous if I wasn't prepared to finally speak out about a crime I know to have been committed whilst I was a schoolboy.

As I now know, you read Simon's journal, so you will have seen mention of the death of a fellow pupil at St Cuthbert's, Xavier Houghton. A death which was ruled an accident.

At the time, and in truth, ever since, I suspected James Wentworth of playing a part in Xavier's death. It is to my eternal shame I allowed myself to be convinced to remain quiet.

Simon was close friends with James – whom I believe you met at the memorial. (I didn't go in the end, which I think you know... I had no wish to encounter James.) When Xavier died, James convinced Simon and me to keep quiet, but when questioned himself, he suggested Simon had been involved; shifting the shadow of blame I assume. From that day to the time of his death, Simon believed I had been the one to point the finger at him.

I have spent many years writing works of fiction, accounts of make-believe crime. No longer. As I boy I was afraid to speak up, as an adult I valued my career and connections too much and fooled myself into accepting the lie of the accident. No longer. Now, is the time to make amends... and who knows, it might even do my book sales some good! (I'm kidding).

Keep sleuthing,
Hugh.

Also by Rachael Gray

A Little Bird Told Me

A Storm in a Teacup

Acknowledgements

Writing a book can be a solitary endeavour, but creating the finished article involves so many talented and generous people.

I remain indebted to my wonderful husband, Steve, who not only reads all my books, but has created a beautiful map of Elderwick for me, so I don't get my locations mixed up. Thanks too, to Mum and Dad for their unwavering support and for being the best parents a person could wish for.

Again, I owe a huge thank you to my BBF (best beta friend), Jessi Porter, an incredible writer herself, who helps me shape my early drafts into something readable. I don't know what I'd do without her.

I would also like to thank Mell and Tom Islip, Martin, Linda, and Keith Rudd and my dear friends Emily Wood and Deborah Sexton for being amazing cheerleaders; the Bloodhound authors, who are always quick with encouragement and advice; the Bloodhound ARC readers for being so generous with their time; my new book friends on Twitter and Facebook; all the lovely people who read book one, as well as the fab bloggers who reviewed and wrote about it; the knowledgeable members of r/Anglicanism on Reddit who helped me with some details for Reverend Christopher Ibori—all errors are mine.

My sincere gratitude to the brilliant Bloodhound Books staff for making all of this happen: Betsy, Fred, Tara, Patricia, Hannah, Lexi; Clare Law, my lovely editor who makes the worst part easy; Mel of Better Book Design, and proofreader, Ian Skewis.

Finally, to all of you who've read *A Turn-up for the Books*, you make the hard work worth it! Thank you. I hope to see you back in Elderwick for book three: *A Storm in a Teacup*, to be published in March 2025.

About the Author

With over twenty years of experience working as a Doctor of Clinical Psychology for the NHS and healthcare charities, Rachael Gray is the author of *A Little Bird Told Me* and *A Turn-up For The Books*.

Though she'll always be a Yorkshire girl at heart, Rachael now lives and writes from the home she shares with her husband in Normandy, France.

Rarely without her nose in a book, her *Elderwick Mysteries* series is inspired by her love of a good whodunit.

She can be found on:
Twitter: @RachaelGray_psy
Facebook: RachaelGray_Psy
or visit her website for the latest book news and offers: https:// welcometoelderwick.godaddysites.com/

A note from the publisher

Thank you for reading this book. If you enjoyed it please do consider leaving a review on Amazon to help others find it too.

We hate typos. All of our books have been rigorously edited and proofread, but sometimes mistakes do slip through. If you have spotted a typo, please do let us know and we can get it amended within hours.

info@bloodhoundbooks.com